CABEDELO

BY
GARE BARGATZE

Warfield
Happy Hollow
Hurricane Creek
Hollow Rock
McGill

Upcoming Titles in the
Your Winding Daybreak Ways Series

Thunderwood
Babylon, A Human Requiem

For more information about the series,
visit the author's website
www.garybargatze.com

CABEDELO

GARY BARGATZE

RIGOR HILL PRESS

Grateful acknowledgment is made for permission to reprint excerpts from:

The Mountain of My Fear and *Deborah* by David Roberts, © 1968, 2012 by David Roberts. Text reprinted with permission of the publisher, Mountaineers Books, Seattle, WA.

Levels of the Game by John McPhee, © 1969 by John McPhee. Reprinted by permission of Farrar, Straus and Giroux, LLC.

ISBN-13: 9781545612590
Library of Congress Control Number: 2017954565

Editorial Credit: POP Editorial Services, LLC

Cover Design by Amanda Wright
Interior Design by Agi Bussanich

Printed in the United States of America

FOR PRIS AND SHEILA, WHO SQUARE THE CIRCLE

1

I NEVER EXPECTED TO return to The Afterlife after will-fully grasping the keys to the gates of hell. Commitments have faded, withered, and slowly settled into the thick, fertile depths of redemptive, unborn dreams. I know the twelve-string is history; but thanks to you the keyboard is once again a loyal friend. And with Armageddon now behind us, I embrace you and your winding daybreak ways.

But back to the beginning, not the very beginning, but the quiet, vital period before The Afterlife, before the broken promises and the extended tours from Leipzig to the Hebrides. The adrenaline was surging as I raced down the marble staircase and exited Redman Hall. It was not the rush of dodging bullets but the intense thrill of sensing the possibilities. The first interview with my graduate school mentor had gone so much better than I could ever have expected. We had so much in common: the same hometown, the same public school, the same classical instruction. One of his old classmates even had the same last name as me.

Professor Taylor was also here on campus as a graduate student back in the sixties at the very center of the burgeoning American existentialist movement. In fact, he helped edit the

Pantheon *Messenger*, arguably the most influential literary magazine of the second half of the twentieth century. He had walked here among the giants of the movement—the novelist Walter Talley; the sensual poet Donald Sanders; the avant-garde dramatist Jeffrey Kline; and Kline's tempestuous lover, Bianca, the tragic Portuguese poetess who spent the last few years of her brief life here in McGill bravely fending off the demons.

There was so much more to the professor. He was not only a brilliant scholar but also the rare academic who could relate on a deeply personal level. He was sincerely interested in hearing my father's story, the father I never knew—my father's enthusiasm to serve the country; his painful decision to leave Pantheon before graduation; the postponement of his June wedding to my mother; the unknown pregnancy; his shipping out under deep cover perhaps to work behind the Iron Curtain; and his final anonymous recognition on the agency's sacred wall of fallen stars.

My graying mentor became even more engaged as I began describing my mother's situation after my father had vanished in the night—facing an untimely pregnancy; withdrawing from Pantheon's undergraduate program; returning home to live with her father; working various day jobs while attending nursing school at night; the temporary suitors; the metastatic breast tumor; the courageous chemotherapeutic struggle; and her relentless determination to survive until the week after my high school graduation.

My mentor's keen interest in my past and his genuine concern for my academic future raised the stakes to another level.

I couldn't afford to let the man down. I would do everything I could to succeed as a graduate student and undergraduate instructor. So after a quick stop at the university library to secure several essays for course preparation, I headed down Main to the legendary Two-Way Café to savor a "volcanic" bowl of the "South's finest five-way chili" before hurrying home to consume the books.

I had luckily found a unique off-campus garret in the shadows of the county courthouse on the seedy north side of McMasters Square. For almost a century, the two-story brick building had housed Grimmig's on the Green, the town's only full-service furniture store. But after a fourth-generation Grimmig suffered a debilitating stroke, the business imploded and the bankruptcy court auctioned the real estate and remaining inventory for pennies on the dollar.

Because of the deep, unforeseen recession of '37 and the subsequent slow economic recovery, the new owner became financially strapped and neglected the structure for almost twenty years, allowing the building to fall into general disrepair. The blighted corner property remained shuttered until the new owner's younger brother returned home to McGill in the midfifties with a fair amount of money from his fighting career and a workable idea: establishing a professional boxing club there serving middle and western Tennessee.

Throughout the forties and early fifties, Bobby Young, or the Warfield Warrior as everyone liked to call him, had been a superb journeyman middleweight who never really got a chance to grasp the brass ring. Over time he became the polishing fight for younger, more talented boxers on their way up the rankings. For almost a decade the aging Warrior went the distance, challenging younger, stronger, quicker rivals as they reached their prime. Satterfield, LaMotta, Fullmer, and Cerdan all mentioned their ten-round brawls with the Warrior as instrumental in preparing them for their grueling quests for the middleweight crown.

With the help of abutting merchants and admiring friends, the retired Warrior quickly transformed his brother's dilapidated shell of echoes into a lively training facility with a comfortable two-room bachelor's loft on the second floor directly above the ring. Over the next twenty-five years, the Warrior built a thriving enterprise running the gym, mentoring young prospects, and promoting professional boxing at the local armory. In fact, the folks around Warfield and McGill still reminisce about the Warrior's fight cards of the late fifties and early sixties, including two top-flight matches headlined by Pappy Gault and Willie Pep.

But it was the Warrior's own courageous battles with metastatic melanoma that most endeared him to his local fans. Such a cheap shot, allowing an undetected irregular pinkish spot to burrow into the Warrior's back and spread to the nodes. He fought the main event first with surgery and then with high doses of radiation. When the final bell rang, the judges declared the Warrior the undisputed champ; he had decisively beaten back the insidious disease. But two years later the gods engineered a rematch with a now much stronger, elusive foe, which quickly spread to his liver and his lungs. Again the Warrior rallied with a powerful regimen of chemotherapy; but this more muscular opponent kept beating him down to his knees. And after a third vicious knockdown, the gods mercifully stopped the fight.

The Warrior passed the thriving business onto his son, Billy, who ensured Warrior Productions and the McGill Fight Club continued its impressive record of growth and profitability. After effectively managing the enterprise from the old loft for several years, Billy, a highly eligible bachelor, finally married in '83 and moved his young bride into a new estate home on the fashionable outskirts of town.

Fortunately, the day the For Rent sign went up on the entrance to the gym was the day I arrived in McGill seeking an apartment for the fall semester. I stopped in and spoke with Billy, who showed me the loft and made only one demand: in honor of his father's memory I was not to alter any of the furnishings, pictures, posters, and memorabilia scattered about the two sizable rooms.

So after that brief stop at the Two-Way for chili, I rushed back to the Warrior's loft to begin drafting the syllabus for the advanced composition course I would be teaching during the fall semester. I always looked forward to entering the club, deeply inhaling the rousing fragrance of leather, liniment, smoke, and honest sweat, and then walking the length of the cavernous first-floor space back to the Warrior's old office where thirteen linoleum steps guided only the most deserving visitors up to the double-bolted inner sanctum above the Warrior's gym.

I now know Proust was right about the plump little "madeleine" cakes and the spoonful of tea conjuring up the unremembered state of his youth: the garden flowers, the waterlilies, the parish church and the good folk of Combray contentedly living out their lives in comfortable albeit rustic dwellings. And for me now, so many years have passed, upwards of twenty, but a certain smell, a touch, a sight or sound can still spontaneously transport me to the solitary sparring ring at the center of the gym; the thick clouds of smoke wrapping about the incandescent lights suspended above the hooks and jabs; the small menu board announcing the training schedule du jour; the dusty, full-length mirrors resting against the wooden bars lining the back wall; the loud clank of free weights crashing onto the sagging floor; the groaning thud from the heavy bags; the rhythmic clicks of the whirring ropes; the cramped dressing room with shattered lockers and drooling showerheads; the valued contenders and the necessary stepping-stones; the blessed daily camaraderie; the holy bedlam of righteous missions; and the profane, scowling, cigar-chomping demands of treasured professional trainers.

Of all the Queensbury demigods, "Birmingham," or "the Buccaneer," was my favorite. He was a short, muscular, tenth-generation Italian in his fifties, whose most distinctive characteristics were a bushy eyebrow, a flattened nose, a black patch sweeping down over his right eye, and a stunning shock of raven hair, which he attributed to a sixty-second workout daily with a profusion of Vitalis tonic.

During the month before classes began, I would stop by the ring every afternoon to watch the last half hour or so of sparring. Birmingham was always there, positioned on the apron shouting instructions to the fourth-ranked middleweight in the world. I would stand at the edge of the bleachers reserved for the press and paying guests until the crowd thinned and the sparring ended for the day. I would then take a seat alone in the third or fourth row to soak up the atmosphere and rich history of the room.

Midway through the second week of my daily visits, Birmingham declared the afternoon session over, climbed down from the ring, walked up the bleachers to where I was seated, and sat down beside me. I didn't know what to expect. During the daily workouts, this screaming dynamo would drive his talented fighter to press beyond the most awful pain simulating the last grueling rounds of a championship fight. As he approached me that afternoon, Birmingham slowly raised the towel draped over his shoulders, wiped the sweat from his ruddy face, and said, "You must be a big fan of the sweet science. I've noticed you haunting the gym every day."

I responded nervously, "I… I leased the old Warrior's loft for the fall and spring semesters, and, ah… yeah, I'm a fan. Been one practically all my life. A neighbor used to take me along with him and his son. We'd sit in the cheap seats at the top of the upper deck. The boxers were about an inch high." I laughed.

"Good memories, huh?"

Warming to the subject, I boasted, "You better believe it. We saw fine fights, and there was one match in particular I'll never forget."

"A professional fight?"

"No, no. Amateur. The Golden Gloves tournament. It was the last fight on the card that February night. The light heavyweights had fought evenly during the early and middle rounds. And as the last round began, the two picked up where they'd left off, fighting nonstop toe-to-toe, absorbing as much damage as each was dishing out.

"At about two minutes of that last round, the maroon-and-gold trunks jabbed and fired a stiff right hand, just as the blue-and-white trunks unloaded a thunderous left hook. The punches landed simultaneously on the chins of the light heavyweights, and they both sailed backward, landing flat on their backs. As they lay on the canvas with arms outstretched, the referee unbelievably counted both men out. And after huddling at ringside for several minutes, the tournament officials declared the match the strangest draw they'd ever seen."

Birmingham shook his head and laughed. "That's a helluva story you've got there, kid. I've been at the sweet science a long time. Never seen anything like it." He wiped the sweat off his brow again, looked over at the clock on the far wall, and said, "I've got to get a shower and get moving. Take care now. See you tomorrow?"

I smiled and nodded enthusiastically. "Absolutely. I wouldn't miss it for the world."

During the week following our initial conversation, I would take my usual place in the stands and watch as Birmingham put his contender through punishing preparations for the November fight in Memphis with the number two middleweight in the world. Afterward, Birmingham would join me in the stands for a chat. Over the days I spent there, I learned a great deal about this highly respected but private, enigmatic man. The real challenge was to decipher Birmingham's highly disjointed, almost Joycean narratives. His biography never progressed in a straight line. Rather, the stories were filled with detours and parenthetical roadblocks, which required significant interpretation each evening as I climbed the thirteen steps to the Warrior's loft.

He launched his history with a couple of mysteries. "Contrary to what you might expect, I wasn't born in the yellowhammer state. And this black patch here covering my right eye? That isn't what inspired my nickname the Buccaneer."

I couldn't help myself. I jumped in with two quick jabs. "So where were you born? How did you get your name?"

Birmingham smiled and easily blocked my punches. "Whoa there, kid! Slow down. We'll get there." He backpedaled and continued at a slower pace. "About a decade after Oglethorpe founded Savannah, Georgia, my family sailed to America and invested heavily in the silk trade, which remained profitable for the next thirty years. As the silk export business gradually died out after the American Revolution, my ancestors abandoned their mulberry trees and planted cotton to take advantage of Whitney's innovative gin.

"Unfortunately, during the Civil War, my family's hundred-acre farm lay directly in the path of Sherman's vicious march to the sea. My surviving family members were forced to pack up their few belongings, forsake the farm, and become squatters, hunkering down in an abandoned two-story charred shell in the city near the Savannah River. Well, they managed to survive that upheaval, opened a small commercial shop, and slowly rebuilt the structure that had been ravaged by neglect and the war."

"Sounds like they endured a lot of suffering but found a way to fight through it," I said.

Birmingham nodded. "Yeah… but in life things have a way of balancing out. For the next sixty years, my family remained unscathed as their friends and neighbors suffered one calamity after another. Eventually you just knew the pendulum had to swing back the opposite way. And during the parching summer of 1933, lightning struck the house and started a fire, destroying it for a second time."

I shook my head and murmured, "Unbelievable."

Birmingham nodded again and said, "Yeah. And wouldn't you know it, it happened at the worst time for my hardworking father and my pregnant mom to lose their home. But the kind folk in the neighborhood did everything they could to help my folks weather the storm. In fact, one of their most generous neighbors was the innkeeper just up the block. He graciously offered my parents a rent-free room in his inn until their house could be rebuilt again."

"A comfortable room in a quaint old inn?" I asked.

He shook his head and responded, "No, not your ordinary, run-of-the-mill historic inn 'serving the community for two hundred years.' No, sir. This was a public house with a checkered past where ferocious pirates and wily ship's masters drank their steaming grog and shanghaied unsuspecting sailors onto shorthanded vessels shipping out for distant seas.... And their room on the second floor was not just any room but the very chamber where the storied Captain Flint of *Treasure Island* died crying out 'Fetch aft the rum, Darby!'" He paused, pointed his thumb to his chest, and added, "So it was in that haunted space yours truly, Tommy Lee Turner, was born. And because of my birthplace there, I received my moniker 'the Buccaneer' decades before this eye patch here graced this pretty face."

I laughed. "You sure had me fooled. I'd have bet the farm it was because of the eye patch." I paused, looked down embarrassed, and said, "Ah, you mind telling me how you got the patch?" And then trying to smooth out the rough edges, I added, "Ah, and how you got your other nickname, 'Birmingham'?"

He smiled and offered a good-natured jab. "You sure do know how to cut off the ring, don't you? Patience, kid, patience." He paused, looked up toward the lights to collect his thoughts, and resumed at his own pace. "Well, on my twenty-sixth birthday, I pulled off the biggest upset of my career at the City Auditorium in Birmingham. I went ten rounds with the number one–ranked welterweight and beat him on points."

"Defeated the number one–ranked welterweight in the world?" I gasped.

He nodded and replied proudly, "Yep, sure did. Got me to 28 and 0. Yes, sir, that fight earned me a future shot at the title…. So boy, did we party that night after the fight. My trainer raised a whiskey and shouted, "Birmingham's been good to us on the way up the ladder. Ten fights here and ten fights won! The city has adopted us as their very own. Let's honor them. Add 'Birmingham' to the back of your robe. What do you say?"

"So fans picked up the nickname off the back of your robe?"

"Yep, sure did; and as they say, 'The rest is history.'"

I jumped in. "Well did you get that title fight? And did you have it in your good-luck town, Birmingham?"

He smiled and responded enigmatically. "Yes… and no."

"Yes and no?"

"Yep, I got the title fight, but unfortunately, it wasn't in Birmingham. The champ insisted on the Garden in New York. And you know how it is, what the champ wants, the champ gets. That's the way it's always been."

"Ah, you said 'unfortunately.' What did you mean by that?"

Birmingham pointed his index finger at me and responded with the slightest tinge of irritation in his voice, "Hold on, kid. I'm getting there."

I lowered my head, eased back against the bleacher, and whispered, "Sorry, sir. Please go on."

After giving me a light fatherly tap on the arm, indicating all was forgiven, he began recounting his brush with fate and fame. "The match had been even throughout the first eight rounds; but seconds before the bell rang at the end of round nine, the champ jolted me with two powerful left hooks, one landing solidly on my temple and the other directly over my right eye.

"When the round ended, I staggered back to my corner shouting, 'I can't see! I can't see!' My trainer pushed me down onto the stool and began checking for cuts around my eye. And finding none, he shouted back above the din, 'You'll be all right! You just got thumbed! Just keep clinching. Stay in close until it clears up.'

"When the bell rang for round ten to begin, he pushed me back out into the center of the ring. But to make a long story short, my sight never cleared up. How could it? Unbeknownst to either him or me, my retina had been ripped from its moorings."

With my curiosity trumping my fear, I jumped in again. "Did you keep on fighting?"

Birmingham nodded and responded in a much more subdued way now. "Yeah, but as every boxing fan knows, champions earn titles by polishing their skills, drawing up fight plans to exploit the opponent's weaknesses, and repeating in the arena what they have executed hundreds of times during tough sparring sessions in the gym. But boxing professionals will always cite you two more qualities: quickly sensing their foe is in trouble and then relentlessly moving in for the kill.

"So somewhere midround the champ sensed I was hurt. He figured out that I wasn't reacting to his punches attacking my right side. He moved to his left and launched stiff jabs and upper cuts to the right side of my head, forcing me back into a neutral corner. One after another the haymakers landed and drove me back against the ropes. As the punches landed, I could hear the groaning 'oohs' and 'aahs' above the roar of the crowd. I desperately tried holding on to stop the onslaught, but the pounding continued until the referee finally stepped in and stopped the fight at two minutes forty-five seconds of the tenth round."

I tried to offer some consolation. "You lost the title, but you fought hard 'til the very end."

"Yeah, but the title wasn't the only thing I lost."

"Not the only thing?"

"That's right. The title was probably the least of the things I lost."

"Of course—your eye."

"Yes, my eyesight and my fighting career. You see, the morning after the fight, I consulted the most renowned eye specialist in the Northeast. He said the retina had been severely damaged and needed surgery right away to save my sight. But despite his reputation, he was only able to restore the eye's ability to register light, with neither detail nor color."

"God, I'm sorry. What did you do?"

"After several weeks of giant mood swings between the far-fetched hope the eye would miraculously heal and the gnawing acceptance of forced retirement, I called a press conference and confirmed what had been speculated following the fight. With my manager, trainer, wife, and two small sons surrounding me, I ended the announcement with an ironic, quivering para-phrase of a favorite poem, Housman's *An Athlete*: 'Now I will not swell the rout / Of lads that wore their honors out.'"

"So what next?" I asked.

"Sometimes it seems when the gods really jab us, they regret their actions and rush headlong into the wreckage, pick us up, and apologetically dust us off. Yeah, that's what happened in my case. As I slowly came to grips with my fate, I began questioning how I would continue supporting my wife and young sons. And that's where the gods entered to atone for what they had allowed to happen in the ring."

"What happened?"

"I got a call."

"A call? A call from whom?"

"The Warfield Warrior. He said he had followed my career for years. Said he listened to the championship fight on the radio, read the accounts of my injury, and watched my retirement on the TV. And then right there on the spot, he invited my wife, Janet, and me to visit McGill to talk about becoming a trainer of top-notch prospects at the Warrior's Fight Club. So a long story short again, we hit it off well; and within two months, I had settled my family in a bungalow on the east side of town and begun demanding the most from my young, aspiring fighters."

"So in a way you had been reborn."

"Yeah, kid, that's a pretty good way to put it.... Yeah, I had been reborn."

So as we sat on those bleachers every afternoon following the sparring sessions, Birmingham regaled me with increasingly more detailed and colorful stories of his days in the ring, his challenging adjustments to retirement, and his totally unexpected afterlife transforming young athletes into genuine contenders. But just when I thought I had exhausted every imaginable question about my new friend, "Shaky" Jake, the Buccaneer's premier cut man, approached early one morning, acknowledged the growing friendship between his boss and me, and then fired off a barrage of his own, representing the queries of everyone working and training in the gym: Why does the Buccaneer suspend training in August every year? Why does he refuse to sanction bouts for September and October? Why does he disappear for several weeks at the end of summer? Why does he leave his wife and children behind in McGill? Where does he go? And what does he do while he is away?

Armed now with Jake's new questions, I got a second wind. As a fighter looking for an opening, I would attempt to force our daily discussions against the ropes, but Birmingham was adept at sensing the pressure, raising his gloves, and skillfully steering our conversations back to the safety of center ring. Only once, just before school began, did I find a slight opening. I fired off a light jab, alluding to his mysterious activities in late August every year. The Buccaneer slowly turned toward me and then forcefully blocked my brief feint with an inscrutable response to my tentative question. "I'm doing the Lord's work." And the tone of his voice strongly suggested there would be no more sparring about that subject anytime soon.

2

AFTER LEASING THE loft and meeting the Buccaneer, I realized I had been dropped into a highly potent metaphor infused with sacrifice and a stoic willingness to face and sometimes accept unspeakable disappointment and gnawing failure. Sport had become for me a compelling placeholder for the human condition with its own worthy body of fiction, non-fiction, and dramatic works demanding serious academic attention.

During our initial meeting, Professor Taylor had granted me significant latitude in shaping the syllabus for my advanced composition course. He had told me he was more interested in the results than the means to the end. As long as the undergraduates learned how effective writers shape their prose, he didn't care which artists and works I chose to demonstrate it.

So with the focus of the course changed, it was back to the drawing board to revise the course outline, the reading list, and the overarching themes for the advanced program. Hemingway would replace Twain. Talese would be in for Forster. Wolfe would substitute for Bacon. And Updike would supplant Huxley in this thorough study of rhetoric based on sports literature. And within forty-eight hours of posting the revisions on the department bulletin board, enrollment in the avant-garde class had risen from seventy percent of capacity to an anxious waiting list of eleven.

Because of my own doctoral work I was forced to schedule the undergraduate course for early Friday mornings. Anticipating the brutality of the predawn wake-up, the night before the first class I had set the clock radio to a soothing folk-rock station, which would gently ease me out of a deep sleep at the dreadful five o'clock hour. But despite the careful forethought, I awoke to the blaring national news at the top of the hour—something about Soviet interceptors blasting a Korean Airlines jetliner, Flight 007, out of the sky and annihilating everyone on board including an American congressman. As I lay curled up in the warm, seductive blankets rubbing my eyes and gathering the will to swing my feet down to the floor, I had the uncanny suspicion that given the flight number, the KGB had mistakenly concluded the passenger plane was on a high-stakes surveillance mission and had given the order to fire on the civilian Boeing 747.

I groped for the switch, silenced the noise, and then rolled out onto the cold tiles. I had once again become the lonely long-distance runner, Colin Smith, shivering my belly off on the icy stone floors at Rexton Towers. I had earlier identified with Sillitoe's borstal lad. I too had been a long-distance runner during my high school and collegiate days. I too had often stood in the doorway in singlet and shorts, nary a dry crust in the gut, staring out at frosted chrysanthemums shimmering in the silver landscape. I too had run five-thousand-meter cross-country races and was ranked high enough in the state to earn scholarship offers from Division 1 schools.

But college cross-country races were so much more challenging than the high school meets. They were consistently more competitive and covered twice the distance. While marathons have often been described as slow roasts over several hours, collegiate ten-thousand-meter races should only be portrayed as the grueling equivalent of running flat-out for thirty minutes while holding your breath.

During cross-country season, punishing competition meant equally painful training sessions almost every morning and afternoon—excruciating 880 speed drills Tuesdays and Thursdays; agonizing hill repeats Mondays and Wednesdays; "friendly" intrasquad races on Fridays; and exhausting fifteen-thousand-meter runs on the weekends. And that was the great mystery for me. Why didn't I ever grasp the metaphor when I was racing all those years? Why didn't I understand the seminal nexus between life and sport until I met Birmingham and witnessed the daily sacrifice in the Warrior's gym?

I suspect it was the endless attention to self, to perfection and victory, and to finding ways of gaining an edge both physically and mentally. Confronting persistent loneliness, fear of failure and unrelenting pain forced me to turn inward. There was never time to fathom the existential truths reflected in my competitors' and my own intense desire to win. I could never step back to objectively interpret the fierce meaning embedded in our athleticism. That would have to wait. I would have to jettison the sport to fully understand its significance. The symbolism would only surface after transitioning from driven participant to fervent witness.

As I walked over to Harris Hall to teach my first class, I experienced the same thoughts and sensations I had felt each time race officials called us to the starting line. I always oscillated between fear and reassuring optimism. On the one hand I dreaded a poor performance, while on the other, I confidently believed no one could have spent as many quality hours in preparation for the blistering races. I knew I was taking a risk. I realized I was trying to do something that few had tried before, stepping out academically onto the high wire far above a packed house of demanding students expecting a good show. When I reached the "Big Tent," the English professors' covert nickname for expansive Harris Hall, I climbed the marble stairs to the second floor, took several deep, calming breaths, and approached the lectern fashionably late as required, seven minutes after the appointed hour.

While scanning the expectant crowd, I briefly allowed my maleness to get the upper hand. I irreverently congratulated myself for the unintended consequences of reworking the undergraduate course around sport literature. Contrary to my expectations, two-thirds of the "lucky few" who made the final cut were incredibly attractive, well-conditioned coeds only a few years my junior. While I didn't understand the correlation between subject and gender, I wryly made a lecherous note to myself to consider a similar approach in the future. During this entire unauthorized diversion of no more than five seconds, I continued smiling broadly as my gorgeous world unwittingly smiled back in kind.

After tackling the mandatory administrative tasks—distributing the syllabus and discussing the guidelines concerning attendance, drop policy, grading, and the "three deadly sins of academic dishonesty"—I launched the groundbreaking class in earnest: "Does sport have a significant role to play in our society? I think I see a hand back there. Rise and state your name."

"It's Mary, sir."

"So, Mary, tell us. Does sport have a significant role to play in our society?"

"Yes, Mr. Lynch. Sport can teach us values and reinforce them."

"Everyone agree with Mary?"

The class nodded in unison.

"Yes, Mary, we all agree. But values related to what?… Who said 'work' back there?… Okay. Rise and state your name."

A young man in the back of the class stood and introduced himself. "I'm Bill, sir."

"Okay, Bill. And what kind of values related to work?"

Bill looked a little less certain now that he was talking for the whole class to hear. "Let's see. Preparation, discipline, effort, and… and… sacrifice."

"Very good, Bill." He smiled at me, glad to be back out of the spotlight. "And values related to what else besides work?" I probed. "I see a hand there. Stand and state your name."

The student rose and responded, "David, sir."

"So, David, what else besides work?"

"Values related to family, sir."

"What kind of values related to family, David?"

"Ah, camaraderie, love, teamwork, ah, working toward a common goal."

"Does everyone agree with David?"

Everyone mumbled, "Yes."

"Very good. Now, anyone think of other values related to sport? Yes, here in the front row. Rise and state your name loudly so the folks in the back can hear."

"I'm Jennifer, Mr. Lynch."

"So, Jennifer, any other values related to sport?"

"American culture, sir."

"How so, Jennifer?"

"Validating the American dream, sir."

"Can you give us a little more? How does sport validate the American dream?"

"Well, talented athletes might have the chance to become professional ballplayers, demand big contracts, live in upscale neighborhoods, and earn praise from their fans. Live the American dream, so to speak."

"Everyone agree?"

The class nodded.

"Very good, Jennifer. Anything else about the American dream? Anyone?" Another young man off to the side raised his hand. "Okay. Rise and state your name."

"It's Thomas, sir."

"Well, Thomas, do you see sports reinforcing any other values related to the American dream?"

"Yes, sir. When athletes break records or perform spectacular feats, they affirm our national character."

"How so?"

"They show American willingness to take on the most difficult challenges."

"Very good, Thomas. That's just what I was thinking of. Now can y'all think of any other important ways record breaking strengthens the culture?" I waited a moment. "No one? Okay, here's a hint. Think of an existing record as a barrier. So what important barrier did athletes break during the last hundred years?

"We have a hand there. Stand and state your name."

"I'm Susan, sir."

"So what barrier did they break, Susan?"

"Ah, I'd say the racial barrier's the most significant."

"Very good! The racial barrier. So over the last century, athletes have informed our beliefs and demonstrated a brave pathway to rightful acceptance. Jack Johnson in boxing. Jackie Robinson in baseball. Bobby Marshall and Fritz Pollard in the National Football League, and Arthur Ashe in tennis. In fact, Ashe is the only black to ever win the singles titles at the

Australian Open, the US Open, and Wimbledon." I saw some smiles as the students made the logical leap with me.

"So let's review. I believe we can all accept the premise that sport has a significant impact on society by teaching strong values and reinforcing them. Some of the values we've mentioned are discipline, sacrifice, love, teamwork, perseverance, and inclusion. Are these values not the subject of world literature?

"If novelists, columnists, dramatists, and essayists focus on these values in their sports writing, don't these works then rise to the level of literature? We've heard the terms 'sociology of sport,' 'philosophy of sport,' 'politics of sport,' and 'sport psychology.' Would it be a giant leap then to use the phrase 'sports literature'? Is it difficult to envision an academic course in applied rhetoric requiring us first to examine authoritative sports literature and then apply the learned principles of rhetoric to our own writing?

"Now we must not lose sight of the stated objective of our advanced course, which is to investigate the technical methods skillful authors use to impose stylistic order on their ideas about life and sport. But my ultimate goal here is to leverage a challenging study of rhetoric into something far more engaging—a serious dialogue about the human condition as expressed through sports literature.

"Among the works we'll read are David Roberts's *Deborah: A Wilderness Narrative*, John McPhee's *Levels of the Game*, Gay Talese's essay 'The Silent Season of a Hero,' John Updike's 'Hub Fans Bid Kid Adieu,' Tom Wolfe's 'The Last American

Hero,' Liebling's *The Sweet Science*, Sillitoe's 'The Loneliness of the Long-Distance Runner,' Harris's *Bang the Drum Slowly*, Michael Murphy's *Golf in the Kingdom*, and Hemingway's *The Sun Also Rises*.

"Since this is an advanced composition course for English majors, the reading and writing demands will be heavy and the expectations for quality work will be high. If you have any questions or concerns along the way, please schedule an appointment. But confidentially, I'll be in my office much of the time and welcome unscheduled visits, that is, if you have a serious matter to discuss.

"For our class next Friday, please read Roberts's mountaineering narrative as your model and write a descriptive essay in which you report your opening paragraphs objectively and then allow the work to seamlessly drift into the subjective world of thought and meaning. Perhaps you'll describe an event in your life, one that has shaped you and provided philosophical insight, for example, into your character, your belief system, your relationships, or perhaps, even your existence. Any questions? None? Okay then, I look forward to our discussion next Friday and then reading your first compositions over the weekend."

As the students filed out, I slowly let out my breath and murmured, "That went pretty damn well, if I must say so myself."

On the following Monday morning the roles were reversed. I was sitting in the student's chair at the back of the room taking notes, and my mentor was at the lectern launching his highly touted Introduction to Graduate Studies, a rite of passage for all English majors transitioning from their undergraduate curricula into the arduous Pantheon doctoral program. After briefly discussing the administrative "rules of the road," Professor Taylor explained he would be lecturing infrequently because he believed we would learn more conducting our own literary research than listening to him describing how it was done.

"Over the course of the semester," he said, "I will be assigning specific projects to each student, exposing you to the latest research tools and providing you with invaluable, hands-on experience in collecting information, assessing the evidence, formulating hypotheses, and drafting scholarly critiques."

He then surprisingly announced, "Class is dismissed. We will reconvene two weeks from today when you will turn in your first assignment." The room was stunned into silence. "Please," he added, "since there are only twelve of you here, if you would remain seated until I call you to the front of the room, I will give you your customized assignments and answer any questions you may have about the exercise."

One after another the professor summoned my classmates to the lectern, revealed their projects, and quietly clarified their questions. The longer I sat waiting for my name to be called, the more anxious I became. I noted several of my peers shaking their heads in disbelief as they exited the room, which I quickly interpreted to mean the exercises were unbelievably tough.

After the eleventh student had approached the lectern, received her assignment, and exited into the hallway, my mentor looked directly at me, smiled, and beckoned me to the front of the room. As he handed me the note card containing the assignment, he smiled again, but this time slyly, and said, "I think you'll find this exercise both entertaining and instructive."

I took a deep breath and, trying not to reveal my nervousness, read the premise statement and multiple questions: "Newsreel LVII of Dos Passos' *The Big Money* contains the headlines, 'Queen Sleeps as Train Departs' and 'Coolidge Urges Advertising.' Marie of Rumania was the Queen. Where was she? Where was Coolidge? And to what exact date was Dos Passos referring with the two headlines?"

I was relieved. I realized the assignment wouldn't be as complicated as I had earlier anticipated while watching my agitated compatriots leave the room. But as we all know, appearances can be deceiving. What I thought would be a simple research exercise of pinpointing the specific date using the *Times Index* devolved into a chaotic fourteen-day nightmare including two all-nighters as the deadline inexorably approached. In fact, I ultimately made the fateful decision to challenge the assertion that there ever was an exact date when the queen slept and the president spoke. I was prepared to take my lumps if the professor didn't like my approach. I knew it was risky, but I was determined to stick to it.

Sandwiched between this initial wake-up call and the final project from hell at the end of the semester were three "conventional" research studies. While I believe the professor misspoke in describing the first and last exercises as "both entertaining and instructive," I would agree the three midterm projects accurately matched his upbeat description.

The first of the midterm exercises was to name a book written by Currer Bell, Smelfungus, J. Milton Sloluck, Huan Mee, and Uncle Harry. Thanks to hard work but mostly luck, I stumbled onto the indispensable Reverend James Wood's 1907 publication, *The Nuttall Encyclopedia: Being a Concise and Comprehensive Dictionary of General Knowledge Consisting of Over 16,000 Terse and Original Articles on Nearly All Subjects and Specially Dealing with Such as Come Under the Categories of History, Biography, Geography, Literature, Philosophy, Religion, Science, and Art.*

This worthy compendium disclosed the identities of forty percent of the professor's real and fictional authors, Currer Bell (Charlotte Brontë) and Smelfungus, Laurence Sterne's name for the irascible author-turned-character, Tobias Smollett, in Sterne's last work, an intentionally sentimental eighteenth-century novel about travels on the continent. As I continued the exercise, however, I realized the professor had listed the five names in order of obscurity and difficulty.

Next up was J. Milton Sloluck, who turned out to be Ambrose Bierce, the author of the brilliant Civil War short story "An Occurrence at Owl Creek Bridge." Following Sloluck was Huan Mee, the pseudonym for the minor authors Walter and

Charles Mansfield, and finally, Uncle Harry, the nom de plume of the nineteenth-century American writer John Habberton. So the answer I confidently submitted for the professor's question was *Jane Eyre*, *A Sentimental Journey Through France and Italy*, *The Dance of Life*, *A Diplomatic Woman*, and *Helen's Babies*. For that, the professor graced my paper with a beautiful A+ in red ink.

The objective of the second "routine" midterm investigation was to introduce me to some of the more obscure literary research tools. The instruction was to identify the Swan of Lichfield, the Water-Poet, Colonel Bath, and the Lady of the Idle Lake.

After a few false starts, I discovered the Swan of Lichfield was the eighteenth-century English Romantic poet and voluminous letter writer Anna Seward, whose six volumes of correspondence with the likes of the Romantic Lake Poets, Robert Southey and Samuel Taylor Coleridge, has attracted considerably more attention than her rarely anthologized minor poetry.

The next challenge was the Water-Poet, whom I eventually learned was a seventeenth-century lyricist and boatman ferrying travelers across the Thames at London. He is remembered primarily for his 1613 treatise, *The True Cause of the Watermen's Suit Concerning Players*, and his 1620 poem, "The Praise of Hemp-Seed." The historically valuable treatise described the ferrymen's grievances against the theater companies when they moved the playhouses across the Thames in 1612, thus greatly reducing the number of theater patrons requiring passage across the river to attend the shows. His

"Hemp-Seed" poem is notable as the first printed reference to the deaths of Shakespeare and Francis Beaumont, which had occurred four years earlier:

> In Paper, many a Poet now survives
> Or else their lines had perish'd with their lives.
> Old *Chaucer, Gower*, and Sir *Thomas More,*
> Sir *Philip Sidney* who the Laurel wore,
> *Spencer* and *Shakespeare* did in Art excell,
> Sir *Edward Dyer, Greene, Nash, Daniel,*
> *Silvester, Beaumont,* Sir *John Harington,*
> Forgetfulness their works would over run,
> But that in Paper they immortally
> Doe live in spite of Death, and cannot dye.

Professor Taylor used the third name, Colonel Bath, to throw me a real curve, which took hours of serious digging to resolve. With the first two names he had conditioned me to look for historical figures, but now he had chosen to dredge up a fictional character, Colonel Bath, who despite his "heroic behavior" remained an obscure minor figure in Fielding's moralistic last novel *Amelia*, which paled in comparison to his earlier picaresque masterwork, *Tom Jones*.

So realizing fictional characters were now definitely on the table, I immediately dove into bibliographies specializing in American and English literature to identify the fourth name on the professor's list. Less than an hour into the mission, I hit pay dirt, discovering the Lady of the Idle Lake was the beautiful temptress, Phædria, who unsuccessfully tried to sway Sir Guyon from his knightly duties in Spencer's epic Elizabethan poem *The Faerie Queene.*

Oddly enough, this second exercise was the source of both pride and embarrassment. I worked hard to identify the four esoteric names and felt a sense of pride when I finally deciphered them. But when Professor Taylor later stood in front of the whole class and announced I was the only student who had successfully completed the exercise and gotten the only A, I lowered my head, slid down in my chair, and wished I was anyplace else but there.

The last of the midterm exercises was a change of pace. It had nothing to do with names. I was to locate a bizarre passage in an unspecified medieval manuscript, explain what was happening, describe the size and significance of the manuscript, and determine if the passage had ever been in print. The unusually repetitious quote was "drunken / dronken dronken ydronken."

After scanning several period and serial bibliographies for leads, I finally identified the manuscript as the fourteenth-century Bodleian Rawlinson D. 913 containing ten secular lyrics in English and two in French. I learned the passage was from a drinking song performed by a drunken fellow, Tabart, who was partying with his sister and two friends, Walter and Peter. The Bodleian Rawlinson D. 913 was a tiny scribbled treasure measuring four by eleven inches, which had been stitched into a miscellaneous volume of medieval manuscripts. Despite its small size, this scrap of paper represented our only connection to "Dronken" and several medieval lyric masterpieces including "I Am of Ireland" and "All Night by the Rose." After further research, I determined all three poems appeared in print in Silverstein's 1971 anthology, *English Lyrics Before 1500*.

As I successfully completed each of the exercises, I became increasingly more confident in my ability to conduct research on a doctoral level. But all of these positive feelings quickly disappeared as I faced the final project. Since Pantheon's rare-book library housed one of the most comprehensive manuscript collections in the South, Professor Taylor required each of us to edit and annotate an original document as a final challenge of the semester.

After receiving our assignments and examining the actual papers in the heavily secured reading room, my classmates and I gathered outside the inner sanctum to compare notes and commiserate. The assigned manuscripts were all various pieces of correspondence from disparate authors including Pound, Poe, Hemingway, Dos Passos, Maugham, and Alfred, Lord Tennyson. Our cunning professor chose only holograph letters for our assignments; none were typewritten. And it didn't take us long to appreciate his modus operandi. Every third word appeared to be illegible. And the pièce de résistance was the plethora of abbreviations, shorthand, and initials distributed generously throughout the handwritten texts.

Only minutes after meeting in the public display room, the moans, groans, and cursing began: "We're screwed. How does he expect us to edit something we can't read?" "The son of a bitch saved the best for last." "Yeah, the icing on the cake!"

Throughout the group rant, I shook my head to demonstrate my empathy for my classmates' plight. But what I really wanted to do was get the hell out of the building as soon as possible. My desire to leave was not based on any burning drive to get started on the project but an attempt to avoid serious embarrassment. For some inexplicable reason, the professor had assigned me a pristine, highly legible letter from Tennyson to a fellow named H. G. Coxhead. It was not *the* Tennyson, Alfred, but his brother, the minor poet, Frederick Tennyson.

On the first pass through the text, I could easily read every word of every line of every paragraph. But of course, the cosmic joke would eventually be on me. While my peers were using magnifying glasses to vainly decipher codelike messages, I was spending all my time desperately trying to determine one of the most important aspects of the document: who in the hell was this letter's recipient, H. G. Coxhead?

In fact, just as with the earlier Queen-Coolidge exercise, I was forced to risk everything by responding I had no definitive answer to a key point of the research. And it was unspeakably excruciating sitting in the last class of the semester knowing that at the end of the period I would be submitting an incomplete paper to, of all people, my graduate school adviser.

When class ended, I remained seated until everyone else had approached the lectern, tendered their final projects, extended pleasantries, and left the room. I rose from my chair and slowly approached the professor, who smiled and asked, "So how did you like the course?"

"It was good, sir. I learned a lot."

"What did you think of the first and last exercises?"

"Honestly?"

Professor Taylor nodded. "Of course, honestly."

"Well, compared to the midterm projects, which were challenging… I'd have to say the first and last exercises were absolute bears."

The professor smiled broadly. "I have to give you credit for taking a risk with the Queen-Coolidge exercise—first contending there was no exact date the queen slept and the president spoke and then expressing your take-away from the project that we shouldn't believe everything we read in print including analyses appearing in the most sophisticated scholarly journals." He chuckled and then asked, "So how did you make out with that other bear—the Tennyson letter to Coxhead?"

I lowered my head and confessed haltingly, "I… I was doing great with the editing until I bumped up against the recipient, that damn H. G. Coxhead. I haven't got a clue who he is. I think his identity's faded away forever."

My mentor now laughed aloud, placed his hand on my shoulder, and gently guided me over to a small table on the far side of the lectern. He picked up a yellowed assignment sheet; and after pointing to a circled number assigned to the Queen-Coolidge exercise, he said wistfully, "I got that bastard right too…. And as far as the mysterious recipient of the Tennyson letter, I still haven't got a clue who Coxhead was. And still today, I occasionally spend time poring over documents related to Italy and the Isle of Jersey where Frederick spent much of his time."

After an awkward pause, I responded, "So you were walking in my shoes as I followed in your footsteps. Why?"

"Because I thought you could handle it," Professor Taylor said quietly. He abruptly moved back to the lectern and began collecting the students' papers, clearly signaling our conversation was at an end. I sincerely thanked him for all his help during the semester and then hurried out of the room.

3

LOOKING BACK NOW so many years later, the first weeks of graduate school were an adrenaline-induced blur. One minute I was receiving the professor's Queen-Coolidge project and the next I was standing again at the front of my advanced composition class assigning a paper based on John McPhee's *Levels of the Game* and leading a spirited discussion of Roberts's mountaineering chronicle, *Deborah: A Wilderness Narrative.*

I slowly scanned the class and began, "Summarizing last week's seminar, we established sport has a significant impact on society. We said sport can teach us values related to work such as preparation, discipline, effort, and sacrifice. We said sport can also teach us values related to personal relationships, for example, camaraderie, teamwork, love, and working toward a common goal. We further agreed sport validates the American dream. When our athletes break records or perform spectacular feats, they affirm our national character of willfully taking on the most difficult challenges without fear of failure. And given the above premises, we then concluded novelists, columnists, dramatists, and essayists emphasizing these strong positive values in their sports writing raise their works to the level of literature.

"Okay. Let's put our theory to the test and move on to a discussion of Roberts's *Deborah*." I spotted Mary sitting with empty desks on either side of her. "Mary, what do you think is the overall structure of the work?"

"Ah, it's a narrative. Roberts, the narrator, tells his story chronologically. He and his Harvard classmate, Don Jensen, undertake a journey of discovery in the summer of 1964, attempting to climb an extraordinarily difficult, unscaled Alaskan peak."

"Thank you, Mary. Did anyone see a second 'journey of discovery' as a subtext?" I scanned the room and found a brunette with her hand raised. "I believe it's Joan, yes? Go ahead."

Joan cleared her throat. "Well, beyond the physical attempt to reach the summit, ah, I believe the climbers experienced an… an emotional journey of discovery about their friendship during their forty-two days alone on the mountain."

"Excellent! So let's pursue Joan's thesis. In an earlier six-day 'practice climb' Roberts said he felt an alliance with Don that went beyond friendship. He firmly believed they made a good team. But, Joan, didn't Roberts suspect there might be seeds of discord already buried deeply within their respective styles and personalities?"

She nodded and replied, "Yes, Mr. Lynch."

"So what did Roberts notice about their styles that could potentially lead to future conflict?"

"Roberts liked to talk, but Don preferred thinking alone."

"Anything else? How about you, Bill?"

Bill rose, paused to collect his thoughts, and responded, "Roberts spoke of the difference in their 'emotional endurance.' At the end of their six-day trial run, Roberts said he felt satisfied with the fourteen-thousand-foot climb. But he said Don was always looking around for more peaks to conquer and was frustrated he hadn't scheduled more time to accomplish his goals. Roberts pointed out that when Don saw a mountain, he felt compelled to climb it."

"Very good, Bill. And… and, David, how much time had elapsed on their *Deborah* expedition before the suspected tensions surfaced?"

The handsome jock wearing a letter sweater rose and answered. "I believe it was about four days, sir."

"That's right, four days. And, Jennifer, what caused the first of the many flare-ups?"

The young lady stood up, smiled, and responded confidently, "Don's repeated use of the word *well-behaved* in describing the glacier's lack of crevasses."

"Strange but true, huh?"

Everyone nodded.

"And, Thomas, what else irritated Roberts about his partner's mannerisms?"

"Small things, sir."

"For example?"

"Like Don's lack of interest in playing chess when they were snowbound. The way Don spooned his food, and, ah, Don's repeated incursions into Roberts's small space as they tried to sleep."

"That's right. And, Susan, how did Roberts describe their relationship?"

Gripping her book, Susan stood and said, "I have it marked here. Let's see. Roberts says they were like lovers or married people, except that, instead of sharing a bond of physical love, they shared a bond of danger and of the mountain."

A snicker erupted from the back of the room. In spite of it, I maintained my professional demeanor and moved on. "Very good, Susan." I then looked around the room for one of the students who hadn't been participating. I noticed a mousy girl in the front row with her head resting on her hand. "Linda, how did the climbers react when they reached the vertical face of the mountain and realized their expedition couldn't succeed?"

The young woman remained seated but engaged and answered thoughtfully. "They reluctantly accepted their fate and gave the mountain its due. Roberts says the mountain had been fair to them by plainly saying 'Stop' instead of leading them on and then forcing them to make the decision and blame their failure on their own weaknesses."

"And, Peter, after surviving the initial stages of a dangerous descent, what did Roberts think would happen to the 'wonderful cohesion of the last few days'?"

"Their shaky civility would end with the absence of danger and hard work."

"Was he right?"

"Yes, sir. They began sniping at each other."

"And how long did it last?"

"Until their first really life-threatening crisis, when Don fell into a deep crevice."

"That's right. And once they both understood the situation and the high stakes, they immediately became an effective climbing team again, focusing solely on Don's survival.... And, David, when Don finally crawled up out of the hole, what did Roberts feel and do?"

"He felt a strong impulse of loyalty. Roberts put an arm around Don's shoulders and told him he had done a great job."

"Yes, that's exactly it. But we then learn another crisis looms. While approaching the edge of the glacier, Don falls into a second hidden crevasse, plunging thirty feet into a narrow hole and smashing his face on a shelf of ice halfway down. So, Thomas, after Don struggled to reach the surface again, he apologized for what, and how did Roberts feel after the apology?"

As Thomas rose to his feet, I could see the wheels spinning at the challenging question. He flipped through his book for a few seconds and then the answer came to him. "Ah, Don apologized for getting blood on Roberts's jacket, and Roberts admitted he had felt love for Don because he had been so courageous."

"Outstanding. So can we all now accept Joan's contention that the climbers were actually on two journeys of discovery—one, the actual physical expedition and the other a difficult spiritual journey to an understanding of their core values and the forceful dynamics of their unique friendship?"

The class mumbled, "Yes."

"Well, can we all agree then that Roberts's narrative rises to the level of sports literature?"

Everyone nodded in agreement.

"Very good. So with the time we have left today, let's discuss the descriptive essays you've written using Robert's *Deborah* as your model. You were to draft the initial paragraphs objectively and then allow your words to effortlessly flow into the subjective world of emotion and meaning. Perhaps you would describe a memorable experience that later influenced your beliefs, your behavior, or your relationships. Do we have a volunteer?" I waited a few moments to see if anyone would rise to the challenge. "No one wants to tell his or her story?" I paused again. "Ah, Bill, I can't see back there in the corner. Is your hand raised? Well, even if it's only halfway up, I'll take it. Come on up to the front of the room and describe your composition and insights."

Bill rose from his chair and walked toward the lectern. His head was bowed and his steps measured. His discomfort was visible in the slump of his shoulders. He turned slowly around, placed his composition on the sloping surface, and glanced toward the back of the room. He then lowered his head again, took several deep breaths, and began speaking, haltingly at first, but more confidently as time passed and the subject turned from disappointment to understanding:

"As you can see, I'm at least ten years older than most of you. My path here to Pantheon was probably not as direct as yours. For better or worse, I left the main highway early on and, ah, shall we say, took some rough back roads along the way—juvenile detention, rehab... and a brief stay in federal prison. I know exactly when things changed. I was eight years old. My best Christmas ever. I got everything I wanted: a Santa Fe freight set with operating milk and cattle cars, a big construction toy, and an honest-to-God, genuine Hank Bauer fielder's glove."

He paused, swallowed hard, and continued, "At least my dad had enough feelings to hold off until the day after that best Christmas ever. I just knew something serious was about to happen. Mom and Dad had gathered my sisters and me in the living room, and the only time we ever used the room was to have serious family discussions. So without any fanfare, my father announced he was joining the military. Said he wanted to be an 'adviser' in some place called 'Vietnam.'

"Well, my eighth and best Christmas ever was the last quality time our father spent with us. From then on, he was either gone or preparing to go back to what soon became a killing zone. His stays at home were always short; and after only a few days he would begin talking, talking about his 'brothers in combat.' He, ah, spoke of their bravery and, ah, his strong wish to be with his men despite the risks. During the early visits home, Dad even told us about wounded soldiers escaping from the hospital tents to rejoin their 'family' on the battlefield.

"Dad's final time home was November 1968. He only stayed a few anxious days and then left again just before Thanksgiving. And it was the following year, on Valentine's Day, Mom received the knock at the door. She showed the military men into the living room. I was at home with the flu. Heard the knocking and, ah, watched the soldiers disappear around the corner. I sneaked down the stairs, crouched in the hallway outside the door, and listened to their conversation. The heater was rumbling in the basement just below me, and I could only pick out a few words and phrases: 'Tet,' 'Hue,' 'brave,' 'saved lives,' 'died quickly,' 'didn't suffer,' 'you can be proud,' 'a true hero'...

"When I knew the men were leaving, I ran up the stairs to my room and stayed there until their car disappeared at the intersection. Not knowing how Mom would react, I crept down the stairs and entered the living room. Mom was sitting on the sofa with her head in her hands, bawling and saying over and over, 'Why us? What will become of us now? How will we survive?' I walked over to Mom, sat down beside her, put my arm around her shoulder, and quietly answered her last question with a teenager's baseless, 'We'll make it, Mom. Everything will be okay.'

"But these soft words of comfort for Mom actually served a second purpose. They also hid a painful sense of abandonment that had been silently growing in me for years and that had become a destructive form of anger, bordering on real rage. The eight-year-old innocently asked, 'Why does Dad have to leave?' The ten-year-old inquired, 'Why does he stay away so much?' The twelve-year-old asked, 'Why does Dad call his army pals his family?' The fourteen-year-old asked, 'Why does he love his other family more than he does ours?' And on that fateful Valentine's Day, the sixteen-year-old demanded, 'Why did you die saving them while destroying us?'

"As the years passed, the fire became embers mainly because of the numbing drugs and the occasional distractions into theft and violence. While I've never been a religious person, I owe my salvation to a holy man I met while I was in prison. I should tell you he was not a visiting minister. He was a twenty-to-lifer who had supposedly murdered his lover's wife as she ran out of the house to tell the church elders of her 'horrible' discovery.

"When the reverend was not on his knees praying for forgiveness, he was hedging his bets with spiritual acts of goodwill toward the rest of us inmates. After patiently listening to my childhood complaints for months, he slowly convinced me to begin living in what he called 'the imminent.' He said I may never understand why my father abandoned our family to join his men in fighting a dead-end war, but at least I should forgive him so that I could freely imagine an unburdened future." Bill paused briefly and then continued, "Now that I've described my background, I'll put my bifocals on here and, if you don't mind, I'll read you the last part of my composition, which I called 'Roberts's Adventures of Self-Discovery.'"

With trembling hands Bill pulled his reading glasses from his shirt pocket, adjusted them on his nose, and began reading. "I used the plural, 'adventures,' in my title because after racing through *Deborah*, I scoured the card catalogue and learned Roberts had written an *earlier* work describing a *later* Alaskan climb up Mount Huntington only a year after the failed attempt to reach Mount Deborah's summit. I was intent on confirming or debunking what I had theorized while reading *Deborah*. And Roberts's earlier work, *The Mountain of My Fear*, rewarded me, validating what I had suspected and in a style so unlike the later wilderness narrative.

"While stylistically *Deborah* was a well-constructed straightforward account, the earlier *Mountain of My Fear* featured sweeping philosophical passages burning white hot with luminosity and intensity. Excuse me if I offend anyone, but it was as if after spontaneously pouring out raw emotion onto the page in the first work, editors or professors influenced him to write fact-based narrative, sucking the very passion out of the telling.

"And what did I learn by reading Roberts's first book? After experiencing the anger, the harsh words, frustration, and bitterness following a failed attempt to reach Deborah's summit, Don Jensen and Roberts were back together again only a year later enthusiastically planning the assault of another dangerous Alaskan peak. But why?

"Throughout the narrative, Roberts attempted repeatedly to explain 'the happiness he could find only in climbing.' He described their protective snow cave as a 'splendid inhospitable space' where there was a 'bonding of brothers, an electric tension... from a kind of communication in which the motions of our climbing were more eloquent than words.' Roberts added that this process of bonding was accompanied by an overwhelming feeling of gratitude toward the other climbers, 'an impulse like love.' And he believed this love for his comrades would be enduring: 'Someday I might be so old that all that might pierce my senility would be the vague heart pang of something lost and inexplicably sacred, maybe not even the name Huntington meaning anything to me, nor the names of three friends, but only the precious sweetness leaving its faint taste mingled with the bitter one of dying.'

"So why did Roberts write his books? I believe it was to tell a story, but more importantly, to share his humanity. In an existential passage worthy of Beckett or Camus, Roberts expresses his deepest emotions:

> Someone will see, for instance, a picture of two men beneath a mountain wall, roped together, apparently trying to climb it, and will thrill somewhat as the climbers themselves did, and wonder what it was like for them. The men in those pictures, so calm and proficient they seem to take on some of the mountain's own implacable cold, still are men, men afraid to die and capable of love.

"There's no question in my mind, Roberts's books transcend sport narrative; they are literature. Quoting the novelist E. M. Forster, 'What is wonderful about great literature is that it transforms the man who reads it towards the condition of the man who wrote it.'

"But a more relevant Forster quote for me is, 'The only books that influence us are those for which we are ready and which have gone a little farther down our particular path than we have yet ourselves.' How did Roberts's works influence me? As if hammering successive pitons into precipitous walls, Roberts's paragraphs inexorably lifted me toward a lifelong objective, a resolution of my enduring doubts about my father's actions.

"I now understand the war was his mountain and the platoon his loyal band of climbers. It was not that my father didn't love us or consider us his family. He supported us financially and provided us a decent place to live. But Dad felt his other family needed him more. They were under attack, in danger of dying, and he wanted to be there to help cover their backs. After Dad was killed at Hue, I always wondered whether he died quickly without suffering. But Roberts even taught me something there. When one of the climbers fell to his death during the Huntington descent, Roberts observed: 'But, though I could not have wanted Ed to die suffering, dying without pain or fear seems to me the equivalent of living without joy. Let us be aware of our end, because life is all we have.'"

Throughout Bill's soliloquy, the room had remained quiet and transfixed. Although time had expired some twenty minutes before, no one had made the slightest move to leave the group. After softly repeating the phrase, "because life is all we have," Bill looked up cautiously from his paper to gauge our acceptance. When he saw the smiles and nods of agreement, his eyes glistened, welled up, and grudgingly allowed a single joyful tear to roll down onto his flushed cheek. As he slowly walked back to his desk, I returned to the lectern, thanked him for his remarks, collected the students' compositions, and half-heartedly announced class was dismissed.

I stowed the students' papers in my briefcase and moved over to the doorway, where I could discreetly observe the poignant scene occurring at the back of the room. The class en masse had risen from their seats, admiringly encircled their older classmate, and begun embracing him. As I surveyed this remarkable scene, I quietly repeated to myself, "Please don't let the moment end. There will be no pictures. Burn it in the memory."

We had traveled up the mountain with Bill to the summit. We had experienced the splendid sunrise in the northeast above a frozen pastel landscape. We had sensed the surprisingly gentle winds brushing against our glowing cheeks. And we had witnessed Bill's exaltation as he scaled the final icy wall and stood triumphantly on the peak. I wondered if Bill's classmates truly appreciated or understood what they had just experienced, a rare display of raw emotional discovery in a public forum. Roberts was right, "the best moments lurk in the tension just before success." I had to admit this might have been the pinnacle for all of us. We could spend the rest of our lives treasuring this rare moment while listlessly rappelling down the mountain to the glacial floor.

4

SEVERAL TIMES DURING my cross-country career I came to the sickening realization I had little stomach for a blistering, hilly competition that day. Ironically, I never faced this overwhelming lethargy *before* a meet; it was always during the second or third mile, after the adrenaline high had begun to dissipate. And despite following the same superstitious, monastic routine before every event (drinking unsweetened tea, snacking on unbuttered toast, and most importantly, staying off my feet until it was time to race), I would inexplicably feel someone pull the plug, sow the doubt, and slow me to a jogger's pace. First, I would try to deny my misgiving; and when that was no longer possible, I would draw on a high-octane mixture of competitive spirit and intense fear of failure to hang with the lead pack for perhaps another mile or two. But when the legs and lungs really began to burn, I would lose resolve, fall off the pace into survival mode, and depending on my mood or the importance of the race, reluctantly accept either my personal failure or an unjustifiable fate.

Since I had never experienced this unsettling feeling outside competition, I tried to explain away the familiar symptoms when they first appeared in my daily life. It was the week following Bill's memorable discovery. I was leading the composition class in a discussion of their next assignment, a paper based on John McPhee's *Levels of the Game*, a brief but compelling account of the semifinal tennis match between Arthur Ashe and Clark Graebner at Forest Hills during the United States Open Championships in 1968.

"Mary, any ideas why McPhee called his book *Levels of the Game*?" I asked.

"Because the narrative actually works on a number of levels."

"For example?"

"Well, besides McPhee's description of the match from the first serve to the final point, there are at least three layers representing critical societal forces: economics, politics, and, ah, race."

"Very good! And, Richard, can you think of any other levels beyond the societal?"

"I was thinking perhaps a study of personality or psychological makeup."

"Excellent! So let's tackle these subterranean levels one at a time. Jennifer, what did we learn about the players on the economic level?"

"They were from opposite ends of the economic scale. While Graebner's folks were middle-class suburbanites—I believe his dad was a dentist—Ashe's family had far fewer resources. His dad had worked odd jobs like mowing grass, cleaning windows, and providing janitorial services."

"Very good. And, Teresa, since both were amateurs, what did the players do to make a living outside competitive tennis?"

"Graebner was a civilian, an assistant to the president of Hobson-Miller Paper Company. He enthusiastically enjoyed selling high-grade printing papers."

"What about Ashe?"

"He had attended UCLA, joined the military, and had risen to the rank of first lieutenant at West Point."

"That's right." I paused to let the note-takers catch up. "Now let's move on to a second significant level: politics. Since Ashe had known and competed against Graebner from their early teens on, how did Ashe describe his off-court friend? Let's see.... Janice."

Janice picked her head up off her desk and straightened her spine. "Ashe used very specific political labels. He said, 'Graebner is a straight, true Republican. He seems to tend that way.... Clark is tall, strong, white, Protestant, middle class, conservative.... He's tight with his money, and he wants to see the poor work for their money.'"

"Yes. And, Mary, how does Graebner describe Ashe's political leanings?"

Mary spoke with confidence. "Quoting him, he says, 'I've never really seen Arthur discipline himself. He plays the game with the lackadaisical, haphazard mannerisms of a liberal.' And I believe I've read that in the sixties 'liberal' was synonymous with the party label 'Democrat.'"

"Very good. And now let's discuss the controversial third level lurking beneath the objective description of the match: race relations in America. To provide a bit of historical context before we begin our discussion of race, do we have any

American history aficionados in the room? I see a hand there.…
Okay, Joan. What had occurred in America only months before
Ashe and Graebner met at Forest Hills?"

"Martin Luther King had been assassinated in April."

"Yes, one of the prime movers of the civil rights movement
had been killed in Memphis. Anything else?"

"Robert F. Kennedy had been gunned down in Los Angeles
in June '68."

"That's right, another strong proponent of equal rights had
been murdered. And, Joan, what did the King assassination
precipitate?"

"Race riots in over a hundred US cities including significant
violence and damage in the nation's capital."

"Yes, and, Teresa, what role did race play in the competitors'
families and in their own early lives?"

"Graebner was born into a family of white professionals
enjoying racial privilege. But Ashe's West African ancestors
had been traded into New World slavery for small quantities
of Virginia tobacco. And when the young Ashe tried entering
junior tournaments in '58 and '59, his applications were refused
or deemed 'too late' for processing."

"Very good, Teresa. So we'll leave the societal layers and
now focus on the personal level. Susan, how does a mutual
friend of Graebner and Ashe describe Ashe's demeanor?"

"I have a quote from the book, sir."

"Fine. Please read it."

"McPhee writes, 'The usual view of him is that he is cool,
even-tempered, and unemotional, and this is right to a certain

extent. His dad taught him to be humble, quiet, to live and let live, and that others are entitled to their opinions. His father was protective of Arthur—because of racial prejudice and because Arthur's mother died when he was young—and Arthur developed a shield.'"

"Yes, that's just the quote I had in mind as well. And, Mary, how does Arthur's behavior compare to Graebner's?"

"Graebner's been described as having been 'spoiled rotten when he was a kid.' They said, 'He's high-strung, and he can be very demanding. His speaking style sometimes sounds abrasive, staccato-like, but he doesn't mean it that way. It sounds pushy.'"

"That's right. So if we believe McPhee chose the title to alert us to the personal and societal levels woven into his narrative, why then would he construct such a complex, multilayered structure in the first place? I see a hand there. Yes, Linda?"

"Because McPhee's providing historical perspective and social commentary."

"But what links the subtexts to the objective description of the game?"

"I have a quote, Mr. Lynch."

"Okay, let's hear it."

"I think McPhee provides the clue early on." She lifted the book to eye level and began to read in a loud, clear voice:

> A person's tennis game begins with his nature and
> background and comes out through his motor
> mechanisms into shot patterns and characteris-
> tics of play. If he is deliberate, he is a deliberate

tennis player; and if he is flamboyant, his game probably is, too. A tight close match unmarred by error and representative of each player's game at its highest level will be primarily a psychological struggle.... Ashe feels that Graebner plays the way he does because he is a middle-class white conservative. Graebner feels that Ashe plays the way he does because he is black.

"Excellent! So in late summer '68 at Forest Hills, it was Graebner's 'steady, accurate, and conservative' game against his friend's carefree, lackadaisical, inattentive style. As they played the final games of the third set, the match statistically couldn't have been any closer. Each player had won a set. One hundred eighty-six points had been played, and each man had won ninety-three. But at that critical point in the match, Ashe began playing creatively with, as McPhee describes it, 'loose, all-out abandon—prudence be damned.' And he hit shots 'as if God Himself had given them a guarantee.' Graebner began hearing the ominous voice: 'I just can't beat this guy. I can't play the guy.' He tried rallying with stronger serves and decisive volleys, but Ashe responded with 'all-time' winners. Graebner double-faulted. He was broken.... So the tennis court is life, and we are the way we play."

As I described Graebner's valiant rally and final collapse during the deciding fourth set, I, too, heard the voice and felt the familiar misgiving, but now in a totally unfamiliar setting. It was an electric flash, so fast my mind could easily have denied its existence but for its previous haunting recurrences during my competitive career. I calmly ignored this first foreboding and continued the lecture, emphasizing the overarching theme of sports literature.

When class ended, I casually requested the students' latest compositions and assigned several model essays for the next project: Talese's brilliant portrayal of DiMaggio after baseball (and Marilyn Monroe); Updike's proof that the gods do answer letters (his eyewitness account of Ted Williams's last home run in his last at-bat of the last game of his storied career); and Wolfe's dynamic rendering of the rise of Junior Johnson and stock-car racing against a raw Appalachian backdrop of moonshine, sermons, courage, "blossomy breasts" and seersucker suits. After the last student left the room, I sank down in my chair, as spent as if I'd run five thousand meters.

Several more times during the semester the flash appeared as I lectured, each spark stronger than the one before and now accompanied by a menacing, enduring rumble of soft thunder. It was uncanny; and the triggers ranged from perceptive paragraphs in the students' own compositions to provocative passages in the model works. A student's observation about the arc of DiMaggio's life stimulated the next occurrence.

During his playing days, DiMaggio had it all: looks, money, fame, and the most beautiful woman on the planet. But after the divorce and retirement, everything changed. Although constantly surrounded by friends, fans, and business associates, DiMaggio was almost always alone. And that perverse twist in his life was a trigger for the devious flash. From my first days on campus until now, I had continuously interacted with my students, colleagues, professors, and friends; but after that first flash, I had begun to feel increasingly isolated and perhaps professionally headed in the wrong direction. I was the inverse of DiMaggio. He had everything and lost it. I had little; but with a dramatic shift in direction, perhaps I could have it all.

With each succeeding flash, the frustration, disquiet, and doubt intensified. But true to form, I, like Graebner, redoubled my efforts and bravely fought to overpower the stubborn misgivings.

The next trigger was Liebling's *Sweet Science*: "Beside when you go to a fight,… you are surrounded by people whose ignorance of the ring is exceeded only by *their unwillingness to face facts*." Next it was Sillitoe's *Long-Distance Runner* with Colin's refusal to play by conventional rules. Then it was Harris's *Bang the Drum Slowly* depicting the doomed catcher's determination to fully live out his last year on earth. And finally, near the end of the semester, it was Hemingway's *The Sun Also Rises*: "Listen Jake,… don't you ever get the feeling that all your life is going by and you're not taking advantage of it? Do you realize you've lived nearly half the time you have to live already?"

Since I had always been adept at hiding my emotions and performing well under pressure, I wasn't surprised my students, professors, and colleagues hadn't detected the psychological warfare that had dragged on into the spring semester. As the flashes continued and strengthened, I instinctively ratcheted up my responses, relying more heavily now on a primal fear of failure. Despite a weakening resolve, I felt I had no choice but to keep fighting; my back was to the wall. What would my mentor think if I left the doctoral program? And more importantly, what would I do for an encore? Unlike Graebner, I was still not broken. And unlike Roberts, I hadn't yet peeked over the icy plume at the daunting crumbly face of the impossible mountain.

Throughout the second semester, I played for time. I was a stunned fighter trying to clear my head, backpedaling with my elbows close in to protect the ribs and my gloves up against my cheeks to block the slashing shots to the head. Adopting this holding strategy actually worked to a point. Playing defense at least allowed time to sort out my feelings about earning a doctorate and joining the academic world.

I knew I enjoyed books, teaching undergraduates, writing critical essays, and vigorously exchanging ideas with students and peers. But early on I began to realize academia was more a friendship than a love affair. And my motives for coming to Pantheon and then stoically remaining in the graduate program were not pure. I had to face reality. I had come to McGill to follow in my father's footsteps, and I had continued in the program because I didn't want to disappoint my mentor, who had invested so much time in helping me succeed. My blunt assessment of the situation: I was breaking one of my mom's valued tenets. I was trying to find a way to run from something rather than enthusiastically racing toward a positive opportunity.

With no immediate resolution in sight, I buried myself in preparing for spring finals and grading my students' final compositions. There had already been many sleepless nights given the workload and the internal pressures incessantly building as the weeks passed with no logical path out of the labyrinth. I fought the exhaustion with caffeine; wonderfully rich, aromatic, yet powerful Turkish cigarettes; and strict adherence to a daily routine. The premise behind the madness was the fewer the variables, the less energy expended in nonessential activities. All my strength would then be dedicated solely to my professional responsibilities and my determined effort to cut the Gordian knot.

I had become Prufrock living out my life in coffee spoons. I would roll out of bed, shower, and immediately head over to our faculty lounge, which fortunately housed one of only two authentic Italian espresso machines on campus. After several shots of that vital energy, I was ready to face the most rigorous professional and personal challenges.

So this day began no differently or auspiciously than any of the others spanning the months since the unsettling flashes began. I had risen at seven, showered, flashed a high sign at Birmingham and the Warrior's son as I exited the gym, and trudged along in the bright May sunlight. I was headed for Redman Hall and my daily dose of the muscular blend. Admittedly, the sameness of the daily pilgrimages was both soothing and reassuring: the same chirping, the same barking, the same chimes, the same aromatic doughnuts frying, the same cop waving, the same child waiting, the same siren wailing, the same music blaring, and the same freight rumbling through our waking town. I climbed the same stairs to the same third floor, moved down the same empty hallway to the same lounge door. I opened it and discovered nothing would ever be the same again.

5

Was the soft, unexpected greeting real or just an imaginary extension of the internal conflict that had now plagued me for going on nine months? No one was ever in the lounge at this early hour. And as I made my customary sharp left turn and headed back toward the espresso machine, I didn't notice anyone sitting at the tables, at least not on the near side of the room. To be honest, the unexpected "Good morning" had startled me, causing me to pivot quickly and peer awkwardly into the shadows at the opposite end of the lounge.

Next came the obligatory feminine apology for frightening me and then my embarrassed, stammering masculine denial of the slightest sense of fear. Drawing now on my limited reserve of undergraduate method training, I nonchalantly dropped my briefcase onto the table nearest the door, switched on the rest of the overhead lights, and strode toward the back of the room to speak with the mysterious stranger.

As I neared the corner table, the dark-haired, dark-eyed beauty lithely rose from her chair, extended her hand graciously, and said, "Hi, I'm Allison." She was dressed casually in a black, scoop-neck top, faded jeans, and leather T-strap sandals highlighting her perfectly rendered dark red nails. "I'm waiting for my husband. He's giving a guest lecture upstairs to grad students on entrepreneurship."

I extended my hand. "Nice to meet you, Allison. I'm Sam. Sam Lynch. I was dropping in for my caffeine fix. So while I'm doing the brewing, could I interest you in a fine espresso or cappuccino? That's if no one's absconded with the fresh milk I've hidden in the back of the refrigerator."

No more than three minutes could have elapsed between the time she accepted my offer and the instant I returned with double espressos and several small tins of Danish butter cookies I had found stashed in a cupboard above the sink. Allison slid the book she had been reading over to the right side of the table, smiled warmly, and motioned for me to take a seat opposite her. Well, how should a relatively shy graduate student open a conversation with a stunning, dark lady perhaps ten years his senior? At least launch the dialogue objectively with your strength; there would be far less chance of a screwup. So I pointed to the book and said, "That's my favorite Capote novel. How far along have you gotten?"

Instead of answering my safe, factual question, Allison immediately enumerated a host of reasons for her reading Capote's autobiographical novel. "I thought *Other Voices* would be fascinating. I admired *In Cold Blood*. I really like Southern Gothic novels. I'd heard the main character, Joel Knox, was born in my hometown, New Orleans, and as luck would have it, I've been involved in the restoration of a mansion similar to Joel's new home at Skully's Landing."

After this surprising underspun crosscourt backhand, I had little choice but to return an easy lob. "Interesting."

To which she straightaway responded with a screaming shot down the line. "What do you believe were the major themes?"

I reacted instinctively and coolly hit a strong backhand within inches of her feet. "Alienation. Coming of age. And, ah, the unintended consequences of pursuing a missing parent." It was not the time to tempt fate. So back to the game plan of keeping it objective and conversational. "So your husband's an entrepreneur. What's his line of work?"

And thank God this time Allison followed my lead and responded to the question. "He's in the music business. Focuses mostly on emerging folk, pop, and new age artists. The Squire has a knack for finding 'diamonds in the rough,' honing their skills through initial albums and then handing his charges off to close associates who, unlike my husband, enjoy managing established artists."

"Sounds exciting. I mean, finding and shaping raw talent."

"It has its pluses and minuses. The biggest drawback, he spends a lot of time on the road, visiting music festivals, boutique clubs, and traditional coffeehouses all over the South and up and down the East Coast. And the job also requires he keep an office in Nashville for negotiating deals with artists and music executives."

"But I'm sure there are upsides."

She smiled and replied, "No question. He's his own boss and has settled in a niche providing a comfortable life."

Sensing a unique chemistry growing between us, I stayed on message and asked, "Where's home?"

"Our plantation's outside of Warfield, about thirty minutes from McGill."

"Wow. A plantation, huh?"

"Oh, we're not working it. The Squire doesn't have the time or inclination to farm the land. Been in and out of the family over the centuries."

"In and out of the family?"

She nodded, "Yes, my husband's ancestors owned and later lost the property. During the Civil War, it was the largest cotton plantation in middle Tennessee. The Squire's relatives used the wealth derived from the land to help fund the Confederate's four-year insurgency after the Union army had captured the major Tennessee cities and forts by mid-1862.

"And the Squire's ancestors lent far more than money and materials to the rebel cause. You see, three of the plantation owner's sons were heavily involved in the resistance. The eldest son ran a risky smuggling trade out of a storefront in Memphis. The middle son rode with General John Hunt Morgan on raids behind Federal lines throughout Indiana, Ohio, Kentucky, and Tennessee. And the youngest boy joined General Nathan Bedford Forrest's forces and fought at Johnsonville and Fort Pillow, where allegedly Forrest's men massacred many of the Federal troops, killing some sixty percent of the black soldiers and thirty percent of the white. Legend has it the youngest son executed two of his own father's runaways after they'd fled to

Memphis, joined a black Federal unit, and were surrounded during Forrest's assault on Fort Pillow."

I interrupted politely and asked, "But how'd they end up losing the land?"

"Well, when it became clear the owner's allegiance was to the South, Union commanders conducted several raids on the plantation, freed slaves, stole animals and supplies, and harshly interrogated the household about the whereabouts of the owner's three 'missing' sons. And after the war ended, the family tried rising up out of the proverbial ashes, but the combination of overall economic destruction from the war and the deadly yellow fever epidemic of the 1870s proved too much to bear and drove the Squire's family into bankruptcy and off their land."

Allison broke off her narrative, looked up, and surprised me by asking, "You read much Hawthorne?"

I nodded quizzically and acknowledged, "As an English major, yes, of course I have."

"You familiar with the theory about Hawthorne?"

"The theory about Hawthorne?"

"Yeah, that he laced his works with gloomy strains of Puritanism because he'd been haunted by his Puritan ancestors who'd persecuted Quakers and condemned witches to death."

I nodded. "Sure, I'm aware of it and believe it's true."

Allison then elegantly meshed this sidebar with the previous story line, comparing the Squire's attitude toward his ancestors to Hawthorne's thoughts about his. "Well, for years, just like with Hawthorne, the Squire's obsessed over his family's role in slavery. Their financial support of the rebels, their participation in the war, and especially the alleged massacre of captured black troops at Fort Pillow."

"I gotta say the Squire sounds like an interesting person. How'd he end up in the music business?"

Appearing increasingly more relaxed, she replied, "Well, after surviving the invasion of Normandy and the liberation of France and Germany, he returned home to McGill, finished his business degree at Pantheon, and then moved to Nashville where he and a college roommate founded a record company in their three-room apartment overlooking the Parthenon in Centennial Park."

I smiled. "A humble beginning...."

"Yeah, but eighteen-hour workdays seven days a week produced the valuable connections they needed. Connections to artists, agents, and well-heeled investors. And before you knew it, a four-story brick building across Fifth Avenue from the Ryman Auditorium replaced their modest apartment near the Parthenon. And for the next two decades the money rolled in as they honed their skills finding raw talent and helping the singer-songwriters mature into established stars.

"Several times a year the Squire returned home to McGill to visit relatives and check up on local charitable activities he'd established, including the Food Bank, the Jobs Bank, and the Venture Bank, which specializes in first-time loans to promising entrepreneurs." "I've heard of them," I interjected. "But I didn't know who was involved. Ah, I'm sorry, please go on."

She smiled. "No problem, Sam. Well, anyway. It was on one of these 'forays into the hinterland' as he called them, sometime during a Christmas lull, that he drove past the old plantation, which had been in the same family since the Squire's relatives forfeited the property after the Civil War. And after checking the land records at the Warfield county courthouse the next day, he headed back out to the estate, drove up the driveway to the old mansion, and knocked on the door. He said a thin elderly female voice asked, 'Who is it?' And the Squire simply responded, 'A friendly neighbor.'

"At least a half minute later the door finally opened, and an older, gray-haired lady probably in her late sixties or early seventies poked her head out into the space between the peeling door and the warped jamb. And after a brief introductory exchange, my charming husband gained the owner's confidence and suggested she join him on the porch to 'sit a spell.'

"Well, over the course of the next two hours, the Squire slowly introduced the topic of purchasing the property. He wanted to better understand the obstacles he faced to closing a deal. He learned the widow's main concerns were, one, she wouldn't have a place to go after closing the sale and, two, she was afraid the buyer would subdivide the land and build 'little boxes' where rebels once bled and died for the rebellion and General Bobby Lee.

"After assessing her objections, the Squire made a unique proposal, calming her fears. He promised to respect the land just as much as she and her family had over the years, and he suggested adding two special clauses to a cash-only contract: one, she'd continue living on the property sharing the mansion with him and his children the rest of her life, and two, he'd ensure the plantation remained intact, never allowing the land to be subdivided or sold off to developers for the remainder of his life. And over several shots of straight Tennessee whiskey, they struck a deal allowing the Squire to reclaim The Afterlife for his children and for his forebears who had fallen on hard times and lost the land."

Feeling much more comfortable now, I interrupted Allison's narrative again. "The Afterlife? An odd name for a piece of property."

But she had a logical explanation waiting in the wings. "The Squire's ancestors compared their fertile tract to a paradise, a heaven on earth. They'd tell folks they were already living in the afterlife without ever having suffered death. So that's the reason for the name with which they'd originally christened the estate and which the Squire restored after purchasing the property—despite having doubts about his ancestors' treatment of slaves who'd ironically considered the place a living hell...."

This sensitive observation appeared to be a good time to change the subject without severing the thread. I smiled and shook my head. "That's quite a story you've got there. But, ah, if I may ask, what about you? How'd you end up at The Afterlife?" When she glanced down, I urged her on. "Don't be shy now, Allison. I'd really like to know."

She looked up and smiled. "I don't know what it is, but I feel much more comfortable talking about other folks' lives and successes than I do talking about my own."

"I know what you're saying. Unless you're an egomaniac you never really feel relaxed talking about yourself. So from one shy person to another, I'd honestly like to hear your story."

Sensing my honesty and empathy, she gazed into my eyes and relented, smiling. "Okay, then. I wouldn't do this for everybody…. I'm a seventh-generation Creole from one of the earliest families to settle Opelousas, Saint Landry Parish, Louisiana. Music's been a great part of my life from the very beginning. While on any given night my dad would be playing the accordion, fiddle, or rub board in a local Zydeco band, my mom might be playing the piano at social events or perhaps teaching music in the front parlor, or rehearsing next Sunday's soprano solo in the Catholic church choir.

"I was truly blessed. I'd been exposed to so many types of instruments and styles of music, ranging from the Louisiana blues to Beethoven. But following my mother's lead, I finally settled on the piano and began writing songs and playing small local venues when I turned eighteen. Well, a couple of years passed, and one evening while I was playing at a local pub, a new customer approached me during the break and strongly recommended I travel to Kerrville, Texas, northwest of San Antonio, and attend one of the largest folk festivals in the country."

"Why's that?"

"You mean why'd he recommend I attend the festival?"

I nodded. "Yeah."

"He believed Kerrville could be very helpful in jump-starting my career. He said there'd be singer-songwriters galore and many styles of music—from bluegrass, acoustic rock, and traditional folk to blues, jazz, and Appalachian Mountain. He said the emphasis there was always on emerging artists; and while the evening stage shows were fine for seeing established stars, he recommended tenting in one of the designated campgrounds where I could jam daily with experienced players and perhaps meet up with one of the many legitimate promoters prowling the grounds for original talent."

"Did you do it?"

"Ah, no. Well, not at first. I thought it'd be a long shot. So I mulled it over the rest of the year, continued writing songs, and rotated every two weeks or so among respected establishments in central and western Tennessee. But the following spring I decided to take the leap. I was encouraged with what was happening."

"What's that?"

"Well, it seemed the more time I spent writing, the more polished my ballads became. And I knew things were changing when I noticed the bar patrons were putting their drinks down and spending more time listening than carousing and shouting across the room."

I laughed. "Been there, done that."

"I know. We've all been guilty at one time or another."

"I'm sorry. Go on."

"So following the stranger's advice, I invested in a tent and camping gear, drove my beat-up 1963 Wagonaire down to Kerrville, and maneuvered my way into one of the largest campgrounds surrounding the festival site. With the help of my neighbors, I erected the tent, built a fire, and grilled my first outdoor meal, which I shared with these kindred spirits. And just as the stranger said, I found myself jamming with top-notch musicians and discussing songwriting with artists from New York to California."

Allison looked up toward the lights. Her expression became wistful and reminiscent. She lowered her voice to a whisper. "I remember meeting him as if it were yesterday. It was the evening of the third day of performances. Most of the musicians in our 'neighborhood' decided to skip the nightly stage show to gather around the campfire and share compositions. When it was my turn to perform, I sang two of my songs a cappella—my upbeat, humorous, 'General Mischief and Mayhem,' and a soulful, confessional ballad about painful breakups, 'Flight from Opelousas.' While the up-tempo, nonsensical 'Mayhem' evoked laughter and applause, 'Flight's' serious subject matter reduced everyone to a reflective murmur, that is, everyone except a baritone immediately to my left who said, 'When we shut up shop tonight, I'd like to speak with you privately.'

"Well, out of deference to families attending the festival with children, the campfire sing-around ended between ten-thirty and eleven o'clock with everyone contributing to a soulful rendition of 'The Streets of Laredo.' As the gathering dispersed, the voice said something about the chill in the night air and then helped me wrap up in my grandmother's shawl."

"The Squire?" I asked.

She nodded and smiled.

"He say anything about your songs or your singing?"

She nodded again. "He suggested we follow a moonlit path down to a small stream running through the campground. As we walked along the bank, he said, 'That second song was haunting. Anguished. Full of truth. I agree with your lyric. We can occasionally touch the hearts of others, but rarely ever really know them. And I don't know if anyone's ever told you, but you've got a helluva voice too. It's sharp, expressive, crystalline. Do you play any instruments?' I kept walking and looking straight ahead. I replied simply, 'Piano and some guitar.'

"As the Squire reached into his pocket and retrieved a business card, he asked, 'You ever thought about a professional career?' I explained I'd always dreamed of it but felt at least up until recently I hadn't written enough quality works to produce a solid album, let alone plan a national tour. I'll never forget—he smiled broadly and countered with, 'I'm willing to risk it if you are.' I nodded I was ready to take the leap and excitedly extended my hand to seal the deal."

"Just like that?"

She laughed aloud. "Yeah, just like that." She caught herself, looked around, and saw that faculty and staff were beginning to show up for their daily caffeine fix. She lowered her voice and continued, "But it gets even better. You see, two years, two albums, and a summer tour later, the Squire telephoned and asked me to drop by his Nashville office 'for a brief chat.' I assumed it was to check on my progress writing songs for the third album. Well, he escorted me into the office, closed the door, and motioned for me to take a seat. He sat down in his executive's chair, leaned forward, stared directly into my eyes, and spoke seriously in his baritone drawl. He said, 'Allison, there's something I've been considering for some time now. You've developed so much professionally in the last two years—think of how much the crowds, the fan mail, and the record sales have grown. In fact, you practically sold out every venue on the tour last summer. So I really believe you're ready now to make the move up to the next level. And as I explained early on, what truly excites me is finding the new talent, nurturing it through a couple albums, and then backing off and allowing my associates to manage the rise to the top.'

"I confess I was stunned and concerned how this drastic change could impact my confidence and career. Sensing my fear, the Squire moved over to where I was sitting, put his arm around my shoulder, and stayed there beside me until the initial shock had worn off. He then returned to his executive's chair behind the desk and resumed his soliloquy. 'Allison,' he said, 'there's something else I've been mulling over for many months. Despite serious temptations along the way, I've never become emotionally involved with any of the prospects I've represented.

"'And as you know, my wife died several years before I met you. I was lonely and spending much of my time caring for my eight-year-old twin boys, Zach and Beau, and my precious four-year-old daughter, Carolina, whom God gave me in exchange for a loving wife. But the more time I spent with you, the more I understood I wanted to be something more than your managing agent. It took everything in me to resist the attraction. I had to remind myself to stay focused on the music and resist my fascination with your beauty, charm, and exceptional talent.

And I successfully made it to this hour, when I can now openly express how I really feel about you.'

"I sat there too stunned to say anything while he made his proposal. 'All I ask is you fairly consider the possibility,' he said. 'I know there's a considerable age difference. I know we've spoken about your unfortunate relationships in the past. I know you would be inheriting a family of five from the very beginning with little or no time for us to bond. And yes, I know there will always be the professional pressures of preparing for tours and traveling for months on end. But please don't reject the idea out of hand.

"'I promise I won't push you. You'll have all the time and space you need to decide the future. So let's spend the next six months enjoying each other's company outside the hurly-burly of the music business. It's something I've dreamed of for some time now, having you curled up close to me on the sofa near the fire in The Afterlife. Are you willing to give it a shot?'"

Allison looked me full in the face. "Well, how did you respond?" I asked.

"I paused," she said with a laugh, "and then said I'd be willing to try as long as he kept his word and didn't pressure me into a life decision. But it didn't take me very long to know where I really belonged. The children were bright, energetic, and clearly accepting of me as a potentially 'hip' stepmom. The Squire was kind, gracious, and true to his word. He never made even the slightest demand. He kept his business trips to a minimum because he wanted to make those next six months all about having fun and living in the moment."

Allison then hinted, or maybe I inferred, that she knew almost immediately she was falling in love with the much older Squire. But it was not the passionate sexual love of her teens and early twenties. It was a much more substantial, rounded, mature blend of respect, intellect, charm, and common interest with a modest degree of physical attraction added to the mix. After all, she had just turned thirty-five, and the Squire was nearing sixty, somewhat eccentric in dress, and usually consumed by business and philanthropic activities.

"So what happened after the six months?" I asked.

Allison beamed and replied, "We had an outdoor wedding and reception in the restored gardens of The Afterlife. The ceremony was a celebration of family. The Squire's twins served as handsome 'best men,' and his daughter 'assisted' me as an adorable bridesmaid. And we even convinced 'Grandma,' the former owner of The Afterlife, to join the proceedings as my matron of honor."

As she transitioned to a description of their honeymoon in New Orleans, the lounge door swung open and a large figure strode in and gazed toward our table at the far end of the room. All I remember about this first encounter with the imposing Squire was the predominance of white—his long, wavy hair, his short boxed beard, his brilliant gentleman's top hat and attire, and especially his broad, gleaming smile with only the slightest hint of yellow gold. As he approached the table, I spontaneously stood and braced for a vigorous handshake from the animated Squire who had extended his hand some ten paces before arriving at our spot.

He was the quintessential entrepreneurial producer-agent—distinguished, wealthy, ruggedly handsome, confident, positive, and imminently capable of sucking all the oxygen out of a room. My pulse quickened as the Squire introduced himself and firmly grasped my outstretched hand. He then immediately turned to his wife and apologized for making her wait so long. He explained the graduate students were so engaged discussing his financial successes he felt he shouldn't impose a time limit on the Q&A.

After reassuring Allison he had already telephoned the estate planner to inform the fellow they would be "a little late," he turned to me, expressed regrets they had to leave immediately, and then quickly escorted his wife to the door. Throughout this brief exchange, Allison remained silent, focusing all her attention on the dynamic Squire. But as she followed her spirited husband to the lounge door, she looked back, paused at the entrance, and smiled as if to say, "Thank you. I enjoyed the conversation and hope we'll meet again sometime."

After Allison and the Squire disappeared into the hallway, I stood at the back table stunned, motionless, and staring down at the empty espresso cups and Capote's *Other Voices, Other Rooms*, which she had left behind. Did our meeting really happen or did I simply layer another menacing level of complexity onto an already daunting internal conflict? How could I have ever imagined this conversation with one of the most beautiful people I'd ever met? That would be crazy. It had to be real. Look at the evidence: the empty cup with traces of lipstick about the rim, the dog-eared novel of alienation and discovery, and the sweet lingering fragrance of freshly crushed roses wafting about the space.

But next, the insistent regressive doubts. Allison had alluded to Hawthorne, who masterfully negotiated the illusive line between fantasy and reality. Was the puritanical Young Goodman Brown holding his wife's pink ribbon or was he the victim of a nightmare conjured up out of inner conflict? Did an ambitious guest seeking fame actually visit a family in the notch that awful night and share their gloomy fate in the landslide? Or should we agree with the deniers who didn't believe "there were sufficient grounds for such a conjecture"? But all this speculation would have to wait. I had papers to grade and final exams to take the following week. I picked up Allison's book, retrieved my briefcase, and headed back to the espresso machine doggedly determined to suspend analysis of this consuming variable and return to my daily routine.

After a productive day poring over Milton and grading lengthy compositions, I stopped by the Two-Way Café to reward myself with comfort food: five-way chili, saltines, and a cold draught beer. I found a seat near the center of the bar directly in front of the Two-Way's showcase, the large antique mirror with the impressive etching of General P. G. T. Beauregard on horseback, cavalry saber drawn above his head, leading his charging Confederate forces into fierce battle at nearby Shiloh, Tennessee.

Since it was early in the week, there were only a few patrons scattered about the room—one fellow at the far end of the bar and several couples milling about the tables quietly discussing Bloomsday and minor league baseball. Over my left shoulder in a dark corner at the back of the room a talented local musician sang and strummed covers of "Pennsylvania Sunrise," "Golden, Golden," and "Roseville Fair." Since I was the only customer listening to his solid renditions, I made it a point of stopping by the small stage on my way out to congratulate the young man on his shamefully ignored performance.

As I walked home from the Two-Way, I began preparing my battle plan for the evening: read Milton's *L' Allegro, Il Penseroso,* and *Lycidas* and then double back to Donne's posthumously published *Songs and Sonnets.* After climbing the thirteen linoleum steps to the Warrior's loft, I sat down on the overstuffed traditional sofa, dragged the thick, heavy anthology out of my briefcase, and wedged myself against the rolled arm with one-of-a-kind throw pillows touting a San Juan fight club and autographed by early Puerto Rican champions Sixto Escobar and Carlos Ortiz.

I made surprisingly good headway through *L' Allegro, Il Penseroso,* and *Lycidas*; but when it came to Donne's lyrics, my pace slowed considerably, not because I was wearing down but because I was becoming more engaged with the remarkable beauty of the lines. And then it happened. The subconscious confluence of three experiences I'd had that day—meeting Allison and her producer husband, listening to the young performer at the Two-Way, and then reading Donne's extraordinary

Songs—mysteriously turned my head toward the front corner of the room where my guitar case stood propped against the wall, untouched since the day I'd moved into the apartment. Trancelike, I placed the open book on the end table next to the sofa and retrieved the beloved instrument I had neglected far too long.

Ironically, my acceptance to Boston's Berklee College of Music and my brief stay there as an undergraduate were based solely on my keyboard skills, not on any raw talent I possessed for the guitar. While I'd received professional training on the piano beginning at age eight, I'd never touched a six- or twelve-string until I reached my midteens. I was completely self-taught listening to Leadbelly, Renbourn, Kottke, and Towner and relied on unconventional fingering and tuning to compose and perform. So I suspect the many years of keyboard practice and pressured junior recitals finally took their toll, and I began thinking of the piano simply as a predictable long-term friend. But almost immediately, the guitar became a passionate lover helping me mine the most unexpected, undiscovered emotions.

I said I'd neglected the guitar far too long, and that goes for the piano as well. After a semester and a half at Berklee, I became the teenage protagonist of *Other Voices, Other Rooms*. I was driven to know my missing father. I wanted to get as close to him as I possibly could by following in his footsteps. I would drop out of Berklee, become an undergraduate English major at a respectable college, and then attend Pantheon for my doctorate in literature. So as I embarked on that long-term, personal mission demanding high levels of focus, determination, and commitment, I mistakenly concluded that practicing, performing, or creating music would be a highly suspect use of valuable time.

But when I sat back down on the Warrior's sofa, opened the hard case, and lifted the guitar out of its protective cradle for the first time in years, I sensed the pendulum was beginning to shift in the opposite direction. The memories began welling up: chancing upon the used instrument on the back wall of a ramshackle music store in a seedy section of Memphis; spending hours alone in my bedroom playing the same chords and short pieces over and over again; and then performing for the first time in public at the highly popular Jefferson County fair.

The old Bavarian acoustic had by now become a certified antique. It was a Framus twelve-string, Model 5/024, mahogany, nineteen frets, floating bridge, with a unique rosette around the sound hole. But what made my Framus Hootenanny even more special was that it was identical to the instrument Lennon had played throughout 1964–65 and in the Beatles' film *Help!*

I was surprised how much memory remained in the fingers, moving automatically from D to the more difficult barre chords and then on to fragments of tunes I miraculously recalled from the past. As I continued playing, I caught the anthology out of the corner of my eye, and the creative juices began flowing. Why not try writing a melody to accompany one of Donne's brilliant works from *Songs and Sonnets*? I placed the thick anthology on the table in front of me and focused on the last lyric I'd read, simply entitled "Song."

Sweetest love, I do not go,
For weariness of thee,
Nor in hope the world can show
A fitter love for me;
But since that I
At the last must part, 'tis best,
Thus to use myself in jest
By feigned deaths to die....

O how feeble is man's power,
That if good fortune fall,
Cannot add another hour,
Nor a lost hour recall;
But come bad chance,
And we join to it our strength,
And we teach it art and length,
Itself o'er us to advance....

Let not thy divining heart
Forethink me any ill;
Destiny may take thy part,
And may thy fears fulfil.
But think that we
Are but turn'd aside to sleep.
They who one another keep
Alive, ne'er parted be.

6

IRONICALLY, HOPEFUL SCENARIOS can intensify ambivalence and uneasiness. Before meeting Allison and the Squire, hearing the musician at the Two-Way, and reading Donne's *Songs and Sonnets*, I'd never believed I was agonizing over a false, improbable choice. I thoroughly understood how I had gotten into the conflicted situation—attending graduate school out of a blind, stubborn respect for a missing, imaginary father and then fighting the growing impulse to pack it in. But I never acted on the urge to leave Pantheon because something in the back of my mind was continually questioning the feasibility of abandoning academia midstream and irrationally embarking on some new, risky, undefined career.

But in only a matter of hours, Allison, the Squire, the Two-Way musician, and Donne had collectively changed the equation, offering a practicable way out of my long-standing dilemma. Ah, but there's the rub. A viable alternative to a life-time of scholarship demanded a consequential decision, thus raising the stakes and my anxiety to even higher levels than before. And there were so many important variables to assess. Could I polish my guitar skills to breakout levels? Could I write relevant, contemporary songs that would get plenty of airtime?

Could I convince a producer to take a substantial risk on an untested artist? And how would I ever explain to my fatherlike mentor I was forsaking a respectable scholar's life to become a globetrotting bohemian troubadour?

Despite wanting to resolve the issue immediately, I understood it would require a rational approach over a reasonable period of time. So I quickly decided to remain at Pantheon and begin tackling the difficult questions that I knew would ultimately define the future. Since I really had no place to go after final exams, I had preregistered for two summer classes to expedite completion of the course requirements before undertaking the doctoral thesis and defending it before the committee. But after picking up the guitar, beginning to practice, and thinking about writing songs again, I felt justified in scaling back to only one advanced seminar, a challenging course on the English Romantic poets.

While the world was suffering famine, tropical cyclones, collapsing dams, and multiple deadly air crashes that summer, I remained keenly focused on the game plan: writing effective essays for the graduate seminar, practicing for hours on end, and even dusting off some of my musical "juvenilia," which I'd unceremoniously relegated to a cigar box when I left home for Berklee. I essentially led a monastic life—no bars, no women, no movies, no anything. I rarely left the loft except to buy groceries, attend classes, or visit the research library.

I focused solely on the holy triumvirate of essays, practice, and songs, that is, except for one Saturday in July when I arrived at the Two-Way for an early breakfast just in time to hear the

British broadcaster's opening announcement on the television: "It's twelve noon in London, seven a.m. in Philadelphia, and around the world it's time for Live Aid." I easily rationalized the diversion. The megaconcert was definitely related to my personal mission, and frankly, when would I ever have another chance to see Dylan, Zeppelin, and Queen performing over the course of a day?

I also caught a break from Professor Taylor, who I was sure would have questioned my priorities if he had been around to discover what I was up to. But fortuitously, he had scheduled a unique trip to Tuscany and Umbria to follow his own passion. Henry James, a favorite of my adviser's, had published the travel essay "A Chain of Cities" in 1909, describing his scenic and artistic exploration of the timeless mountainous villages of Assisi, Perugia, Cortona, and Arezzo on the narrow, twisting road between Florence and Rome. The professor was tracing James's steps, leaving me to enjoy a musical phenomenon in peace.

When fall classes began after Labor Day, everyone was back in his place. The professor was teaching and mentoring. I was studying, lecturing, practicing, and writing. The Warrior's son was closing a deal to bring a bantamweight championship fight to Warfield. Birmingham was putting his young fighters through their paces after returning from another of his mysterious trips back East. And according to the gossipy

McGill Herald Weekly, the Squire was "visiting" Nashville to sign his latest phenom while Allison was in rehearsals for the first phase of her upcoming "Hallowed Walls" tour beginning in late September in Napa Valley and ending in Santa Fe just before the Thanksgiving holidays.

As the semester progressed into November, I'd never felt more comfortable with what I had undertaken and what I was actually accomplishing. I had tackled four major challenges, two academic and two musical, and I was succeeding at all of them. The graduate courses on the rise of the novel, contemporary English theater, and the American transcendental movement were surprisingly stimulating primarily because of the lively exchanges between the outstanding young professors and my highly motivated classmates.

My advanced composition course, Musical Forays into Literature and Drama, was loaded with remarkably bright, energetic undergraduates, who expected far more creativity from the course work and from me than I had ever anticipated. As far as the music goes, any spare time beyond the graduate studies and the lectures was devoted entirely to demanding practice sessions and serious attempts at meaningful songwriting.

And there was a unique synergy between the academic and creative worlds; the harder I worked at the music, the better I performed in class and vice versa. I speculated the reason for the beneficial interaction was that working hard musically led to greater relaxation and better performance in the graduate studies and the lectures, and that this psychological calm, in turn, greatly increased my confidence in playing and writing songs.

By Thanksgiving I had surpassed the guitar metaphysics of my earlier years and was now playing complex, experimental riffs across changing chords and harmonies. And after bravely venturing into the creative abyss, I proudly possessed two greatly enhanced younger works and five new songs, including "Missing You," "Skully's Landing," and "Missouri Fever." Unlike almost everyone else on campus, I really had no place to go for the Thanksgiving break. So I took Mom's advice about making lemonade from lemons and omelets from broken eggs and decided to make the most of the day.

I had read in the *McGill Gazette* that the Squire's Food Bank would be distributing holiday dinners to shut-ins the day before Thanksgiving and then sponsoring a sit-down meal the following day in the basement of Saint Paul's Episcopal next door to the Food Bank warehouse. So why not go over to the church on Thanksgiving and help with the preparation and the cleanup after the meal? I would be doing some good for the community; and perhaps, if lucky, I would reconnect with Allison and the Squire.

But circumstances are never as simple as when we first imagine them. When I awoke on Thanksgiving morning and pulled the curtain back, I was greeted to deep blowing drifts and horizontal snow. My first impulse was to climb back into bed because who in their right mind would risk going out in a freak blizzard? My second thought, however, was perhaps this could be one of those rare moments of truth when the gods actually reward us for crashing through the barriers. So I resolved to shower, trim the beard, don the winter parka and boots, wrap Allison's book up in a small plastic bag, and stride out into the fierce storm determined to help the homeless and hopefully spend a little time with real music professionals who might reciprocate someday.

After trudging six difficult blocks through the driving snow, I arrived at old Saint Paul's around nine o'clock, found the outside stairwell leading down to the church dining area and kitchen, and entered the snowbound building. At the far end of the massive kitchen on the wall above a fieldstone fireplace, the prophet Micah's stirring words aptly described the bustling activity occurring throughout the room: AND WHAT DOTH THE LORD REQUIRE OF THEE, BUT TO DO JUSTLY, TO LOVE MERCY, AND TO WALK HUMBLY WITH THY GOD.

Aluminum pots, skillets, and pans of all shapes and sizes hung from the rafters and from large swinging wrought-iron hooks bolted into the plaster walls. Henry Ford would have been proud of this productive assembly. Six parishioners stood on either side of three long tables preparing the afternoon meal. There was an elegant division of labor: table 1 prepared the turkeys and cornbread stuffing for the oven; table 2 was responsible for vegetables, salads, and homemade cranberry sauce; and table 3 worked diligently on the pumpkin pies and rich, dark chocolate cakes. I thought, "This is one of those rare moments when we witness scripture transformed into sacred action."

Unfortunately, these were hard times in McGill requiring so much more beneficence than ever before. The oil and gasoline shocks of the seventies were followed by a rare double-dip recession in the early eighties, which sent joblessness skyrocketing to the highest levels since the Great Depression. While liberal economic policies had moderated unemployment a bit, the number of chronically unemployed living in shelters and on the streets remained unacceptably high. And if it were not for the kindness of strangers and generous souls like the Squire, Allison, and the Saint Paul's parishioners, the ill-fated would likely starve or freeze to death on the streets.

After unzipping my parka and cleaning the thick condensation from my wire-rim glasses, I moved from the warm, busy kitchen into the spacious dining room, which was surprisingly already overflowing with folk who had been transported over from the homeless shelter near McGill General. While some of the parishioners were handing out hot cider with cinnamon, others were setting up sound equipment in the back corner for a Thanksgiving sing-along to entertain all of us while the food was simmering in the ovens.

I scanned the room and discovered Allison and the Squire were missing. Catching the attention of one of the church members, I said, "So sorry to bother you. Have you seen Allison or the Squire this morning?"

"Oh no, honey, not yet," she said with a warm Southern drawl. "Apparently the storm kept the Squire from getting out of Nashville in time for dinner. I believe he'll be joining the festivities once the Highway Department clears the main roads."

"Oh, that's too bad.… Ah, what about Allison? Is she around?"

"Allison," she said, "arrived earlier this morning in the teeth of the storm. That's thanks to Chief Holland's reliable four-wheel-drive." She motioned upstairs and said I would probably find Allison in the office wing adjacent to the auditorium reserved for Sunday services.

I thanked the woman and did my best not to skip with excitement as we parted. I located the stairs, climbed to the first floor, and entered the cavernous hall dimly lit by a dozen or so recessed lights strategically placed to illuminate the emergency exits. At the far end of the auditorium, near the pulpit, I noticed a door on the left stood partially open, allowing a bright shaft of light to flood into the darkened space. I walked down the center aisle, stopped beneath the elevated lectern, and called out Allison's name.

"I'll be out in a minute," she responded.

I sat down in a front pew and swung around to admire an excellent replica of a Chagall stained-glass masterpiece, which had been installed in England's ancient Chichester Cathedral in the 1970s. On the right-hand side of the rose, cerulean, and brilliant white window, a figure held a testament of praise. At the midpoint of the panels, two worshippers raised a golden menorah, and near the top of the work King David strummed his harp and surely sang one of his most celebratory Psalms:

> Praise ye the Lord. Praise God in his sanctuary: praise him in the firmament of his power.

Praise him for his mighty acts: praise him according to his excellent greatness.

Praise him with the sound of the trumpet: praise him with the psaltery and harp.

Several minutes later, Allison pushed the office door open wider and entered the auditorium accompanied by two thin, stooped older women. As she approached, she appeared puzzled, obviously trying to place me almost six months after our meeting and now in a totally different setting. I blurted out short phrases trying to help her recollect: "Spring semester," "faculty lounge," "graduate student," "waiting for your husband," "Truman Capote," and the clincher, "*Other Voices, Other Rooms*." Allison then smiled broadly, thrust her hand out, and said, "It's really good to see you again." I responded, "likewise," and explained I had dropped by to help out with the Thanksgiving dinner and hopefully to spend a few minutes afterward getting caught up since we had last spoken. She turned to the women, informally introduced me to "Anna" and "Jennie," and then suggested the ladies go on downstairs ahead of us, promising we would follow along shortly.

After the women disappeared into the hallway at the back of the auditorium, Allison clarified the situation. "Anna and Jennie are homeless widows who prefer living on the streets. They're afraid they'll be abused in the public shelter. As the storm intensified last night, church members found them and finally persuaded them to stay at the shelter after promising to spend the night there with them providing 'protection.' I'd brought them upstairs here to shower and dress in some winter clothes Grandma had donated. We'd gotten a call from one of the parishioners this morning saying they had two widows at the church in need of 'new' clothing."

I smiled admiringly and said, "You and the members here are doing what my mom called 'the Lord's work.'" I paused and then added lightheartedly, "And I think it's high time I get downstairs and pitch in either with the meal or the sing-along."

As we walked up the carpeted aisle toward the vestibule, Allison made my day. She said, "Once we've finished straightening up the place after dinner, let's sit down and get caught up on the past six months."

By the time we got downstairs to the kitchen, the industrious church members had already finished preparing and loading the stuffed fowl, sweet potatoes, green bean casseroles, and pumpkin pies into the large stainless commercial ovens. Allison smiled, shrugged her shoulders, and said, "Well, if we can't be of use here, let's go see if we can help out with the sing-a-long."

As we entered the room, the Saint Paul choral director and a half dozen of the regionally renowned choir were stepping up onto the risers in the back corner. Several minutes later the director turned toward the excited guests, waved his left arm back and forth to quiet the crowd, and encouraged everyone to sing along. He then raised and lowered his baton to signal the initial beat of a familiar Thanksgiving hymn, "Come Ye Thankful People, Come":

Come, ye thankful people, come, raise the song of
harvest home;
All is safely gathered in, ere the winter storms begin.
God our Maker doth provide for our wants to be supplied;
Come to God's own temple, come, raise the song of
harvest home.

I stared at the floor, embarrassed, as the director announced the next hymn, "Thy Bounties, Gracious Lord," and then waved his baton vigorously:

Thy bounties, gracious Lord,
With gratitude we own;
We bless Thy providential grace,
Which show'rs its blessings down.

As the choir prepared for a third existential moment, I continued looking down, smiling ironically and silently questioning, "Doesn't anyone here grasp the juxtaposition of the audience to the verses?" The director then raised his arm and launched a third awkward assault, "My God I Thank Thee":

My God, I thank Thee, Who hast made
The earth so bright,
So full of splendor and of joy,
Beauty and light;
So many glorious things are here,
Noble and right.

Just when I thought the unwitting insensitivity would never end, the director approached the microphone, alluded to "a consummate artist in attendance today," and then encouraged everyone to welcome Allison to "our makeshift stage." As the welcoming applause crescendoed, the singer-songwriter beamed confidently, stepped up onto the platform, and headed for the old Baldwin upright positioned stage left.

In sharp contrast to the choir's traditional Thanksgiving Day hymns, Allison opened with B. F. White's upbeat, revival spiritual, "The Morning Trumpet." And after hearing only the first few bars, I knew the Squire had perfectly captured the essence of her strong mezzo-soprano: sharp, expressive, and crystalline. She continued with a second lively spiritual, "Now Let Me Fly," which had all of us tapping our feet and singing along:

> Meet that Hypocrite on the street,
> First thing he does is to show his teeth,
> Next thing he does is to tell a lie,
> And the best thing to do is to pass him by.

Allison then effortlessly transitioned from the light-hearted to a soulful study of forgiveness and redemption with a haunting interpretation of the familiar folk hymn "Amazing Grace," highlighting the rich, unique timber, texture, and color of her voice.

> Amazing Grace, how sweet the sound,
> That saved a wretch like me.

I once was lost but now am found,

Was blind, but now, I see.

She paused briefly as if to allow the hopeful message to permeate the hall, and then announced, "I'm gonna close out my set with a new piece, which I'm thinking of adding to my tour performances after the first of the year. Now, I'm a little nervous, you hear?" she joked while strumming the opening chords. "I've never played this song in public but I think this has to be the ideal venue, trying out a new song in a church full of the most forgiving people in Tennessee." She paused until the applause and cheering died down and then continued, "I heard this last piece recently on a Canadian singer-songwriter's latest album release. There are several well-known biblical allusions buried in the lyrics. And I like the message that even an imperfect love for others can help us overcome our greatest difficulties and fears."

As Allison introduced her final number, I got an idea. I asked the guitarist if I could borrow his twelve-string for a few minutes. After holding the instrument up discreetly to catch Allison's attention, I first pointed to the guitar, then to me, and finally to the platform. She understood the message immediately and subtly motioned for me to join her on the stage. When Allison had finished her introductory comments, I stepped up onto the platform, asked her for a low E, and then nodded I was ready to accompany her on the still unidentified song.

She played the beautiful opening bars and then sang in perfect pitch. I began playing and joined her in singing the hallelujahs of each chorus. She looked over toward me, smiled, and shook her head incredulously out of a sense of surprise, joy, and artistic respect. At that moment I felt somewhere deep inside of us our souls were merging. It was an intense emotion, one that would have to be buried beneath layers of convention; after all, she was married to a caring husband who had launched her career, was stepmother to three young children who had longed for a new mom, lived in a mansion surrounded by every amenity you could imagine, and enjoyed the love and respect of hundreds of thousands of fans, who admired her fairytale life and meteoric rise toward the top. When we had sung the last hallelujahs, she rose from the piano bench and signaled for me to join her at center stage. We embraced momentarily, turned toward the applause, grasped hands, and bowed slowly and deeply. I whispered to myself, "What a glorious way to end the beginning of a memorable day."

After the guests had feasted and boarded the church buses for the snow-packed ride back to the shelter, those of us left at the church pitched in to wash the dishes, clean the dining-room tables, and strike our rudimentary set. Anna and Jennie had remained behind. Since they had expressed reluctance to return to the shelter without "proper protection," Allison had offered to put them up at The Afterlife for a few days until the snow melted and the nighttime temperatures had moderated a bit. When all the parishioners had left for home, Annie and Jennie migrated to the warm, inviting hearth to await the Squire's arrival from Nashville. He had telephoned the church earlier to say he was on his way to pick up Allison and the holiday meals the members had prepared especially for him, the children, and Grandma, who had graciously offered to stay behind with the twins and Carolina because of the severe weather.

After Anna and Jennie had settled in next to the glowing fireplace, Allison and I moved to the dining room and sat down at one of the tables nearest the kitchen where we could attend to the ladies and hear the Squire's knocking when he arrived. I opened the conversation with an apology. "I'm sorry, Allison. I have something of yours I need to return." As I pulled *Other Voices* from the protective wrap, I explained, "I searched everywhere here for an address or telephone number...."

Allison cocked her head to one side and teased, "You'd better be glad I'd just finished reading that when you walked into the faculty lounge that morning or you would've had hell to pay."

I slid the book across the table and changed the subject. "Well, Capote was the first thing we had in common and now this today."

She shook her head and replied, "You never told me you played or sang. You just don't know how rare and magical that 'Hallelujah' was for a professional expecting performances to usually fall within limits, never below average, and seldom exceeding our own expectations. But once in a while we performers capture the lightning before enthusiastic audiences and then spend weeks, months, or even years trying to replicate the soaring feeling of the spark arcing to flame. But here we were today covering a complicated new song totally unrehearsed in a church dining hall filled with the homeless who had been bused over from the town shelter for, of all things, a Thanksgiving Day meal to celebrate their many blessings. Somehow, someway we sparked the fire in them and in ourselves. I can't explain what happened, but I'll never forget it. This was really special."

"So how'd you find out about the song?" I asked. "My understanding is that it hasn't gotten any airplay here because Cohen's label had refused to release the *Various Positions* album in the US."

"Ah, the Squire received an advance copy of the LP. Foreign talent agents and promoters know the Squire's made lucrative business deals and promoted top-flight concerts in the Midwest and the South. He brought the vinyl home from Nashville. Suggested I listen to it and then we'd discuss the tracks. After playing the record several times, I felt comfortable bringing the topic up over dinner. The Squire said he believed every song on the album was strong but felt there was one in particular that had a chance to be remembered, to be great.

"He then asked me to pick the song I thought would endure; and with so many potential candidates, I chose a piece other than the one the Squire had in mind. He then revealed his counterintuitive choice, 'Hallelujah'—a song that he believes if it were ever released in the US, would still never get airplay. It lasts over five minutes, has difficult, ambiguous lyrics, and contains interwoven sexual and biblical references, which would offend over half the population. But he quickly added, notwithstanding the commercial drawbacks, he believed 'Hallelujah' was a great song that I should strongly consider adding to my concert repertoire."

Allison then returned the favor. "So how did you find out about the song? As you've said, it's virtually unknown here."

"It was just by chance. One of the undergraduates in my advanced composition course, Musical Forays into Literature and Drama, had returned home to Montreal over a weekend for his brother's wedding, heard the Cohen piece playing in a suburban record store, and immediately purchased the newly released album. Over the past three years, he had become a Cohen aficionado, having rescued all six of Cohen's earlier studio albums from various used-record bins across the continent. His fourth assignment of this semester was to draft a brief composition comparing and contrasting thematic materials from a descriptive essay to those of a contemporary piece of music of his own choosing.

"His composition was provocative and brilliant. He selected Heywood Hale Broun's 1921 essay, 'Sport for Art's Sake,' which had appeared in the Pulitzers' *New York World*; and then because he was a Cohen fan now armed with the singer's first studio album in five years, he chose Cohen's bluesy rock anthem, 'Hallelujah.'"

"But why the 1921 Broun piece?" Allison asked.

"That's funny. I had the same question. So after handing him back his paper with a solid 'A,' I asked him. He explained his grandfather had met the wildly popular Georges Carpentier of France, the light heavyweight champion and heroic subject of

Broun's essay, during the boxer's promotional visit to Montreal in May 1920. And from that point on until the day he died, the grandfather never stopped retelling the story and proudly showing every family member the autographed program validating his account of that memorable day."

"So what did the student have to say? In the essay, I mean."

"In the opening paragraphs of his composition he first set the scene—July 2, 1921, Jersey City, New Jersey, heavyweight championship fight, over ninety thousand spectators comprising boxing's first million-dollar gate, first radio broadcast of a mass event, and a key landmark launching the 'Golden Age of Sport.' It was a much smaller World War I ace, Carpentier, fighting the long odds against the larger 'Slacker,' Dempsey, who unlike his heroic opponent, had allegedly avoided the military draft.

"In summary, it was David versus Goliath and for just eleven seconds of the second round the crowd felt they were witnessing a miracle. Carpentier nailed Dempsey with a straight right hand, which caught the champion flush on the jaw. Dempsey rocked back, then forward, and his arms dropped helplessly at his side. For a brief moment the champ was vulnerable; and Carpentier swung a powerful right-hand uppercut that missed. Broun observed sardonically, 'We know of course that when the first prehistoric creature crawled out of the ooze up to the beaches… it was already settled that Carpentier was going to miss that uppercut.'

"The champ held on until he regained his senses and then stayed close to Carpentier the rest of the fight. In the next two rounds, Dempsey wore the brave Frenchman down with terrific body shots and finally knocked the challenger out in the fourth round. Broun reported, 'A gorgeous human will had been beaten down to a point where it could no longer function.'"

Allison interrupted. "But where does 'Hallelujah' come in?"

I laughed. "Hold on. I'm getting there."

"Sorry. Go on."

"Well, after establishing the facts, my student emphasized Broun had used the word *fate* four times throughout the essay and then provided several quotes showing how Broun had moved from the objective to the unbelievably existential. Paraphrasing now, Broun writes: 'The surprising revelation which came to us on this July afternoon was that a thing may be done well enough to make victory entirely secondary.... It was the finest tragic performance in the lives of ninety thousand persons.... All of us who watched Carpentier know now that man cannot beat down Fate, no matter how much his will may flame, but he can rock it back upon its heels when he puts all his heart and the shoulders into a blow.... Eugene O'Neill and all our young writers of tragedy make a great mistake if they think that the poignancy of the fate of man lies in the fact that he is weak, pitiful, and helpless. The tragedy of life is not that man loses but that he almost wins. Or, if you are intent on pointing out that his downfall is inevitable, that at least he completes the gesture of being on the eve of victory.... We feel that one of the elements of tragedy lies in the fact that Fate gets nothing but the victories and the championships. Gesture and glamour remain with Man.'"

I paused and smiled. "And now we get to Cohen's song. My student argued the artist had created a hallelujah chorus for our imperfect world. He believed Cohen had woven the David and Bathsheba and the Samson and Delilah allusions into the lyrics to emphasize man's ability to overcome horrific missteps and still achieve a semblance of redemption. In both biblical narratives, sexual desire led to a string of tragedies, sincere contrition, and ultimately to God's forgiveness.

"He then quoted the optimistic last verse—you know, the one you'd mentioned in your lead-in this morning. He used the lyrics to conclude Cohen had actually composed a joyous affirmation of life despite knowing full well man 'cannot beat down Fate,' which 'gets nothing but the victories and the championships.' The student ended his composition with several quotes from Samuel Beckett's existential works, 'I cannot go on; I must go on' and 'Try again. Fail again. Fail better.'"

I paused and then impulsively asked Allison, "Do you think it was fate or coincidence, our meeting in the faculty lounge, debating Capote and singing Cohen's obscure song?"

Allison pointed into the air and replied, "It depends on what they had in mind. But does it really matter, if we live in the moment?"

I nodded and then ventured into the future. "I've been doing more than practicing guitar and rehearsing covers of Cohen's songs over the summer. Whether it was fate or coincidence, our first meeting and discussion of *Other Voices* had a profound impact on me and inspired me to retool earlier works and compose new songs, including 'Missing You,' 'Skully's

Landing,' and 'Missouri Fever.' Would you consider reviewing them?" I should have stopped there but perversely felt I had to add a teasing tag line: "The titles disclose the primary sources of my inspiration."

I held my breath, feeling our six-month friendship was now at a critical juncture. Our conversation would either stall out with polite, "Don't call me—I'll call you" pleasantries or find lift and carry us on to uncharted destinations. But I didn't have to wait long for the verdict. Allison responded enthusiastically, "Your timing's perfect! The Squire and I will be off the road from now until the beginning of the year. We'll have plenty of time to review your work." She paused, smiled, and added, "I'm really looking forward to running through all the pieces you've written, Sam." She pulled a business card out of a side pocket of her large leather handbag, struck out the business number, substituted her private line, and said, "Telephone me later this week to arrange a visit to The Afterlife."

The sharp knocks at the basement door startled Anna and Jennie from their brief naps near the fire. Allison jumped up, unlocked the door, gave her husband a bear hug, and said she was really happy he had gotten home safely. As I walked back into the kitchen, Allison was introducing Anna and Jennie to the Squire, explaining their difficult situation and informing him she had offered to put the ladies up in the mansion at least until the weather improved.

While turning toward me for introductions, Allison said to the Squire, "You remember Sam. Y'all met in the faculty lounge at Pantheon after your guest lecture on entrepreneurship."

The Squire, who rarely forgot names or faces, responded, "Of course I do! How's life been treating you, Sam?"

I smiled and responded, "Could be worse, sir."

Allison then turned to the Squire and said, "I've invited Sam out to our place in the next few weeks for a business meeting. I'll explain on our way home tonight."

She left us briefly to retrieve everyone's coats and the Thanksgiving dinners from the refrigerator. When she returned, she looked over at me and said, "How about a ride back to your apartment so you don't have to trudge through the drifts."

I smiled and replied, "Thanks for the offer, but I promised the church elders I'd be the last to leave—to make sure the fire was out and lock the basement door behind me…. Y'all go on and get Anna and Jennie to your home where they'll feel safe and warm."

I walked everyone to the exit, said my good-byes, returned to the kitchen, and stared into the glowing, crackling embers. I didn't mind staying behind to secure the building; in fact, I looked forward to sitting alone again for a few minutes in the darkened auditorium. I climbed the stairs, settled into an aisle seat on the back row, and scanned the immense space illuminated intermittently by the recessed lighting positioned above the exits.

Although I was alone, I felt connected to something much larger than life. I had felt this way before as a young man. Whenever I faced an intractable issue, I would step outside beneath the sweep of stars, lie back on a nearby knoll, and survey the shimmering constellations. I believe it was the enormity and immutability of the vista then that calmed me, allowed me to gain perspective and focus confidently on resolving my problem.

My first impulse was to stay in my comfort zone, reset the time line, and make my decision perhaps a week or two after visiting the mansion and gauging their reactions to my keyboard skills and the original compositions. But after standing on that tiny stage that morning and holding my own with a consummate professional, I was determined now to reject the familiar impulse to kick the can down the road again.

So even if I ended up traveling thousands of miles and playing small venues or living out of a car and busquing for loose change near churches and train stations, I would accept my fate no matter what the result of the upcoming meeting at the mansion. After all, it was more than ten long months ago that I'd first experienced the electric flash that had inexorably devolved into cruel, daily bouts of vacillation, guilt, frustration, insomnia, and fear.

To be honest, I was wearing down. How much more painful could decisive action be than the smoldering purgatory I'd endured all these months? While there would be a real risk of bombing during the audition, I was choosing what I loved over what I felt was duty. From then on, music trumped literary scholarship. I would run to daylight. And with my decision now firmly in hand, I confidently descended the stairs, doused the lingering flames, locked the door behind me, and walked home beneath the cold, clear expanse of approving stars.

7

AFTER THE ANTIQUE knocker banged several times, a pleasant, self-assured little girl answered the door and escorted me into a large antebellum ballroom featuring crystal chandeliers, gleaming parquet, and a vintage grand Steinway positioned beneath a spectacular wall of ceiling-high windows. She explained her father was on a conference call and her stepmother had been delayed with a meeting of local restaurateurs supporting the family's food bank in McGill. She pointed in the direction of the piano, asked me to take a seat in one of the chairs nearby, and said she would let her father know I had arrived.

As I approached the windows to view the calming panorama of stonewalls and rustic barns, a cheerful voice rang out from across the room. "You must be the young musician Allison spoke so highly of after the Thanksgiving Day dinner at Saint Paul's." While gliding across the floor, the elegant, gray-haired lady wiped baking flour off her hands onto her bright yellow apron, extended her arm, and declared, "I'm Grandma. Welcome to The Afterlife." Following traditional rules of Southern hospitality, she next tempted me with freshly baked biscuits, homemade butter, and rich, thick sorghum, which convention dictated I politely accept without hesitation. She then graciously asked me to follow her to the kitchen, which conveyed the time-honored meaning I had passed the matriarch's initial screening and had been provisionally accepted into the inner circle as one of the family.

Grandma's invitation to the kitchen, the warm, buttery biscuits, and her fascinating stories about the historic plantation were true blessings that helped me pass the time and remain calm while the minutes turned into an hour. As she began relating a very promising tale about a former pastor and an elder's second wife, the Squire strode into the room, extended his hand, and genuinely apologized for the "unavoidable delay." "Nevertheless," he said, winking at Grandma, "it appears Allison and I left you in good hands," and he nodded toward the plate of biscuits. Grandma returned a doting smile. The Squire then put an arm around my shoulder and invited me to return to the ballroom for our informal get-together.

We sat down in a couple of the gold empire side chairs near the piano and made small talk—first about the unusual wintry weather, next about Allison's imminent arrival, then onto the children's anticipation of Christmas, and finally about the remaining restoration projects planned for the mansion, the outbuildings, and the surrounding land. As the minutes ticked by, the Squire repeatedly glanced toward the door across the room anticipating Allison's appearance at any moment. But when she hadn't returned home by the time he'd completed the description of a second comprehensive improvement project, his affable Southern charm gave way to a polite but driven entrepreneurial tone. "Since my wife has obviously been delayed longer than expected, why don't we get down to business? Did you bring the compositions?"

I nodded. "Yes, sir."

"Well, we can have a look at the lyrics now, and Allison can run through the melodies when she gets back."

While lifting the folded papers from my breast pocket, I realized the Squire was unaware I played piano, which must have been his primary reason for delaying the audition. But now I had fully grasped the situation. Allison's absence had become one of those critical moments Mom had always talked about, advising me to sense the opening and seize the opportunity. I calmly rose from my chair, gestured toward the piano, and suggested modestly, "I'm no Allison, but I can sing the lyrics and play the melodies for you."

He responded humorously with the slightest hint of embarrassment, "I agree you're not as good-looking as she, but let's see what you can do with the vocals and keyboard."

I sat down at the piano, shuffled through the drafts, inhaled deeply, and launched into the long, mysteriously dark instrumental opening of "Skully's Landing." As the chords transitioned from a minor to major key echoing the narrative's measured move from exploration to hopeful discovery, the Squire discreetly shifted his body away from the piano and stared out the windows toward the bright slant of winter light playing on the trunks of the shaggy bark hickories. My immediate reactions to this subtle move ran the emotional gamut: Was he rejecting the work out of hand? Was he somehow relating the music creatively to the glistening landscape? Or was he attempting to focus more intently on the meaning beneath the complex lyric?

But I'll never really know what he thought of my solo performance. As the Squire gazed out over the icy wonderland and I continued playing, Allison quietly stole into the ballroom through a side door behind us, approached the piano, leaned in to read the lyrics, and joined me for the upbeat chorus following the second verse. She then slid around to my left, motioned for me to give her room on the bench, sat down, and flawlessly transformed my solo into a vocal duo for four hands. And after singing backup for her on one of my earlier works, I moved over to one of the chairs next to the Squire, allowing the professionals to assess the strength and commercial viability of my latest songs.

The tenor of the meeting changed as I sat silently off to the side watching the masters start, stop, debate, repeat, discuss, and then move on to the next work. It was as if I, the parent, had been invited into the operating room to watch highly trained surgeons performing investigative laparotomies on each of my children one at a time. Clipped phrases like "Try that an octave higher," "That's awkward for the right hand," and "That doesn't work, but how about this?" offered few clues either to how they felt about my work overall or to the outcome of the audition.

But when Allison had finished a soulful, uninterrupted run-through of "Missing You," she gazed directly into the Squire's eyes and offered her assessment. "I believe the pieces deserve a hearing. How about you?" The entrepreneur smiled and was off to the races. Everything now was about "how," not "if." I couldn't believe what I was hearing. Their conversation quickly moved from my songs to exclusive contracts, potential albums, regional solo tours, opening for Allison, and perhaps even performing duets with her on the big stage. And after a very early celebratory libation of Mr. Jack on the rocks, the Squire drove me back to McGill, gave me a hearty, congratulatory handshake, said he would be in touch, and drove off quickly toward his philanthropic Venture Bank.

The heady weeks following the meeting with Allison and the Squire were filled with celebrating holidays, teaching classes, grading compositions, writing term papers, studying for final exams, and entertaining grandiose visions of signing stacks of album covers for adoring fans after sold-out concerts. But as everyone knows, things never really work out the way you imagine. As the weeks passed into months, I found every reasonable explanation for the lack of communication with the pair. First, I was sure it was the holidays getting in the way; next, it had to be the business demands of the New Year with the Squire returning to Nashville and Allison heading back out on the road; and then it must be the contracting process, which I understood was complicated and required a great deal of time to structure equitable deals.

And everyone also knows that nothing ever really breaks until tiny voices begin whispering in the back of your mind, "What the hell were you thinking?" and you begin to pull in the horns, cancel confessional meetings with your mentor, commit to another semester of teaching, enroll in three additional graduate school classes, but keep the dream on life support by landing short-term gigs at local clubs around Warfield and McGill. Such was my life when about halfway through the spring semester, I returned home to the gym after teaching the latest iteration of my composition course and found a sealed envelope on the tile floor inside my apartment. It was a note from Allison asking me to call her the next morning. She said she had news.

Of course, I didn't sleep well that night; I lay there counting the hours until I could telephone to find out what was going on. But when I finally made the call the next morning, Allison would only say coyly it was good news, and the Squire wanted to see me at the mansion around three o'clock that afternoon. I was lucky enough to hitch a ride with one of Birmingham's corner men who lived over that way, and after a mostly silent drive, I climbed the mansion stairs promptly at three o'clock.

Allison answered the door, smiled, stepped out on the porch, and for the first time warmly embraced me. "You made it!" she said. "Here, come with me." She hooked her arm around mine and guided me back through the labyrinth of hallways toward the stately ballroom. "The Squire is awaiting your arrival," she said with self-conscious pomp. As we approached the grand piano now bathed in brilliant sunlight streaming in through the massive windows, the Squire rose from his gold empire chair and extended his hand. "Welcome back to the mansion, Sam."

He immediately began choreographing the seating. He pointed to a second empire chair and said, "Sam, you take a seat here next to me; and Allison, you take your place there at the piano." He paused, sat down next to me, and launched his sales pitch in earnest. "Now, Sam, I've been in the rough-and-tumble music business for years. I've learned the painful lessons of what works and what doesn't. And of course, the objective here is always to succeed." He looked directly at me and asked, "Agreed?"

I smiled anxiously and replied, "Yes, sir. Agreed. That should be our number one goal every time."

"Well, Sam, I'm sure you'll find what I'm about to say frustrating, but you can do with it whatever you think is best."

I knew this was the mandatory windup before the major league pitch. And then it came hurtling toward me. The Squire continued, "I would recommend you take small steps. Continue writing songs, which Allison can record. Begin playing smaller venues on the regional circuit; and occasionally perform duets with Allison especially during concerts in western Tennessee and neighboring states.

"While I believe you have a good voice, Sam," the Squire rationalized, "I don't think it's either unique enough or strong enough to be a commercial success. On the other hand, your songwriting is both unique and commercially viable, which I believe would help you draw sell-out crowds to smaller venues in the South and also help you generate substantial income through Allison's recordings."

They both leaned in awaiting my response. I sat there silently for a few seconds allowing the shock to wash over me. I took a deep breath. And then calling on everything within me to respond without my voice cracking and fully revealing the disappointment of a shattered dream, I said, "Ah, since you're the pro at this, sir, I guess you're laying out the best path forward."

And as you would expect from a wily sales veteran, who sensed my pique, the Squire chose a strategic blend of proof of concept and significant ego stroking to seal the deal. He gazed into my eyes, smiled, and responded, "We have a surprise for you, Sam." He looked over at his young wife and said, "Allison, show Sam what we have in mind."

She opened the demo with a cover of one of my seriously revised earlier lyrics, followed it with an incredible interpretation of "Missouri Fever," and concluded the minisession with a soulful rendition of "Missing You." Throughout the three performances, Allison looked deeply into my eyes conveying that same blaze of light we'd first shared that earlier Thanksgiving Day.

As the last few chords reverberated across the vast space, the Squire interrupted the dreamlike atmosphere with the salesman's typical follow-up question: "Now wasn't that the best damn music you've heard in ages? These are the songs we want to include on Allison's next release. What do you say?"

I paused and then admitted that the Squire had been right all along. "I agree with your assessment, sir. I wrote the lyrics, but Allison truly owns the songs. And I want to be up front with y'all. It'll be several months before I could ever think of touring and writing songs again. I have to finish teaching my composition course, schedule a final meeting with my mentor, and find another place to stay, since my lease will be up at the end of the school year."

Within seconds the quintessential salesman responded, "While we can't do anything about the composition course or your mentor, I'm sure we can help you with the housing issue. Come on, Allison, let's give our new partner the grand tour of the property."

We quickly exited the ballroom, exchanged brief pleasant-ries with Grandma in the hallway, and then left the mansion via the impeccably restored country kitchen. The Squire first guided us to a scenic overlook above a remarkable expanse of fertile gardens, lush pastureland, and rolling hills, and then suggested we follow him along a summit walkway to a much narrower trail, which abruptly disappeared into a thick forest of cathedral pines. As we walked along the winding forest path, strong rays of afternoon sunlight occasionally pierced the dense canopy animating a host of playful woodland sprites darting above the laurel, fern, sorrel, and lush carpet of apron moss.

We must have hiked at least a half mile into the dark, primal woods before spotting a small ellipse of intense light pulsing at the far boundary of the forest. I speculated silently what lay beyond the woodland—perhaps a meadow, a pasture, or a field of wheat, rye, or corn? But when we finally reached the daylight, we stepped out onto the rugged pristine shoreline of an enor-mous lake. The Squire immediately turned to his right, guided us up the rocky shore about a hundred yards, and pointed east-ward toward an isolated two-story log house set back from the water on the crest of a small rise.

The salesman smoothly wrapped his arm around my shoulder, smiled broadly, and said, "Now isn't this the most inspiring place you've ever been? It's a paradise on earth. And just imagine—what if we were to air the cabin out a bit, spruce it up inside and out, and clear away some of the underbrush and tall grasses surrounding the property? Now, I know it doesn't have electricity, running water, or indoor facilities, but doesn't the beauty of the place, the raw spiritual solitude, and the magical vista inspire the soul to song?" Before I could form a reply, he had moved toward the flagstone steps leading up to the rustic porch wrapping around the front of the cottage. He pulled a key from his white linen jacket, unlocked the door, and motioned for Allison and me to join him in the cabin.

As we entered the great room, the Squire was busy unlatching the shutters and opening several lakeside windows to counter the mustiness and allow the bright afternoon sunlight to flood in. Every piece of upholstered furniture was covered with a white tarpaulin, giving the house a ghostly feel. The real estate agent now went to work describing all the positive aspects of the interior: the privacy of a large upstairs bedroom; pine paneling throughout the house; antique wide-plank flooring; primitive American portraits and landscapes adorning the walls; a massive fieldstone fireplace to the left; a turn-of-the-century blue enamel cookstove with eight burners and two warming cabinets on the right; and a back wall lined with shelves teeming with countless nineteenth- and twentieth-century histories, biographies, and first-rate fiction.

"Beyond the exceptional vistas and the inviting interior, there is also a unique and compelling history associated with this place," the Squire said, before launching into a dramatic soliloquy. "It seems a few years before the Civil War, my great-great-grandfather built the lodge as a hermitage for hunting, fishing, gambling, and carousing with relatives and fellow landowners. But after the Union forces learned his two youngest sons were actively involved in the Southern resistance and had put substantial rewards on their heads, my great-great-grandfather turned the hidden refuge into a hideout for his sons, who then only left the "rebels' den" to conduct raids with Confederate Generals Nathan Bedford Forrest and John Hunt Morgan. When the war ended, his two sons came out of hiding and took up residence in the mansion for a time. And family rumors have persisted that the youngest son later returned to the cabin to live out his life with his only surviving child and several sharecroppers, after the economy soured, the fever hit, and the bank foreclosed on the highly leveraged Afterlife property. This home has been an inspiration to me and I would be so pleased if you would live in it," the Squire concluded.

How could I resist such a potent sales pitch? As we began walking back through the forest toward the mansion, I responded. "I want to thank y'all for your generous offer. And I'll accept it with the proviso that I must first complete my graduate classes, finish teaching the advanced course, and then speak with my mentor about my future plans."

The Squire hugged me and shouted, "Well, welcome to the family, Sam!" He then held me out at arm's length and gazed into my eyes. And now adopting a quiet, serious tone, he said, "I promise you, Sam, you'll never regret your decision to leave teaching for the music world."

Allison jumped in. "When we get back to the house, let's check our calendars and establish a date for your big move out here from the fight club."

"Now just to be clear, I don't think we should count on anything before June 15 at the earliest," I responded.

The Squire slapped me lightly on the shoulder and said, "June 15 will be just fine.... just fine."

Contrary to my expectations, the pending career change never impacted my performance in the classroom either as a teacher or as a graduate student. Since I realized these would probably be the last classes I would ever take and the last undergraduate course I'd ever teach, I pulled out all the stops. And there was one graduate course in particular I wanted to ace, Contemporary American Studies, my demanding mentor's signature course. When the prospects for a music career looked rather bleak at the beginning of the semester, I threw caution to the wind and shouldered the pressure to impress my mentor a second time.

The final assignment for Professor Taylor's course was to draft a "creative essay" analyzing Leonard Bernstein's use of an innovative cross-disciplinary approach in his 1973 Norton Lecture Series at Harvard to answer Charles Ives's metaphysical question on the future course of music, "Whither music?" We were to demonstrate how Bernstein applied linguistics, elementary physics, aesthetics, and poetry to a study of the broad sweep of musical history. After receiving the challenging assignment, I followed my usual oblique method to inspiration and response: end the day at the Two-Way Café with a heaping bowl of chili, head home for some light reading of the local sports pages, and then strictly adhere to an early lights-out.

As I lay in the dark loft above the Warrior's gym gazing out at the blue humming flashes of neon touting the greasy spoon next door, I began outlining my final academic paper. What was Bernstein trying to say? Schoenberg had led contemporary composers over the cliff into a rejection of tonality and blind acceptance of the serial method:

> But the frightened over commitment of the new converts caused this spate of new music to emerge for the most part sterile and dry; there was so much ordered precomposition involved, amounting almost to a mathematical takeover.

Bernstein believed modern music had "acquired the musty odor of academicism." And it was that single word, *academicism*, that inspired my next move. I would use my last essay as a subtle precursor preparing my mentor for the difficult news I would soon share with him that I was leaving academia for a life in music. But how could I begin telling him I had been pursuing the wrong thing for the wrong reason? I had chosen Pantheon's PhD program not because of a passion for literary scholarship, but because I was desperately chasing my father's ghost. Somehow I would have to weave the admission into the paper. Perhaps by quoting Thoreau on desperation and the limitless possibility of change:

> The mass of men lead lives of quiet desperation. What is called resignation is confirmed desperation.... So thoroughly and sincerely are we compelled to live, reverencing our life, and denying the possibility of change. This is the only way, we say; but there are as many ways as there can be drawn radii from one center. All change is a miracle to contemplate; but it is a miracle which is taking place every instant.

My goal was to let the professor know I was not running from him or the program but toward something I truly loved, toward daylight, toward a resounding, affirming yes.

While I had spent much more time completing the assignment than expected, I still succeeded in handing the paper in on time at the end of our last scheduled class. All I could do now was finish grading the undergraduate compositions and wait for the professors' feedback in my English department mailbox. So with classes over and my adrenaline stores completely exhausted, I allowed myself a little R&R. I took my customary seat in the fourth row of the bleachers, watched some fast-paced sparring, and waited for my old friend, Birmingham, to finish for the day.

But somewhere in the back of my mind, I realized this was not a casual visit to relax and catch up on things. The Buccaneer had earned his reputation as one of the best trainers in boxing by consistently preparing fighters to go the distance both physically and mentally. I guess I subconsciously wanted Birmingham to make me mentally tough for the upcoming meeting with my mentor. Before dropping the bomb on Professor Taylor, I wanted first to see how the Buccaneer would react to the news that I was changing careers, saying good-bye to the loft, and moving on to The Afterlife to write songs and be near the Squire's wife, whom from the first moment on I found intellectually stimulating and physically attractive.

When he had sent his latest top-ten prospect to the showers for the day, Birmingham climbed down from the ring apron, strode up the bleachers, and took a seat beside me. He slapped his right hand down on my knee and inquired, "How you doing, Sam? Long time no see."

"Hanging in there, Buc. My elbows are in and my gloves are up. Haven't been stopping in for the sparring because I've had too much work and far too little time to get it done."

As he wiped the beaded sweat off his forehead with the terry towel he had draped over his shoulders, Birmingham probed, "So to what do we owe the honor of this visit today?"

I turned, looked him directly in the eye, and answered, "Could I speak with you seriously for a few minutes?"

He responded in his usual upbeat manner: "Sure, kid, anything for the fight club's number one fan."

I immediately moved to the center of the ring and opened the conversation with the easy stuff. "I'll be moving out of the loft sometime around the middle of June." In response to Birmingham's raised eyebrow, I added, "No complaints here. I understand where the Warrior's son is coming from—you know, wanting to open a small museum above the gym honoring his father and the strong legacy of boxing around Warfield and McGill." Birmingham's face relaxed. I then quickly dispensed with the pawing jabs and began throwing crisp hooks and straight right crosses. "Buc, ah, I'm thinking seriously about dropping out of the doctoral program and taking up the Squire's offer to become a singer-songwriter full time."

Birmingham backpedaled and countered, relying heavily on the many years he'd spent preparing his charges for the next big fight. "Do you understand the new demands? Have you done the heavy lifting? Do you see a real opening?" And before I could respond, he continued, "If you can honestly answer 'yes' to these questions, then you should take the risk and deserve praise for stepping in the ring."

And then I launched the haymaker. "But there's more, Buc. The Squire's offered me a place to stay out at his plantation. And I'll... I'll be spending a lot of time on projects with his wife, who is stepmother to his three children." Answering the unasked questions, I explained, speaking rapidly as I unburdened myself, "I met Allison in the faculty lounge one morning by chance and then spent Thanksgiving Day with her at Saint Paul's feeding the poor. And honestly after that, nothing's been the same. I've had the feeling there could be much more than friendship and artistic camaraderie. I see it in her smile, in her clear hazel eyes. I'm not a religious person, Buc, but every time I've been near her, I've felt inspiration… love… and a powerful attraction on a… a deeply spiritual level."

The Buccaneer didn't respond immediately. And he chose his words carefully. As usual, he avoided the morality of the situation and focused solely on the potential impact such a relationship could have on everyone involved. He couched his subtle warning in a humorous boxing maxim as old as Queensbury. He simply said, "Women weaken legs."

I nodded to let him know I understood his message—boxers don't mix pleasure with business, and I should do the same. It was his indirect, avuncular way of advising me the move to music and The Afterlife were probably okay, but getting involved with the wife of the fellow who would control my livelihood was not a smart thing to do.

Birmingham stood up slowly and motioned he would have to be going. He placed his thick, arthritic hands on my shoulders, gazed into my eyes, and said, "I'm going to really miss seeing you around here, kid. Stop by when you're in town and share some of your latest stories and songs."

I didn't have to wait long for the verdict on the Bernstein paper or for an appointment with Professor Taylor. He actually beat me to the punch. Below the "A," he had scribbled, "If possible, please drop by the office this week between one o'clock and three." I chose Tuesday at one o'clock. While I felt some trepidation, I was now determined to get the dreaded meeting behind me and close this chapter of my life.

After entering ivied Redman Hall, I trudged up the staircase to the top floor and proceeded down the narrow hallway to room 311. I paused, took a deep breath, and then knocked lightly on the thick oak door. My mentor responded, "It's open! Come on in!" I slowly turned the knob and entered. Everything was in its usual place. The professor was seated behind his massive oak desk surrounded by bookcases, the visitor's chair was still piled high with open books, and strong afternoon sunlight flooded into the room highlighting the antique chessboard resting on the wide marble sill of the lone window at the back of the room.

From our first meeting on, every succeeding visit had reinforced my belief that nothing ever changed there. It was as if the office had become a museum, a sanctuary, or perhaps a sacred shrine. As I approached the desk, he stood up and shook my hand. "Congratulations on your final paper. It was outstanding.... Oh, here," he said, noticing my helpless look, "let's move some of the books off the chair. Put them over there on the bottom shelf and take a seat."

After I'd sat down in front of his enormous desk, Professor Taylor smiled and opened the conversation with an observation and an implied question: "If I were a gambling man, I'd bet you've woven a message into the fabric of your last essay. Anything important you want to discuss today?"

The many months anticipating this dreaded moment must have drained any lingering anxiety from me. I remained unexpectedly calm and replied, "Yes, sir. First of all, I want to thank you for all the support you've provided me as a graduate student and a teaching associate. I'll never forget the coaching and advice you've shared over the last two years. But I think it's time now to cross the Rubicon from, ah, creative analyses to, ah, inspired creativity. I've decided to leave the doctoral program and focus on a career in music. You see, I've met an artist, fallen in love with her, and have developed a passion for writing melodies and lyrics, which she can record and perform on tour before thousands. But honestly, I've never felt as passionate while studying and teaching literature. I now realize I came here pursuing a doctorate for the wrong reason. I was vainly chasing my father's ghost…."

The professor shifted uncomfortably in his chair trying to absorb the unsettling message. An antique wall clock pounded the seconds and screamed the quarter hour as we sat facing each other staring blankly into the charged silence. My mentor finally broke the ice with an ironic reminiscence. "Believe me, I empathize with your decision. I too fell in love with a beautiful artist. I postponed a serious career in academia for years, before finally finding my footing and rehabilitating my professional credentials. And what do I have to show for the experience? A poem, a note, the chess set behind me, and the bittersweet memories of what was and what might have been." He paused and added, "I wish you all the best. And I want you to know my door will always be open to support you any way I can." Professor Taylor gazed into my eyes, smiled warmly, and said, "I've only got one request."

I responded simply, "Anything for you, sir. What is it?"

"When you have your first legitimate, large-venue concert, I'd like two seats. Third row, center."

I immediately and enthusiastically replied, "Consider it done!"

The professor pushed back from his desk, rose slowly, and walked over to where I was standing. He extended his arms, firmly grasped my shoulders, and whispered, "I'll miss you, Sam." He then escorted me to the door where we embraced and parted professionally perhaps for a last time.

8

THE TRIP FROM the fight club out to the lake house was a journey back in time. Allison had picked me up at the apartment in the family van and driven me out to The Afterlife, where we transferred my meager belongings to the bed of a restored Confederate wagon for the last half mile to the cabin. Over the past two weeks a series of unrelenting storms had rendered the narrow forest road practically impassable for modern vehicles with rear-wheel drive and one-wheel traction. And as would be expected, the foul weather had continued on into my moving day, draping a thick, heavy layer of threatening clouds over the tops of the hardwoods and hemlocks that framed the mysterious entrance to the Squire's woods.

After a rough, zigzag ride through the forest, we finally reached the craggy shoreline where powerful whitecaps crashed one after another against the tall, metamorphic boulders. As Allison slowed the wagon to a stop, several brilliant flashes of lightning arced against the charcoal sky, announcing the leading edge of another strong summer storm. We quickly jumped down from the wagon, tied the reins to a low-hanging branch, and shuttled several hand-me-down suitcases and four bulky duffel bags from the wagon to the historic lodge.

We struggled mightily with the swollen window frames but managed to get them down and locked before the June deluge really rolled in. But the afternoon light the small panes produced would never suffice either for unpacking or for navigating safely among the heirlooms scattered about the open space. Not to worry. The past would save us again. Allison moved along the left wall to a writing desk, found some safety matches stashed behind a secret panel, and lit an antique kerosene lamp. And within minutes I would have sworn I was appearing live on stage among the floodlights. She had located and fired up four additional lanterns to fully illuminate the main room.

When we could see properly, Allison proudly launched an extensive tour of both floors, demonstrating that she and the Squire had kept their earlier promise to air the cabin and spruce it up a bit inside and out. "Since the rain refuses to let up, come over here with me to the side windows." When I joined her, she said "See there? We cleared the tall grasses and underbrush away from the house so you'll have a good view." She then led me up the narrow curving stairs to the second-floor bedroom where she pointed out, "We whitewashed the walls, dressed the rope bed with fresh linens, and dusted all the furniture from top to bottom."

"Looks fit for a king!" I said. "But you really didn't have to go to all the trouble."

As she turned toward the stairs, she looked back over her shoulder, smiled, and said, "A promise made is a promise kept. And besides, nothing's too good for a close friend and partner."

Returning to the ground floor, Allison playfully pointed to the colorful upholstered furniture and shouted, "Voilà! As you can see, we've performed a successful exorcism of the tarpaulin ghosts covering the sofa and chairs." She next moved over to a side wall, ran her finger along the edge of one of the picture frames, and declared lightheartedly, "Incredibly spotless portraits and landscapes!" She then strode over to a large cabinet next to the blue enamel cookstove, opened the cabinet door, and added, "And for your dining pleasure, a fully stocked pantry with a wide variety of canned fruits, vegetables, and meats, which we'll supplement regularly with Grandma's fresh-baked breads and handpicked produce from our extensive gardens."

I shook my head, turned to Allison, and said, "Unbelievable. What can I say?"

She tapped me teasingly on the arm, smiled, and replied, "'Thank you' will be quite enough."

With the grand tour winding down and the summer storm moving beyond the plantation, Allison peered out the window and said, "I had better take this little break in the weather to ride back home before the next wave gets here."

I nodded and agreed reluctantly, "Yeah, I hate to see you go, Allison, but it's probably a good idea."

As we walked down the flagstone steps toward the shoreline, she said, "Now remember, the Squire will be leaving for Nashville tomorrow morning and I'll be heading back out on the road at the end of the week to finish the tour. So if you need anything at all, go talk to Grandma. She'd love to see you and bend your ear for a while."

I laughed and then turned serious. "Hey, I really want to thank y'all for taking me in."

Allison smiled and replied, "It's our pleasure, Sam. We're really happy you're here."

I wrapped my hands about her small waist, lifted her up onto the wagon bench, and untied the woefully drenched horse, which had dutifully endured the brunt of the frightening thunderstorm. As she pulled on the reins to maneuver the wagon toward home, Allison humorously demanded, "I expect to see a wagonload of new songs when I get back home from the tour."

I clicked my heels, extended my arms, and bowed deeply. "Madam, at your service. Your wish is my command." I walked alongside the creaking wagon up to the edge of the forest, waved broadly when she flashed a warm smile over her shoulder, and then stood there at the haunting entrance to the dense woods longing for my Mistress Brown as she slowly disappeared among the mischievous sprites dancing in the muted forest light.

With my momentous moving day behind me, I quickly settled into a false security of the routine. I now understood Brahms, who spoke of being on holiday and stepping lightly to avoid crushing countless tunes scattered beneath his feet. Every sight and sound at the cabin inspired a lyric or a melody:

the ancient lake, the pristine landscape, the burnished sunsets splashing rainbows across cerulean skies, the dazzling blankets of shimmering stars, the kerosene shadows dancing on midnight walls, the creaks and groans of restless logs and the resident spirits darting in and out of my diaphanous dreams.

Yes, everything was so much easier than I had expected. While I had always considered melody writing a mysterious, joyful, beguiling gift, I had found the composition of lyrics a painful, meticulous internecine warfare. But for the first few months on the plantation, everything flowed effortlessly from vision to pen, scattering hints of conflicted feelings for Allison among evocative images of this panoramic solitude.

In the back of my mind, however, I knew this run would never last. Mom had warned me early on that change was the only constant in life. And while growing up, I'd unfortunately experienced Mom's truism a thousand times. So this initial burst of inspiration lasted until the fall. And when I reached the inevitable writer's block, I didn't panic. I knew I would have time to recover, since I had already crafted a respectable number of songs for Allison and the Squire's homecoming in early November. Somehow, someway the juices would begin flowing again, allowing me to meet a second target date I'd set for the upcoming year.

And the gods treated me kindly. Before long, inspiration returned. It was late October, almost to Halloween, when a rare autumnal thunderstorm finally broke the unusually warm weather we had experienced throughout the fall. I was upstairs in the bedroom reading by candlelight when a single flash of lightning turned night into day and produced an immediate jarring crash of thunder, signaling the onset of a deluge. Several minutes into the downpour, I began hearing rain splattering onto the wide-board floor. I rolled out of bed, grabbed the candleholder from the nightstand, and began tracing the leak back to its source, which appeared to be a thin seam running between the ceiling plaster and one of the original hand-hewn beams. I quickly realized the only way to stop the substantial flow was to find a way up into the attic.

After carefully searching the bedroom ceiling without success, I found a small attic door hidden in my narrow walk-in closet at the far end of the room. I rushed back out into the main space, grabbed a chair, and excitedly returned to the closet to pursue the leak. I set the candleholder on the floor, jumped up on the chair, and began pushing up on the attic door as hard as I could. But the thick wooden slab wouldn't budge. Since it appeared someone had intentionally nailed the door shut, I called a retreat for the night, opting to catch the flood in a large galvanized bucket while planning an all-out assault on the attic fortress for one hour past daybreak.

I soon learned it was a mistake to postpone the attack until sunrise. I didn't sleep well. The incessant drip tortured me throughout the night. So instead of lying in bed until dawn, I got up, marched downstairs, and assembled the tools I would need to breach the stubborn barrier. I was on a mission not only to plug the leak but also to determine why the attic had been hermetically sealed. Was there something special up there that was not to be seen?

Hurrying back upstairs with tools in hand, I jumped up on the chair and began hammering the crowbar into one corner of the door. I needed to gain a toehold. Fifteen tough minutes later, I concluded there really must be something up there that someone didn't want anyone to see. The attic door had not only been cleverly nailed shut but was uniquely constructed of black locust, one of the hardest woods on the planet. Finally, after forcing a small opening between the thick timbers and the frame, I began the monotonous, backbreaking exercise of chiseling away the remainder of the boards an inch at a time.

Despite the adrenaline surging through my body, I had expended so much energy holding the hammer, chisel, and crowbar in the air that once I had created my opening, my aching arms could no longer pull me up through the jagged hole into the attic. I would have to storm the bastion with the twelve-foot wooden ladder hanging on the wall outside the house. Down the stairs I went, retrieving the ladder and returning to the room once more. When I finally managed to ram the ladder up through the dark opening, I shouted out triumphantly at the secretive carpenter and his personified handiwork, "Now give up your ghosts!" I grabbed the brass candleholder and began cautiously climbing the slick, loose rungs toward the stronghold.

When I popped up through the opening and held the candle high, all I could see were rough-hewn beams, massive cobwebs, and large, gray rats scurrying away from my frightening light. I stepped off the ladder onto a ceiling beam like an acrobat approaching the high wire and scanned the four corners of the attic space. Nothing there… nothing there… nothing there… and nothing—whoa, what's that? Light reflected dimly off what I presumed was a piece of metal. I immediately stooped down to avoid the low rafters and eagerly began stepping across the thick beams toward the glowing object.

As I neared the reflection, I became increasingly excited; I could now make out the shadowy outline of an antique stage-coach trunk. It was a nineteenth-century beauty with fancy tooled leather, several iron bands circling the exterior, large decorative studs securing the bands to the frame, and a thick brass lock protecting the valued contents from even the most rapacious intruder. Or so I thought. After the shock of discovery had worn off, I began questioning how I would ever break the substantial lock to get at the contents. But what the hell; why not try the latch before planning a second assault that day? When I compressed the levers on both sides of the lock, the pins unbelievably receded and the latch snapped open. Perhaps the mysterious owner felt anyone persistent enough to crash the attic door deserved to view the riches stored within.

And this Jenny Lind indeed held exceptional treasure, which all at once unlocked the past, absolved the present, and signaled a promising future. When I lifted the heavy lid, I first discovered a complete Confederate cavalry officer's uniform, including a woolen, cadet-gray shell jacket with bloodstains near the right shoulder, a pair of gray wool trousers with a wide vertical yellow stripe running the length of the leg, and a cadet-gray stag hat with yellow rope and acorn trim, ostrich plume and a brass emblem pinning the raised brim on the right side to the crown.

I reverently lifted the neatly folded uniform out of the trunk and draped it over the ceiling beam directly behind me. Now back to the remaining items in the trunk. The next layer down consisted of the officer's weaponry: a .44-caliber steel blue Navy revolver, a sawed-off double-barrel shotgun with leather sling, and a doubled-edged saber with leather handle, wire wrap, solid brass guard, and elegantly curved shaft engraved with the motto, "Draw me not without reason. Sheath me not without honor."

One by one, I carefully removed the weapons and placed them on the beam next to the officer's uniform. Now back again to the contents. I lifted my candleholder directly above the opening to illuminate the bottom third of the trunk space, where the authentic treasure had lain undisturbed for a century or more—layer upon layer of thin bound volumes dated clearly on the spine beginning in the early 1860s and running through the end of the war in 1865.

I spent the next half hour transporting the journals over to the attic opening, stacking them neatly on the beams nearby, and then gingerly carrying them down the rickety ladder by the armful. After moving all the notebooks down to the bedroom, I returned to the attic a final time to stow the weaponry at the bottom of the trunk and carefully place the rebel's uniform on top. With so much going on, I decided to hold off on tracking down the maddening leak until another deluge forced my hand most likely the following spring.

Needless to say I spent the rest of the week reading, taking notes, and jotting down potential lyrics inspired by the first installments of Charles Summerfield's early days as a Confederate cavalry officer. I traveled with him and his small ad hoc band of rebels as they conducted guerrilla raids cutting Union telegraph wires, destroying railroad tracks, burning bridges, demolishing warehouse supplies, and spreading a general fear among the Feds patrolling western Tennessee. The early passages were filled with bravado, especially after hooking up with Robert's Raiders and engaging the enemy in small battles and skirmishes at Rising Sun, Burnt Bridge, Hatchie Bottom, the Iron Works, and Galloway Switch.

But as the war dragged on, this youngest son of the country gentleman who had owned The Afterlife began writing more introspectively, describing the continual suffering of all the people in the region—black and white, rich and poor, civilian and soldier. But in a way, the passages were all over the map. While on the one hand, there were lengthy descriptions of everyday hardships including unrelenting diseases, widespread hunger, painful separations, and countless deaths, on the other hand the young warrior would offer rousing accounts of burning depots and killing "despotic occupiers" in defense of his beloved home state.

As I continued examining the war entries well into November, I noted that by April 1864 a bleak mixture of horror, despair, and futility had overwhelmed both the descriptions of daily hardships and the gallant passages depicting his heroic defense of the homeland. With at least a hundred horsemen now under his command and reporting directly to the celebrated Wizard of the Saddle, General Nathan Bedford Forrest, I believe the young officer felt compelled to provide extended accounts of major engagements.

He first reported the attack on the Johnsonville Depot in early November 1864, which resulted in the destruction of four Federal gunboats, fourteen transports, and twenty barges; the capture of twenty-six artillery pieces and one hundred fifty prisoners; and damage to over six million dollars' worth of Union property. Later that November he describes the bloody battle of Franklin, where after fierce hand-to-hand combat, he scraped up a half bushel of brains from around the front steps of the family homestead. He then details the harrowing escape after the battle of Nashville where he and his men protected the remnants of General Hood's disorganized, barefooted forces as they retreated southward in the freezing rain toward the Tennessee River on the last Christmas Day of the war.

But it was his detailed description of the fierce attack on Fort Pillow in April 1864 that debunked a family legend and absolved a soldier of all charges. Perhaps it's best to let the officer tell the story in his own words:

> The first months of 1864 were filled with a number of coordinated raids on Federal supply lines and skirmishes with small contingents of Yankee soldiers who in battle had become separated from their battalions.

During this period, I was in continual contact with my fellow guerilla leaders and mid-level officers in General Forrest's command. Toward the end of March, the General summoned all of his west Tennessee cavalry leaders to a meeting scheduled for three o'clock near Union City. I arrived early to catch up with old friends. It was really good to see my old commander, Robert, and the troops. They didn't look any the worse for wear, were in fine spirits and spoiling to take the fight to the Bluebellies. At precisely three o'clock the General stormed into camp, dismounted, shook each commander's hand heartily and led us into his large headquarters tent.

The General said he had recently gotten disturbing reports from folks around Jackson that Union soldiers from Fort Pillow had repeatedly robbed them, harassed them and disparaged the wives and daughters of our good soldiers with the most disgusting epithets. The General described the Union force strength as two battalions, one white and one Negro, and then loudly announced we would all mass west of Jackson on April 9 to attack and capture Fort Pillow and 'summarily suppress the evil and grievances.'

By eight o'clock in the morning on April 12 all our forces were in place, and General Forrest signaled our sharpshooters to begin firing down from the surrounding hills into Fort Pillow. As the suppression fire continued, the General asked Robert, his second in command, and me to ride up with him onto a boulder-strewn overlook to survey the battlefield. While we were there, the General had three horses shot out from under him. After each of these Yankee affronts, the General got up, dusted himself off and ordered another horse be brought up to his position.

During the early afternoon, our infantry field officers reported they had succeeded in blocking the Bluecoats on three sides and pinning their backs to the Mississippi River. If our troops continued applying the pressure, Lincoln's boys would have no choice but to either surrender or be annihilated. Knowing his forces had maneuvered the Union troops into an untenable position, the General ordered Robert to carry a message down to the fort's commanding officer requesting an unconditional surrender. After an exchange of several clarifying communiqués, the Union officer finally refused to give up the fort. General Forrest responded with an immediate order for an all-out assault on the doomed Union stronghold.

But Robert and I were in for a surprise. The General commended our troops for having been at the point of the spear over the last six months. He said our forces would be held in reserve ordering Robert's men to follow him up to a bluff overlooking the battlefield and sending my men to seal off the Memphis Road to prevent any Union reinforcements from surprising us from the rear. I was given specific orders to hold my position until the firing stopped, the bugle blew, and my lookouts saw our Stars and Bars flying over the fort.

Not long after my horsemen had established a formidable blockade on the Memphis Road, I heard the bugler's signal, the sharpshooters' opening rounds, and then the thunderous yell of our troops sweeping down the surrounding hills toward the vulnerable fort. It was the most frustrating day of my career. I could see nothing of the battle. But I could tell we were winning; because as the battle progressed, the tumult of screaming and gunfire diminished. We were driving the Feds down the steep embankment toward the Mississippi.

I next ordered two of my soldiers to mount and ride back down the road toward the garrison and report back when they saw our Stars and Bars flying above the fort. Only twenty minutes after sending them down the road to reconnoiter, they were racing back up the incline excitedly reporting the Federal flag had been lowered and ours had been raised to the heavens. But I didn't immediately give the order to mount and move out; I could still hear faint sporadic gunfire emanating from somewhere near the beach. So following orders, I waited until the firing had completely stopped before commanding my troops to advance toward the sacked fort.

By the time we entered the garrison, uninjured Federal troops had already begun tending to their wounded and stacking the dead against the back wall of the stockade. We made our way down to the beach where I understood most of the brutal hand-to-hand combat had occurred and where we now witnessed the most bizarre incident of the war. As the Federal troops began burying their dead under our oversight, we witnessed several miraculous resurrections. Several of the "dead" rose from their shallow graves as the Bluecoats shoveled dirt in upon them.

At this point in the journal, the young soldier had inserted an extra page written sometime after the war had ended. He was elaborating on these mysterious rebirths and defending the General and the rest of his command:

These extraordinary resurrections were probably the basis for the inaccurate allegation that our troops buried Federal soldiers alive. God be my witness. After my arrival on the battlefield, I never saw General Forrest or anyone in his command order our troops to do anything other than treat the captured, wounded and fallen with the deepest respect. And concerning the malicious reports of hearing mysterious gunfire during the night suggesting we had executed Federal prisoners, I summarily dismiss the charges as damned lies. I never heard a single shot within the encampment from dusk to the following dawn.

As I read his contemporaneous account of Forrest's attack on the fort, I became increasingly excited but admittedly uneasy. I remembered Allison's unusual comparison of the Squire to Hawthorne and her revelation that her husband suffered strong feelings of guilt about his forebears' actions during the Civil War. But now I had convincing evidence debunking the local legend that the plantation owner's youngest son had executed two of his father's runaway slaves after Forrest's successful assault on Fort Pillow. In the journal the young soldier clearly stated he was nowhere near the battlefield until after the shooting had stopped. And from the moment he reached the riverbank, he was always in the company of Federal and rebel officers, who would have condemned and officially reported such a cowardly, unlawful act.

So throughout his adulthood, the Squire had carried a heavy burden of ancestral guilt that ironically and unfortunately was based on battlefield fiction. But is "unfortunately" the right word here? Haven't the gods made foolish the wisdom of this world? Didn't the Squire's false guilt drive his good deeds: restoring The Afterlife for educational and charitable causes and creating the highly effective Food Bank, the Jobs Bank, and the Venture Bank for deserving entrepreneurs? Would he have played the part of philanthropist if the guilt hadn't been there driven by a cunning fabrication?

I knew it wouldn't be very long now until Allison and the Squire returned home to The Afterlife for Thanksgiving and Christmas. I pondered my situation. Should I tell them what I had learned? If so, how would they feel if they knew I had rummaged through the trunk and read every last word in Charles's journal? And how would I disclose my secret? Should I invite them out to the cottage or carry a representative sample with me to The Afterlife? But either way, wouldn't they expect to take immediate possession of the trunk and its contents? Wouldn't I then risk losing access to the journals forever and sacrificing this mother lode of inspiration for a thousand songs?

9

THE FOLLOWING APRIL was indeed the cruelest month, with unexpected deaths bookending Allison's latest album release on the fifteenth. There had been no premonitions. No one was looking over his or her shoulder saying, "When will the good times end?" As planned, Allison had finished the grueling yearlong tour, the Squire had returned home from Nashville, the children were out of school on break, and the extended family, which now included Grandma, the caretakers, and me, had celebrated another rewarding Thanksgiving at Saint Paul's and then an iconic, joyous Christmas at The Afterlife. There were roaring fires, layers of colorful presents, and a traditional Norway spruce decorated with handcrafted ornaments, multicolored bubble lights, and old-fashioned garland made with uncooked cranberries and large popped kernels of white corn.

But it was not just the festive holiday season that had lulled us into a false sense of well-being. Only hours after learning Allison and the Squire had returned to The Afterlife, I was proudly standing on their stately front porch clutching an overflowing portfolio of new compositions. It was as if they had clairvoyantly anticipated my arrival. Only seconds after I pounded the large brass knocker, they appeared at the main door together, spotted the bulging folder pinned under my left arm, and enthusiastically invited me to join them in our customary meeting place, the antebellum ballroom with the ornate Steinway positioned beneath the stunning wall of ceiling-high windows.

After a brief exchange of updates and pleasantries, Allison teasingly broached the subject of new compositions. I didn't reply; I just smiled broadly and handed her the thick packet of lyrics I had written at the cabin while they were away. Allison quickly took a seat at the piano and eagerly began examining the contents of the portfolio. The Squire and I took our usual places in the empire chairs beside the Steinway and made small talk until Allison had finished scanning the songs and begun playing the pieces one after another. When she had completed the initial run-through, she leaned around the corner of the keyboard, smiled warmly, and declared with a laugh, "Well, it looks like you've earned your keep."

She then turned to the Squire and with great enthusiasm, began discussing the possibilities. The entrepreneurs were off to the races. I listened in disbelief as they rapidly developed a plan to join two of my earlier compositions with four of my latest songs and six of Allison's, which she had been tweaking on the road; assemble a strong Nashville backup band (drums, fiddle, piano, guitar, and bass); begin initial rehearsals over the holidays; and then head into the recording studio sometime in February targeting an early spring release.

When they paused to catch a breath, I jumped in. "I'm dying over here. Either of you care to tell me which of my songs made the cut?" Allison and the Squire laughed and then explained. Besides the earlier "Missouri Fever" and "Missing You," Allison had chosen my "Ridgeline Whispers," "Moonlight Jester," "Miracle Sky," and "Blind Metaphor." What immediately struck me about her selections was the remarkable consistency in their tone and thematic makeup. She had chosen lyrics infused with intertwining threads of longing, difficult choices, isolation, resilience, survival, and redemptive, bittersweet resolution—all inspired by Charles's journal.

"Have you given any thought to a title for the album?" I asked Allison. This would be her fourth studio album, a crucial moment in her career. Allison smiled and said, "There's only one option befitting the collection. It has to be *The Afterlife*. Most of the songs were written here on the property, and in one way or the other, they all explore how we live out our lives after suffering unspeakable pain and loss."

I smiled. "I like it," I said. The Squire nodded his approval.

The next several months were some of the most fulfilling of my life. Since the band members and she would most likely need help unraveling some of the thornier passages, Allison suggested I temporarily abandon the cabin and come live at The Afterlife proper until the postproduction process had been completed. I must admit it felt strange at first, sitting in the antebellum ballroom day after day listening to Allison and her veteran backup band stopping midchord to discuss the real meaning of this line or that in each of my songs. And during these deliberative breaks, I would lose myself in their interpretations, preferring one over the other until I remembered I knew the true meaning of the lines in question; I had written the lyrics myself.

But it was my occasional one-on-one interpretive sessions with Allison that I loved and feared the most. If she hadn't chosen music as a career, I suspect she would have ended up a sleuth, a scientist, or a literary PhD. She had a probing mind that demanded certitude. She would ask me to interpret a passage; and of course, I would willingly comply. Her first request would be followed by impossible questions of inference and nuance: "What were you *really* trying to say there? What were you feeling when you wrote the lines? Did you have a specific person in mind?" And there again's the rub. How could I tell her how I felt without risking everything? How could I ever reveal she was the "you" in "Missing You"? The soft, alluring voice on the silvery ridgeline? The elegant queen to my playful but reticent fool? The summer vista of sweeping stars? The compelling but veiled metaphor for my deepest love, my inspiration, and my passage to creative fulfillment? But as the long days of rehearsal passed, I became increasingly comfortable, gradually letting my guard down, more openly answering her multifaceted questions, and pushing my once tentative responses right up to the indistinguishable line between flirtatious propriety and oblique confession.

Once the studio recordings were "in the can" and the technicians had begun preparing the final mix and dubbing it down to the master tape, Allison, the Squire, and I began planning the tour promoting the new album. We agreed to schedule the concerts in two phases: a regional minitour in late spring and early summer to work out any unexpected technical and performance glitches and then a demanding countrywide tour beginning in mid- to late summer and continuing on up to the week just before Thanksgiving.

Allison and the Squire suggested I join the band at least for the regional tour. They believed having a local songwriter on stage playing backup and singing duets with the star would add a "bit of sizzle" to the regional performances. I immediately accepted their generous offer. How could I ever refuse such an opportunity to gain the exposure I needed to ensure my own successful gigs in the future?

Everything was happily tracking for the mid-April album launch when the gods abruptly but characteristically intervened on All Fools' Day. No one really became alarmed until the mantel clock struck four and Grandma still hadn't appeared to begin preparing the evening meal. She had an ironclad rule to always start preparations at the final stroke of three. "Has anyone seen Grandma?" The Squire asked. "It's not like her to start cooking dinner after three o'clock."

We all shook our heads and mumbled in unison, "No… neither hide nor hair."

After unsuccessfully canvassing us about her whereabouts, the Squire said, "We'd better fan out, find her, and make sure she's all right. Allison, you and I will check the house. Children, y'all check the barn and stables. And, Sam, you check the flower garden and the greenhouse. Everybody clear?"

We all nodded and shouted, "Yes, sir!"

As the Squire turned toward the door, he spurred us on. "Well, let's get going then. There's no time to waste!"

Sad to say, fifteen minutes into my search, I found Grandma. She was suspended facedown among her beloved coral and crimson tea roses, which she and her mother had nurtured since her early childhood. After hesitating momentarily as I absorbed the shock, I rushed up the path, gently lifted Grandma up and out of the bushes, and then lowered her onto the lawn surrounding the clusters of decades-old roses. I knelt beside her and checked her thin neck for a pulse. There was none. Our Grandma was dead. But thankfully, she must have died quickly and painlessly. Despite the deep, oozing scratches on her cheeks from the razorlike thorns, Grandma appeared to be only napping. She didn't look any different now than when I would catch her dozing off on the porch in the steep slant of an autumn sun.

Leaving Grandma to recline comfortably in the garden, I ran back to the house, located the Squire, and reported, "I found her!"

Before I could explain, the Squire jumped in with a barrage of questions. "Where is she? What did she say? Is she all right?"

I lowered my head and stammered, "She's . . I'm sorry, sir. She's passed away."

He appeared stunned at first. He didn't speak; he just stood there shaking his head. And then, as if trying to undo the undeniable, he finally asked, "Passed away? Are you sure?"

I nodded and whispered, "Yes, sir. I'm sure. There was no pulse."

"Where is she?"

"I found her in the flower garden, sir. I believe she was tending her roses."

He paused; and then as if a switch had gone off in his head, he became the Squire of old, taking charge and giving orders. "Sam, before anything else, go to the barn and stables, round up the children, and bring them back here to the house. I don't want my darling Carolina or the boys wandering over to the flower garden and discovering Grandma. I'll call the police. They'll want to investigate, since Grandma died outside the hospital. And after that I'll have the unpleasant task of finding Allison and breaking the news."

Following Reverend Williams's wise counsel, the Squire and Allison transformed Grandma's funeral into a dignified celebration of her long and worthy life. Allison chose the music to reflect Grandma's predilection for jazz, folk, and blues. Among her eclectic choices were Knopfler's haunting "Going Home," Staines' celebratory "River," and Ellington's soulful "Come Sunday." And the Reverend Williams delivered a memorable funeral sermon weaving illustrative stories from Grandma's life throughout the scripture he had chosen to commemorate her good deeds:

> When one finds a worthy woman,
> Her value is far beyond pearls....

> She rises while it is still night,
>
> And distributes food to her household....
>
> She reaches out her hands to the poor,
>
> And extends her arms to the needy....
>
> She is clothed with strength and dignity,
>
> And she laughs at the days to come.

When the ceremony ended in the ballroom, the Squire, four neighbors, and I carried Grandma's casket out the funeral door and up the near hill to the extraordinary melting pot of a family cemetery containing the diverse remains of Union and rebel soldiers, sharecroppers and slaves, and the distinguished distant relatives of both Grandma and the Squire.

Regrettably, out of necessity it was back to business the day after Grandma's funeral. We were bumping up against the album launch, and so much still had to be accomplished: signing off on the liner notes, ensuring timely distribution of the records to retailers, and making the required rounds to the regional DJs encouraging maximum airplay for the lead cuts on *The Afterlife*.

When things finally settled down several days after the LP rolled out, Allison dropped by the ballroom unexpectedly. I had been spending my mornings there rehearsing piano arrangements for the regional tour. As she approached, I nodded and continued playing the final lines of "Missing You." As the last longing notes reverberated about the room, Allison slid one of the empire chairs up next to the piano bench, eased down into the plush chair, and complimented my songwriting. "That's one of the most evocative pieces I've ever performed or recorded."

I smiled and replied, "That really means a lot coming from you."

Following a few seconds of awkward silence, Allison's engaging smile faded and her relaxed demeanor stiffened into uncharacteristic apprehension. She obviously felt uncomfortable with what she was about to say. She leaned in toward the keyboard and haltingly said, "I've... I've got a big favor to ask of you."

As she paused, I jumped in enthusiastically, "Anything for you, Allison. What's up?"

She lowered her head and mumbled, "Well, Sam, I know that we invited you to join the band for at least the regional tour, but Grandma's death has turned everything upside down. We really wanted you to go along. The Squire and I felt you would be a real asset. But with Grandma now gone, me on tour, and the Squire working in Nashville, we... we don't know anyone we can trust to take care of the children. I hope..."

I raised my finger to my lips to stop her midsentence. I leaned in and said caringly, "Allison, I fully understand your concerns. I will happily stay with the children while you're on tour. It's no problem at all."

She rose from her chair with a bounce, walked over behind the bench, draped her arms down over my shoulders, and whispered, "You're a godsend, Sam; and ever since we met, you've brought me nothing but the best of luck."

Anticipating their departure in early May, I had spent the better part of an afternoon the following week at the lakefront hideaway packing summer clothes and, much more importantly, retrieving key volumes of the soldier's secret diary, which would provide countless story lines for future songs. As I was returning to the mansion along the wooded path, I spotted Allison racing toward me on her favorite buckskin quarter horse, Captain Bell. Allison pulled back heavily on the reins, gracefully swung down from the saddle, and began walking beside me.

After some teasing banter about my ragged flop hat and jeans, Allison smiled coyly and said, "I have another big favor to ask of you."

"Shoot!"

"Ah, since the Squire and I will be separated for most of the next two months, we'd like to pack a bag on the twenty-eighth and head over to Nashville for some quiet time—you know, away from the children and the business—before the regional tour begins."

While my heart sank thinking of the two of them going away together for "some quiet time," I lightheartedly responded, "No worries on this end. Enjoy yourselves. I'm ready and willing to take up the mantle at a moment's notice."

As the Squire strode into the room, he spotted the pile of suitcases Allison had packed for their brief Nashville getaway. He stopped, looked over at his young wife, and said, "My God, Allison. Nashville's not the start of your tour. This is just a short stay. You've packed enough for an army."

Allison put her hands on her hips good-naturedly and stood her ground. "Now you know we have to look our best when we're out and about. You never know who we'll run into... And besides, we'll be going to the Grand Ole Opry on Saturday night."

The Squire shook his head, picked up the bags, and headed outside.

As her husband disappeared onto the front porch, Allison turned and shouted up the stairs, "Beau! Zach! Carolina! Hurry down here and say good-bye. We're getting ready to leave now." The children scampered down the staircase, gave Allison a big hug, and then made a beeline for the front door to find their father, who was outside packing the car.

As Allison and I exited onto the porch, she looked over and gave me some last-minute instructions. "Now remember, Sam, Beau cannot have peanut butter. He's allergic to nuts. And Carolina must have her seizure medicine twice a day after her meals, once at breakfast and then again after dinner. Be sure she gets it now, you hear? If anything were to ever happen to her, I don't know what the Squire would do. He just dotes on her so much." Allison paused to mentally run through her final check-list again and then concluded with the catch-all admonition, "If you need us for anything, Sam, just call. I left the hotel number on the board next to the refrigerator."

Trying to alleviate her concerns, I put my finger up to my temple and tapped the side of my head several times. "No worries, Allison," I said. "I've got it all stored up here. You don't have to worry about a thing. Y'all just go to Nashville and enjoy yourselves." She smiled, tapped me on the arm, and descended the steps where the Squire and the children were waiting.

After giving their parents a final hug, Beau, Zach, and Carolina ran back up onto the porch and stood there with me waving until the Squire and Allison made the big turn onto the highway and headed east toward Music City. I took a deep breath, tousled Beau's hair, and whispered to myself, "Now it's up to me to make sure nothing goes wrong while the two of them are away."

During our first evening meal together after the parents' departure, Zach gleefully asked, "Hey, Sam, guess what?"

I laughed and responded, "Okay. I'll play along. What, Zach?"

"We have the day off tomorrow!" Beau and Carolina thrust their arms in the air and cheered the revelation.

"Okay, okay. Pipe down!" I said and then asked skeptically, "So, Zach, why do y'all have the day off tomorrow?"

"The election."

"The election?" I looked him straight in the eye and replied, "You're pulling my leg, right? It's not the time of year for that."

Sensing my doubt, he insisted, "Honest, Sam, we do have the day off. It's a special election for the senate, and they'll be using the cafeteria for the voting."

I paused, laughed, and then gave him a thumbs up, signaling that I bought his story and that I was happy that they had the day off. And I really was being honest with them. While on the one hand I would have to spend the day entertaining, on the other, I could continue the slow, complicated process of bonding with them. My objective from the outset was twofold: letting them know I was not there trying to replace their inimitable Grandma but rather trying to be a decent fellow, something of an older brother, supporting them anyway I could.

So what better way to illustrate the point than allowing the children to sleep late the next morning and before waking them prepare their favorite Southern breakfast—country ham and Acadian beignet topped with copious amounts of powdered sugar. When the first servings of ham and fritters were ready for the plates, I climbed the stairs and knocked on the children's doors. "Carolina, are you up?" I called. "Zach, Beau, breakfast is ready!" I waited until I heard murmurs, then headed back downstairs to deep-fry a second batch of New Orleans' finest beignet. Several minutes after receiving the summons to appear, Zach and Beau raced into the kitchen, perched themselves atop the tall stools lining the granite counter, and began devouring the irresistible fritters at an alarming pace.

After draining and dusting the next batch of beignet, I went back upstairs, knocked on Carolina's door, and loudly promoted the ham and fritters again. There was no response. I shouted her name: "Carolina?" There was no answer. After knocking even more aggressively, I slowly turned the crystal knob and pushed the door open just enough to allow the hallway light to slant across the darkened room.

Since the thick drapes were fully drawn, I could barely make out her small frame facing the wall with her knees tucked up close to her chest. I pushed the door back all the way, approached the bed, and called her name again. "Carolina, wake up. Are you okay?" I then gently shook her shoulders; still no response. I could feel the adrenaline surging as I pulled the child away from the wall and discovered her eyes were only partially closed. While instinctively putting my fingers up to her neck, I was praying, "Please let her just be sleeping." But the gods ignored my heartfelt prayer. There was no pulse, and her body had already lost its warmth.

I softly lowered her head onto the pillow, ran down the hallway to the master suite, and telephoned the operator to report the emergency. I next hurried downstairs to forewarn the twins their sister had fallen ill and that a paramedic team would be arriving shortly. When the volunteer firemen arrived, I explained the situation, escorted them up the center stair-case to Carolina's bedroom, and stood in the doorway as they worked frantically over her lifeless body, hoping against hope that somehow they would find a way to revive her.

After fifteen torturous minutes, the fire captain strode over to the doorway to address me. He removed his helmet, stowed it under his arm, and said, "There's really nothing we could have done. All signs point to her having died sometime during the middle of the night. Did she have any medical problems you know of? Children don't just up and die without there being some underlying cause."

Still in a state of shock, I shook my head and mumbled, "All I know is that she was taking seizure medicine mornings and nights."

"Well, that's at least a clue. I've seen this once or twice before where children were being treated for seizures. It's a damn shame.... In any event the coroner will want to do an autopsy." He paused, looked around the room for a few seconds, and then moved on to another topic. "When we arrived, I believe you said that you were looking out for the children while the parents were away. Did I hear that right, you know, with all the commotion going on?"

"That's right, sir. They're in Nashville for a brief stay."

He pulled out a pen and small notepad and asked, "Do you have the contact information handy so that I can inform them?"

"Yes, sir." I paused, looked away, and continued, "But I... I feel it's my responsibility to let them know what's happened to little Carolina."

The fire captain shook his head and responded, "That's mighty brave of you, son, and I don't envy you one bit having to make that call. It's never easy, no matter who it is. But informing the parents of the death of a child has got to be the hardest by far."

I nodded, swallowed hard, and didn't reply. I knew that if I said anything, the quaver in my voice would give away the fear and dread coursing through my veins.

When the paramedics had finished loading Carolina's body onto a gurney, I asked the captain to give me five minutes to get her brothers out of the house so they wouldn't witness the horrific scene. The paramedics complied, and I quickly escorted the twins out to the family garden under the ruse of their helping me pick fresh vegetables for a healthy midday meal.

Once I saw the ambulance pulling out of the driveway onto the pike, I turned to the boys. "Hey, fellas, I think you've harvested enough now. Why don't you stay outside a while and shoot some hoops. I need to call your parents about Carolina's illness." The boys shrugged and went to find the basketball while I faced my dark task.

After entering the house, I eased out of the brave, light-hearted character I had been playing with the boys and faced the situation. I slowly climbed the stairs, walked down the hallway to Carolina's room, and stood in the threshold staring at the abandoned dolls, the crumpled sheets, and the empty bed. Ironically, her bedroom now seemed so much more alive. During their frantic efforts to revive Carolina, the paramedics had thrown open the curtains, allowing the spring light to dance among the memories and animate the mystical space.

I reluctantly turned away, continued down the hallway, and entered the darkened master suite to make the call to Nashville. I sat down on the edge of the bed next to the telephone and buried my head in my hands. Like a twitch, I repeatedly ran my fingers through my hair as intense waves of emotion crashed over my confidence and resolve. How would I explain the inexplicable? How would Allison and the Squire react to the horrific news? Would they blame me, since their child had died while in my care? How would Carolina's death affect my relationship with Allison? What would this tragedy do to my career?

I took several deep breaths attempting to regain my composure. My hands trembled as I picked up the receiver and dialed the number they had given me "just in case I really needed to get in touch." Fear surged through my veins. As the phone began ringing, I prayed to the gods Allison would answer. I selfishly wanted her to be the one to break the awful news to the Squire. I knew I couldn't bear his heartrending reaction. His "little Carolina" had been the light of his life.

When I heard the soft, tentative "Hello," I asked, "Allison, is that you?"

She must have detected the quiver in my voice and responded, "What is it, Sam? What's wrong?"

I began stammering uncontrollably. "I'm… I'm so sorry. I… I had no idea. She… she seemed okay last night before going to bed. It's… it's Carolina. I found her this morning… unresponsive. I… I immediately called for paramedics. They examined her and said… said there was nothing they could do. She… she's dead."

Allison didn't reply. There was a long silence, and then I believe she placed the receiver down near the telephone. I heard her voice and then the Squire's. At first the dialogue was eerily quiet with slight pauses between question and response. But quickly the exchanges became frenzied and clipped. I couldn't take it any longer. The last thing I heard before hanging up the phone was the Squire's long, excruciating, guttural scream.

10

THE GODS ALWAYS seem to know where to find the loose threads that unravel the soul. Despite their unbearable loss, Allison and the Squire managed to maintain their composure throughout the obligatory ordeal of the viewing, the funeral, and the twilight burial near Grandma in the Afterlife cemetery. Frankly, I've never envied the minister's ceremonial task of rationalizing untimely death for bereaved family members. While it must be challenging preparing and delivering credible eulogies for the elderly who've lived long, productive lives, it must be next to impossible justifying the aneurysm and the unexpected death of a seemingly vibrant, healthy child.

But there was the Reverend Williams valiantly attempting to strike the right chord for the second time this bleak spring month. Contrary to liturgical protocol, the sensitive prelate based Carolina's eulogy on Wordsworth's lyrical "We Are Seven" rather than on a germane passage from the divine scriptures:

> —A simple child,
> That lightly draws its breath,
> And feels its life in every limb,
> What should it know of death?

So the clergyman was raising the bar, signaling he would tackle the Sisyphean question head-on: why do the gods tear our children from us? But the reverend had already unwittingly engineered failure into his funeral sermon. Secular philosophy and reason were out; he was a holy man compelled to rely on the Bible to address the thorniest of existential issues.

He quoted Zechariah, who prophesied of a New Jerusalem where "men and women of ripe old age will sit in the streets… and the city will be filled with boys and girls playing there." He cited Isaiah, who spoke of the new heaven and earth where "the sound of weeping and of crying will be heard no more. Where never again will there be an infant who lives but a few days, or an old man who does not live out his years." He referenced the Old Testament psalmist who offered God as a "refuge and strength, an ever-present help in trouble." He included Saint Paul, who suggested a similar consolation in the New Testament: "I consider the sufferings of this present time are not worth comparing with the glory about to be revealed to us. We know that in everything that God works for the good with those who love him." And he shared Saint Matthew's story about Jesus:

> At that time the disciples came to Jesus and asked,
> "Who is the greatest in the kingdom of heaven?" He
> called a child, whom he put among them, and said,
> "Truly I tell you, unless you change and become
> like children, you will never enter the kingdom of
> heaven. Whoever becomes humble like this child

is the greatest in the kingdom of heaven. Whoever
welcomes one such child in my name welcomes me."

As I sat among the mourners staring out through the ceiling-high windows beyond the Steinway, I synthesized the pastor's well-intentioned assertions based solely on Judeo-Christian doctrine—there would be children in the afterlife; they would no longer die prematurely; God comforts bereaved parents; and the Almighty works in mysterious ways for the good of true believers. While no one would argue the minister's predictable assurances were in any way inappropriate for this solemn occasion, many must have left the services feeling the clergyman had overpromised and underdelivered. He had failed to tackle his own highly visible initial question, "Why?," which we all wanted answered with devout conviction.

The first casualty after the funeral was Allison's yearlong tour; and the second was the Squire's lucrative agency business in Nashville. During the months immediately following Carolina's death, Allison and I noticed a radical change in the Squire's mood and behavior. This once expansive, larger-than-life personality had become increasingly irritable and withdrawn, found excuses to avoid Nashville, stopped eating dinner with the family, slept until late in the afternoon, and made daily sunset visits to his beloved Carolina's grave. As he became increasingly gaunt, humorless, and incommunicative, Allison repeatedly encouraged him to seek professional help. But this proud, physically strong Southern gentleman politely dismissed her concerns, declaring he would work through this temporary setback on his own.

Given all the challenges the Squire had faced throughout his life, Allison never really lost hope her resourceful husband would eventually find a way to subdue the demons on his own; that is, until we heard the harsh, incessant knocking at the front door during a violent thunderstorm in early September. The Squire had left earlier in the day "to drive around again to clear his mind," and Allison and I were working in the ball-room tweaking several ballads, while the boys were in school during the first week of their fall semester. Perhaps sensing there was something threatening in the loud, insistent rapping, Allison asked me to find out who was paying a visit in such dreadful weather.

I slowly swung the heavy door open. There before me I discovered a burly pair of highway patrolmen in bright orange slickers flanking either side of the screened entrance. The senior officer was the first to speak.

"We're here to speak with Allison Summerfield."

"Of course. Come on in."

Dumbfounded, I escorted the troopers down the long hallway to the ballroom where Allison was now standing beside the piano. When she saw the patrolmen entering at the far end of the room, she shouted anxiously, "Officers, is there any-thing wrong? Has my husband been in an accident?" Neither answered but kept advancing toward her across the parquet floor. The loud heel strikes of their long leather boots echoed ominously about the enormous room. As they neared the piano, the older officer responded enigmatically, "Excuse me, ma'am, your husband's, ah, resting comfortably at McGill General."

This first mysterious, unsettling response was the most reassuring news we heard the rest of the afternoon. The officer's account spiraled downward in a quiet monotone: "Some people said they saw your husband leave his car at one end of the bridge over the Duck River, you know, near Grave's Bend. They said he walked toward the center of the bridge in the pouring rain, climbed up over the wall, and, ah, just jumped. Two fellows who'd been fishing and taken cover under the bridge when the storm blew in saw your husband hit the water, pop up, and start floating toward them.

"They untied their boat from the pier, paddled over, and dragged him in over the side. They said he was out cold, but breathing. They said the Lord must have been with him. He hadn't swallowed a lick of water. They cranked up their motorboat pronto and headed straight for shore. While these boys were getting to shore with your husband, the fellows who saw him jump off the bridge ran down to the riverbank near Gerry's Bait Shop to help out when the boat landed. But even before the men in the boat had reached the shallow water with your husband, they were already shouting out orders to everyone on shore: 'Call an ambulance! Call the state police!'

"My, ah, partner here, ah, this is Ed. We got the call from dispatch. We were already out this way investigating some downed trees and power lines. We got over to the bait shop lickety-split. Got there even before the ambulance from McGill

General. We checked your husband out and saw he was out cold but didn't seem to be in any real danger.

"After we got him loaded in the ambulance, we started talking to people. We first spoke with the fellows in the boat and then with the eyewitnesses at the bridge, who showed us your husband's car. And that's where we found this note he'd left on the driver's seat."

The patrolman handed the folded sheet of stationary to Allison, who slowly sat down on the piano bench, took a very deep breath, hesitantly opened the note, and began reading. When she had finished examining the contents, she extended her shaking hand toward me and said with a palpable hurt in her voice, "Here, read the note. It's okay. He didn't address it to anyone in particular. It's sort of a personal message to the world." She then buried her head in her hands and murmured quietly, "Why didn't I understand the degree of suffering? Why didn't I heed the warnings?"

I sat down in one of the empire chairs near the piano and began reading the Squire's excruciating words of explanation:

I'm sorry. I've tried. The pain's just too great. I can't take it anymore. Wishing it will not bring her back. I hate the vulnerability, the fear, and the shame. When any of you've suggested I get help, I've sensed your disappointment, your judgment and criticism of my failures. Going to a psychiatrist after what they did to my Dad, dragging him away in the middle of the night to an institution for the rest of his life? That's not for me. Sorry for everything. Forgive me. With love to all. Goodbye.

The next few months oscillated between hope and despair. The extended hospitalization, the intense therapy, and the cutting-edge antidepressants seemed to be working well enough to allow the Squire to return to The Afterlife. In fact, he had begun talking about returning to the agency in Nashville and rescheduling much of Allison's postponed transcontinental tour. He even felt strong enough to celebrate another Thanksgiving with the homeless at Saint Paul's. But during the long, dark winter days between Thanksgiving and Christmas, the pendulum began swinging back the other way.

"I'm really getting worried again, Sam," Allison said, as she entered the kitchen, where I was getting a bite to eat.

I could see the concern on her face. I put my sandwich down and motioned for her to take a seat across the table from me.

As she eased into the chair, she continued speaking in a stream-of-consciousness way. "All the symptoms are coming back, Sam: the irritability, withdrawing from everybody. He's not eating right, and he's back out at the graveyard every sunset visiting 'his Carolina.' We're going to have to do something.... Fool me twice, shame on me.... With him in his current state, there's no use suggesting that he see the psychiatrist or return to the hospital to get checked out."

"What do you think we should do?" I asked.

"I don't know for sure; but maybe if I got him to see our general practitioner for his loss of appetite, the doctor would detect his condition and persuade him to return to the psychiatrist or the hospital for follow-on help."

"I'd give it a shot. I think it's got a good chance of working out—you know, having the doctor on your side to convince him to get help."

"Yeah, well, I guess it's worth a try. I'll start working on him when he wakes up from his nap."

And Allison's strategy worked flawlessly. That is, until the oft-forgotten law of unintended consequences spun her diversionary plan out of control. During the elevator ride up to the twelfth-floor medical suite, Allison and I couldn't help but notice the Squire's acute agitation. He was trembling. He paced and muttered incomprehensible phrases under his breath. To no one's surprise, the doctor recognized the Squire's significant depression during the fifteen-minute interview and recommended he return to the hospital for further evaluation and perhaps a change in medications. But not long after completing the examination and leaving the room to speak privately with Allison, the doctor heard strange, unusually loud noises coming from behind the closed door.

The physician raced back to the exam room but found the door had been jammed. "Open the door, sir! Open the door, Mr. Summerfield!" he shouted. But there was no response. After what seemed to be an eternity, the doctor managed to dislodge the obstruction—a metal chair the Squire had wedged against the knob—and burst into the room just as the patient thrust his right leg out the open window. The physician was convinced the Squire had every intention of jumping from the twelfth-floor suite. He spoke with a soothing voice and advanced slowly toward the window. "Now hold on there a minute, sir. Let's talk this out. There's no need to do this. Your family needs you."

The Squire shouted back, "I've had enough!" and swung his left leg around to clear the wide sill. The doctor lunged toward the Squire and, grabbing his long white hair, managed to pull him back into the building. Within an instant, the nurses, Allison, and I all piled into the room and held the Squire down while the doctor telephoned for an ambulance.

I don't know whether it was bravery, instinct, or shock that allowed Allison to maintain her composure until the emergency crew wheeled the Squire out of the suite and into the elevator. Once the elevator doors had closed and the floor numbers began to tick down, Allison leaned her head against my shoulder, began sobbing uncontrollably, and whispered, "Why? Why now? Why?…"

So much had happened in such a short amount of time. Grandma's fatal heart attack. Carolina's tragic death. The Squire's cruel relapse and hospitalization. It was almost too much to bear. Nevertheless, Allison and I were determined to create an old-fashioned Christmas for the twins, who missed their father deeply and mailed him get-well wishes every day.

We succeeded in finding everything on their extensive wish lists, including the extremely scarce Optimus Prime action figure, which could be transformed from a conventional cab-over truck into the powerful iron-armed leader of the Cybertronic Autobots. Even the weather worked in our favor. The week before Christmas we took advantage of an unusually heavy snowfall to harness Allison's favorite draft horse, Old Mike, to an antique sleigh and drive the boys out to the far reaches of The Afterlife to find the most perfectly sculpted Scotch pine for the family room. And adhering to the Squire's favorite holiday traditions, we encouraged the boys to help decorate the tree, wrap small gifts for the shut-ins and homeless, and collect canned goods for the Squire's Food Bank in McGill.

Following a poignant afternoon visit to the hospital on Christmas Eve, Allison, the twins, and I drove back to The Afterlife, where we all pitched in to prepare a hearty feast of some of the boys' favorites: buttery oyster stew, baked glazed ham, cornbread dressing, mashed potatoes and gravy, and the indispensable pecan pie with huge scoops of vanilla ice cream melting on the side. After returning the kitchen to a spotless condition, which the twins said would have made even Grandma proud, we retired to the family room.

I cupped my hands together, put them up to my mouth, blew warm air into them, and shouted to the twins, "It's cold in here! Let's build a fire. What do you say?"

Zach and Beau jumped up and down and cried, "Yes! Yes! A big fire!"

"Well, get some logs and kindling from the box and stack it neatly on the andirons. Remember, the kindling goes on first, next the smaller logs, and then the bigger ones. And when you've got that job done, we'll hang our stockings, sing a few Christmas songs, and then it'll be off to bed with y'all. So let's get to work!" I looked over at Allison and winked. She nodded and responded with an approving smile.

It was well past their bedtime when we ushered the boys off to bed, tired and happy. That's when the real work began. First Allison and I had to retrieve all the boys' gifts we had hidden about the house. "You got the second-floor list?" I asked.

"Yeah, and you the first-floor list?" Allison replied.

I nodded, held the piece of paper high above my head, and answered, "You better believe it!"

As she turned away toward the stairs, she said, "Well, let's get started then. Last one back is a rotten egg!"

While I had two fewer gifts to retrieve, Allison beat me back to the family room by more than five minutes. As I turned the corner and entered the room, she said playfully, "Well, I always thought men were better hunters; but look at you there dragging up the rear."

I piled my armload of gifts onto the sofa, laughed, and replied lightheartedly, "With all due respect, Your Honor, in my defense I would classify our activity more as 'shopping' than 'hunting.' And with that being the case, I would have to conclude, young lady, that you would have a distinct advantage over me, that is, my being a man. Come on now, everyone knows that shopping is in a woman's wheelhouse."

Allison wagged her finger teasingly and responded, "Well, I guess we'll just have to call our case 'moot' and put it on appeal. In the meantime, we had better get to work wrapping all these gifts." She paused, looked me in the eyes, and asked, "Serious now, have you done much wrapping?"

I laughed and answered, "Hey, I'm not totally incompetent. I can hold my own."

She extended her arm and said, "Well then, here's a pair of scissors, plenty of tape, and a package of stick-on name tags. The wrapping and tissue paper are over there on the table. So how about you taking the crystal radio kits, wristwatches, and board games, and I'll wrap the rock tumblers, action figures, metal detectors, and Million Color Drawing Sets."

"Sounds like a plan. Let the good times roll!"

We dispatched with our respective duties at a steady pace, but once we had finished wrapping this mother lode of gifts for Zach and Beau, we still had to undertake the most difficult and time-consuming task of all: assembling two Motobécane touring bikes with exquisitely etched handlebars, Italian saddle seats, and high-performance derailleurs. In a sense we became a world-class surgical team with Allison reading the directions and handing me the specified nut, bolt, screw, or washer and me positioning the part and tightening it into place. As this transfer of bicycle parts continued well into the night, the touches became softer and the gazes longer.

While I finished tightening the last bolts on the bicycles, Allison excused herself to change into something more comfortable. When she returned, she was wearing a plush, dark-green terry cloth robe. She had removed her makeup and loosened her dark hair, allowing it to flow down gracefully around her shoulders. She moved over to the curved sofa facing the fireplace, collapsed onto the thick cushions, and drew her long legs up under her. Then she sighed, closed her eyes, and slowly dropped her head back onto the top cushion. It was the first time I had seen her trying to relax since the Squire's latest setback.

"It's been a helluva month," I said. "How about a whiskey on the rocks with a splash of branch?"

"Sounds good, Sam."

I made the drinks, handed her a tumbler, and sat down beside her. Tall, yellow, blue-tipped flames continued licking up through the glowing hickory logs. We clinked our glasses. "Merry Christmas, Allison," I said.

"Merry Christmas, Sam. Thanks for all you've been doing to help us out."

"Believe me, that goes both ways."

Allison slowly ran her fingers around the rim of her glass and reflectively murmured, "Merry Christmas." She then gazed into my eyes and whispered, "Yes, we must make this a merry Christmas. For the boys and… and… and for ourselves. Who knows what lurks after the first of the year. Everything could unravel. Honestly, I don't think the doctors know how to treat the Squire. Each new medication looks promising for a week or two and then stops working. God, what if he could never come home and get back to work again? What would we do then? Without the Squire and his connections, there'd be no tours, no recordings, and no income from the agency. Perhaps the ups and downs and the hectic demands of the holidays have taken their toll, but for the first time I really feel overwhelmed. Alone. Afraid we could lose The Afterlife and everything we've worked so hard to achieve."

As Allison spoke, her voice began quivering and tears welled up in her eyes. Without thinking, I began stroking her hair and promising the improbable. "Everything will be all right. I'll think of a way to help out with the bills."

She smiled appreciatively through the tears, moved gently toward me, and rested her head against mine. I stretched my arm out along the back of the sofa, grasped her shoulder, and pulled her even closer to me. We then sat there motionless among the shadows staring into the hot, rhythmic fire.

Her touch, her tears, and her vulnerability finally moved me to confess what I had been feeling for many months. "Allison, ah, you once said we have to live in the moment. So I have some things I need to say. I... I know I could be risking everything, but I believe you should know that as long as I live you'll never be alone. What I feel today is what I've sensed almost from the moment we first met in the teachers' lounge and discussed Capote and your early career. I experienced a connection with you far beneath the words and phrases. I don't know exactly how to describe what I had never really felt before. It was as if our souls were loosely mingling and then merging. And then when the summer passed without seeing you, the memory lingered and sparked the first of my many Allison lyrics, 'Missing You.'

"But it was during that first Thanksgiving at Saint Paul's performing together, I knew then exactly how I felt. I remember the very moment. You had motioned me up onto the tiny stage. I began playing a borrowed twelve-string and singing backup on the hallelujahs. God, what a sweet spot in time. Until then, you didn't know I sang and played; and I didn't know you had become aware of Cohen's latest song. As we approached those last lines, you looked over toward me, smiled, and shook your head perhaps out of surprise or happiness or professional respect. When you gazed into my eyes, I felt our souls becoming one. I... I knew then I had fallen in love with you.

"So after moving out to the cabin, I began writing for you. Not just songs for you to record but *for you* in the sense of capturing my intense feelings and hoping that one day I could explain the underlying themes of isolation, longing, and redemption. In fact, during the prep sessions before you recorded 'Missing You,' 'Ridgeline Whispers,' 'Moonlight Jester,' 'Miracle Sky,' and 'Blind Metaphor,' you asked a number of dangerous questions: 'What were you feeling when you wrote the lines?' 'What were you *really* trying to say there?' 'Did you have a specific person in mind?'... More than once I came close to revealing everything—explaining that you were the 'you' in 'Missing You,' the sensual voice of the rolling ridgeline, the gracious monarch to my taciturn fool, the silvery sweep of stars across the summer sky, and the vital metaphor for my inspiration, my creative fulfillment, and my deepest love."

I never moved away from Allison as I bared my soul. I continued holding her, caressing her shoulder, and staring into the fire. But it was now time to interpret her silence. I took a deep breath, pulled my head back from hers, and gazed into her eyes. "I . . I hope I haven't offended you, or made you uncomfortable on this special night. But I… I just had to tell you."

Allison remained silent as tears welled up in her eyes and began flowing down her cheeks. She slowly raised her arms, cradled my head in her hands, and whispered, "No, no. After all we've endured, how could your expression of love offend me or make me feel uncomfortable in any way?" She leaned back against the sofa, inhaled deeply, and said, "I didn't plan on saying anything, but under the circumstances I believe I owe you a response. So where to begin? Yes.… Thanksgiving Day at Saint Paul's. The concert and the conversation after everyone else had left. I was struck with how much you reminded me of an early lover of mine, a gifted pianist and lyricist, who left for Paris after agreeing our timing wasn't right."

Allison paused and left me to fill in the blanks. How did she really feel about the musician? Were there any regrets the relationship dissolved? Was Allison trying to tell me the timing might not be right for us? Or did she believe you can go home again? You can recapture at least some of the feelings of a first love.

She lowered her head and said: "Do you believe you're the only isolated artist who has ever sat at a typewriter and succumbed to the longing and the loneliness?" She paused again, leaving me to decipher another message. Is she telling me to man up—that there are a lot of lonely writers and composers and the isolation helps them to focus and dig deeply into their creative reservoirs? Or is it possible that despite her marriage to the Squire she has had similar thoughts of missing and longing?

After a moment, Allison looked up, gazed into my eyes, and said, "Let me explain with an analogy. Say there was a captivating object in the middle of the room here. You're in the far corner over there, and I'm over here on the other side of the room in the opposite corner. So we are viewing the object from different angles, but the object itself remains the same. It loses none of its characteristics, its value, or its beauty."

Allison paused a third time; but now she appeared to be waiting for a response. And again, all I had were questions. What were our different angles of vision? On several occasions, Allison had described me as "the romantic" and she "the cautious one," who had endured several difficult relationships prior to marrying the Squire. So is she contending that while our experiences influence our perceptions of the object, they can never impact the object's intrinsic splendor or worth? Which brings me to the key question—what does the object represent? Unspoken mutual love and respect? The real possibility of a lasting relationship? If so, is this her "cautious" way of saying she has also fallen in love with me?

Following a few seconds of awkward silence, Allison rose from the sofa and said, "It's very late. We'd better get to bed. The boys will be up early to open presents."

After tending the fire, we stood for several minutes with our arms locked around each other's waist, lost in our own thoughts as we admired the foiled layers of presents and the magical shimmering tree. As we turned and climbed the elegant staircase to the second floor, Allison slipped her arm around mine, and we continued on down the hallway arm in arm toward my bedroom door. When we reached the entry, I stopped to say farewell but felt a gentle pull, suggesting this was not where I would be spending the night.

Allison led me into her room and over to the four-poster bed. She turned toward me and looked up into my eyes. I slowly leaned in, gently kissed her on the lips, and said, "I really love you."

She moved her arms down from my waist, loosened the belt on her terry robe, allowed it to drop from her shoulders onto the floor, and whispered, "Show me."

Her face, arms, and full breasts were now bathed in the soft moonlight slanting through the frosted casements on the far side of the room. I lovingly swept the hair back from her eyes, embraced her, and kissed her tenderly again and again.

As we slowly eased down onto the large, soft bed, I continued kissing her, sliding down from her lips, to her neck, to her breasts, and then to her inner thighs. She moaned, grasped the back of my head, and firmly pulled me in toward her. Allison's breath quickened, her breasts firmed, and her stomach undulated in rhythmic waves of hopeful pleasure. Slowly, slowly the tension, the expectation grew within her. She breathed in deeply once, twice, arched her back, and then welcomed me into her love. The mingling had ended; the merging had begun. Time vanished; commitments faded; cares disappeared. As the pulsating movement slowed and became more focused, she firmly locked me in place, signaling it was now time for our shared release; and every move we made was hallelujah.

11

THE FOLLOWING SPRING we learned March could easily rival April as the cruelest month. The Squire remained hospitalized, showing signs of improvement followed by relapses into sadness, weight loss, agitation, and suicidal thoughts. As the revenue stream from royalties disappeared, the unpaid bills mounted. I continued writing songs for Allison based on the secret journals, but for what? Allison and I had no way to perform the lyrics or to record them. It was obvious to both of us the gods were applying the squeeze and we would have to find a new, viable way to combat their unprovoked war of attrition.

After a day of soul searching, Allison and I hit on the idea of retrieving the Squire's valuable Rolodex from his Nashville office and mining it for names of potential agents who could put me on the road performing and making money. As she handed over the Squire's custom key ring loaded with more than two dozen keys, she smiled and said, "Looks like the odds aren't good you'll ever even get in the building."

The next morning I partook of a hearty breakfast and readied myself for the event that could change my life. Allison packed a small overnight bag for me, gathered the boys on the top steps of the front porch, and waved hopefully as I drove off to Music City in their vintage family van. When I arrived in Nashville, I sensed the gods were once again shaping the battle-field. The mission was way too easy. First, I found a rare, highly prized parking space in front of the Ryman Auditorium on Fifth Avenue directly across the street from the Squire's office building. Second, facing at least twenty-five-to-one odds, I immediately chose the key that opened the front door. And third, when I switched on the office light, the critical objective of the mission, the Rolodex, was sitting squarely in the middle of the Squire's desk, as if waiting for me. I remember thinking the gods were up to something and there would surely be pay-back for my brief run of good fortune.

I must admit I didn't collect the Rolodex and leave imme-diately. I believe it was the overwhelming sense of melan-choly that compelled me to stay. The blinds were drawn tight, allowing only small slits of bright sunlight to enter the dusty space. All the decorative plants had withered except for a large golden barrel cactus, which had been programmed millennia before to endure such severe neglect. Despite the lively photos, gold records, and music memorabilia scattered about the room, the office projected a sickening feeling of loneliness and aban-donment. It was as if I had entered a colorful spiral shell after the unfortunate occupant had been forced out of its protective chamber into the raging sea. So helping in the only way avail-able to me, I opened the blinds, watered the plants, grabbed the Rolodex, and left, locking the door behind me.

When I returned home to The Afterlife, Allison greeted me at the door. The boys were back in school, and the house was quiet. We headed straight for the dining room table, where I dumped the Rolodex overflowing with index cards. "How in the world are we going to get through all of this?" I asked.

She looked at me. "If I know the Squire, he has notations on the backs of all of these cards. We'll use that to narrow our search."

Allison was right. The front of each card listed just what you would expect—the person's name, company, and contact information—but on the back were notations about family, personal interests, and most important, musical interests. We sorted out the agents, then reduced the list to five candidates who might want to hear from me. The next day I was on my way to Memphis to record a demo tape.

Several weeks passed before I received the first of five curt rejection memoranda. So it was then back to the Rolodex to broaden the search criteria. For good luck we chose the next thirteen most likely candidates. Unfortunately, out of this subsequent baker's dozen, we received positive feedback from only one agent, who according to our research was the youngest and least experienced of all the representatives we had contacted. It was our only lead, so we pounced on it.

The following morning I spoke to the New York–based Mr. Gallagher's secretary by telephone and arranged a meeting with him for the next week in Nashville at a downtown hotel, where the agent was already scheduled to attend a major singer-song-writer convention. When I arrived at the hotel with my six- and twelve-string guitars in tow, I telephoned Mr. Gallagher from the lobby. A squeaky voice answered, "Gallagher here."

Overcoming the shock of the agent's unimpressive voice, I responded, "It's, ah, Sam Lynch, sir. I arranged a meeting with you for today through your secretary last week."

"Oh yes, Sam, I was expecting you. Take the elevator up to the top floor. You'll find me in the presidential suite at the end of the hallway. You can audition. And then we'll talk turkey."

When the agent opened the door, my first reaction was "My God, the high-pitched voice on the phone certainly doesn't match the physique." Mr. Gallagher was no more than twenty-five years old with obvious Irish ancestry in his genes. He was handsome, at least six feet five inches tall, muscular with long, copper hair and striking blue eyes. His firm handshake and broad, infectious smile engendered confidence, rapport, and trust.

He ushered me into the expansive corner living room opening onto a balcony with panoramic views that stretched from the Greek Ionic state house to the Parthenon in Centennial Park.

"Samuel, I've heard the demo tape. Now I would like to experience your songs live and unplugged, as they say. Then I'll feel more comfortable providing feedback and discussing the future."

"Of course. Let me just get set up here." Taking a deep breath to steady my hands, I removed my guitars from the hard cases, tuned them, and played three of my new lyrics based on the secret Afterlife journals, "Memories at the Beauregard," "Juda's Prize," and "Living Out Our Days."

When I had finished performing the three songs, my critical audience of one smiled, applauded heartily, motioned for me to take a seat next to him, and then began his all-important critique. "First of all, the lyrics are outstanding," he said. "They create a natural tension where relevant contemporary themes flow naturally from the nineteenth-century subject matter. Your voice is good, but not great. And honestly, I would question pitching you as an artist who could fill large venues. Smaller sites would be the way to go; but they present a completely different set of challenges. Less space equals less audience equals less exposure equals less record sales equals less revenues equals less income for you and me.

"But I think I have a proven win-win way out of the box. I have an artist or two in your situation who have played smaller venues, sold a lot of records, and made decent money. But not here. Not in the States. They've gone overseas. You see, Europeans love anything American, especially American singer-songwriters. You would have to do some traveling, but the folks and especially the ladies are very hospitable. A lot of free room and board, if you know what I mean."

He reached into his vest pocket and pulled out a piece of paper. "I have management and booking ties to agents in Ireland, the UK, and the rest of Europe. Here's a sample itinerary of one-night stands for one of my American artists touring Ireland and the UK as we speak: Mayo, Galway, Clare, Donegal, Kerry, West Cork, and Dublin in Ireland and Bolton, Newbury, Briston, Manchester, London, and the Isle of Wight in the UK. You see, there's more travel, but much more opportunity. It won't make you rich or make you famous; but it will keep you comfortable. Sound like something you could live with?"

Despite his youth and relative inexperience, Mr. Gallagher's opinion rang true. It echoed the Squire's earlier comments about my work, my talent, and my optimal venues. While I didn't want to leave the States and be so far away for such an extended period, I felt I had no choice but to keep my promise to Allison of helping her any way I could. While nodding my agreement to his proposition, the confident Mr. Gallagher opened his briefcase and produced a lengthy, fully prepared contract, which I briefly scanned and signed.

When I got home Allison was putting the boys to bed. I had just poured us a double whiskey when she entered the family room, and we sat down on the curved sofa together.

"So how did it go?" she asked, taking her glass of whiskey.

I opened with the good news. "Well… I signed on with Mr. Gallagher, who has been consistently successful in booking his clients into profitable venues."

Allison leaned in, stretched her arms around my neck, kissed me lightly on the lips, and said, "Thank God! I had all the faith of the world in you. I knew you'd succeed."

I hesitated and then turned to the devil in the details. "Ah, you need to know something, Allison."

"What's that?"

"If all goes according to plan, I'll be leaving in May. I'll be traveling across Europe for seven months and returning to The Afterlife just in time for Christmas."

Allison slowly collapsed back against the sofa and stared blankly into space, trying to absorb the implications of my pronouncement. After almost a minute of reflective silence, she turned toward me and asked a series of questions: "Are you sure this is the only way? Are you okay with the many months on the road overseas? Does this make sense financially?"

"Do I really have a choice, Allison?" I responded. "You have to remember the Squire's assessment: good but limited talents unlikely to draw large crowds. And that's exactly where Mr. Gallagher came down. That's why he recommended Europe. Folks over there are more forgiving, especially when an American's performing. And as for your specific questions, yes, I believe it's the only way. Yes, I'll survive, but it'll be very tough not seeing you for the next seven months. Yes, there will be enough income for all of us to share and survive." I paused, gazed into her eyes, smiled reassuringly but thought to myself, "And no, I haven't got a clue how many of these forays into the wilderness I'll have to endure to keep us afloat."

May came too soon. Before I knew it, Allison was driving me over to Berry Field in Nashville for the first leg of my trip to Cologne, Germany, where my European tour would begin. Since I knew our separation would be painful, I asked that she just drop me off at the terminal, say a quick good-bye, and then drive away. But Allison insisted on staying with me on the observation deck until they called my flight. We didn't say much; we just held hands and stared out at the busy panorama unfolding below us.

When the inevitable announcement finally came, we spontaneously gripped the other's hand more tightly, slowly turned, and embraced. I then held her out at arm's length, gazed into her eyes, and whispered, "I love you so much. I'm really going to miss you, the boys, and The Afterlife."

Allison leaned in, put her head on my shoulder, and said, "Take care of yourself, Sam. We'll be looking forward to having you home for Christmas, and I promise you it will be the very best celebration of your life."

I took her head in my hands, kissed her passionately, and then gently pulled away. I picked up my small overnight bag, walked to the top of the stairs, turned around, smiled, and bravely waved good-bye.

The sun had finally broken through the stubborn low-hanging clouds as I stepped out of the taxi the following afternoon and dragged my guitars up the long set of stairs to Heinrich Böll Plaza in Cologne. Since I had gotten some sleep on the overnight flight from New York, I was rested, full of energy, and ready to explore. I had asked the airport cabbie to wait for me while I dropped my bags off at the Pension Jansen near the university and then to drive me over to the Ludwig Museum situated between the eastern choir of Cologne cathedral and the majestic Hohenzollern Bridge spanning the Rhine.

As I strolled along the tree-lined plaza, I paused, standing metaphorically at the midpoint of a continuum arcing almost eight hundred years of Germanic history and culture. The contrast was striking. To my right, a massive medieval edifice of ribbed vaults, pointed arches, and flying buttresses; and to my left, contemporary stacks of rectangular galleries with wave-like roofs and smooth, zinc-clad metal flowing down over the textured façades and supporting walls of warm red brick. I couldn't help but think I, too, was at a midpoint between past and future. What that future may be was yet to be revealed.

Since I had more than an hour of free time before a scheduled sound check at six o'clock, I dropped my guitars off at the Ludwig Museum and walked over to the main portal of the imposing Gothic masterpiece on lively Cathedral Square. Staring up at the largest façade in Christendom, I realized the countless stone carvings of creation, forgiveness, and redemption manifest the medieval builders' dreams of creating a heaven on earth, an earthly refuge to offset the ever-present threats of famine, plague, and war in their frightening world.

To reinforce their elaborate architectural allegory, the designers had positioned the enthroned Christ high up on the main portal, echoing John's apocalyptic vision in Revelation: "And I saw a great white throne, and him that sat on it, from whose face the earth and the heaven fled away; and there was found no place for them." Fourteenth-century worshippers would have understood the builders' message sculpted into this western façade and would have carried the external metaphor with them into the vast interior—the heavy ornate doors representing the heavenly gates, the tiny vestibule symbolizing the threshold to the last judgment, and the darkened passageway through the nave toward the brilliant stained-glass windows at the far end of the cathedral signifying the straight and narrow path leading the righteous to the everlasting Almighty.

I lost myself in exploring the cathedral's treasures, including the thirteenth-century gilded reliquary containing the remains of the three Magi. It was glorious. But when I realized nearly an hour had past, I rushed back to the Ludwig, picked up my guitars in the reception area, and headed over to the temporary exhibition hall where my first concert would begin in less than two hours.

Everything about the gallery was ideal for an unplugged performance: the acoustics were outstanding; the room was small enough to allow aficionados to thoroughly study my technique; and the venue was culturally stimulating to both eye and ear, combining live concerts with stunning twentieth-century masterworks lining the walls.

The abstract expressionist paintings exhibited there demanded immediate attention. They had been painted on a grand scale, with the smallest canvas measuring five by five feet and the largest six by eight. They were highly varied, ranging from Pollock's dynamic action drip paintings to Rothko's serene color-field work. And they were uniquely provocative, with color (or lack of color) and form (or lack of form) producing an intense emotional response among observers.

So standing no more than a hundred yards apart, this impressive Ludwig concert hall and the Archbishop's Church of Cologne were in fact counterintuitive foils emphasizing the strengths and rationale for the other—contrasting the resilience of centuries-old, weathered, gray-to-black sandstone and basalt with the nascent energy of months-old, gleaming zinc-clad siding; contrasting the soothing, mystical darkness of the soaring Gothic space with the lustrous white walls of modern possibilities; contrasting the medieval sense of refuge from external threats with the contemporary enthusiasm for an exploration of the difficult, the inconsistent, and the incendiary; and contrasting a high and holy place bearing witness to the continuity of religious faith with an iconoclastic site concerned with existential absurdity, angst, and the absence of God.

As I stood in the hallway outside the gallery listening to my unintelligible introduction in German, I felt unusual waves of adrenaline surging through me. I hadn't suffered stage fright in years. Perhaps it was because I was launching the first concert on my inaugural tour, or being in a foreign country for the first time and having limited knowledge of the language, or performing in such an upscale venue. But one thing I knew for sure was not the source of my anxiety: knowing how much was riding on the Cologne concerts. Because in an odd way, repeatedly reminding myself that Allison was depending on me finally cleared my head and steadied my hands. By the time the host had concluded his lengthy introduction, I was envisioning my confident entry into the gallery, my opening remarks to a young, supportive audience, the first joyful chords of "Miracle

Sky," the quiet final lyrics of "Ridgeline Whispers," and then the boisterous standing ovation as the last soulful notes faded to silence at the end. The performance, by all measures, was a success.

It didn't take long, however, to realize Mr. Gallagher had front-loaded the amenities on the tour. After spending two nights at the highly respectable Pension Jansen and performing two concerts in the world-class Ludwig Museum, I was subjected to much less elegant accommodations for the rest of my months on the road. To be blunt, I was totally reliant on the kindness of strangers for my room and board, and the venues from there on out were predominantly pubs, association halls, and summer beer gardens when the oompah bands weren't playing. So the usual drill was this: arrive at the central train station; find the friendly family producing the show; ride with them to their modest apartment above a small pub; try to communicate with them using hand signals; walk downstairs for the concert; eat pot luck dinners; sleep on the sofa or the rollaway; return to the station; board the train; travel to the next stop; find the stranger producing the show; and so on, day in and day out.

That's not to say I didn't meet some very pleasant, well-intentioned supporters who treated me very well. The real problem was not the people but the sheer demands of the routine, doing the same things over and over again for days on end—smiling, performing, shaking hands, signing autographs, pushing albums, and smiling again. Another counterintuitive aspect of the tour was the profound sense of isolation despite interacting daily with large numbers of people. While invited guests and family members would be conversing at a postconcert buffet, I would be sitting there silently eating my dinner neither understanding the animated dialogue nor knowing what to say. Station after station; town after town; day after day; disconnected for seven straight months.

Besides continually reminding myself I was doing this for Allison and the boys, I relied heavily on the unique history associated with many of the concert venues to motivate and mentally engage me. After leaving Cologne, I traveled southwest by train to Koblenz at the confluence of the Rhine and Moselle Rivers where a victorious Julius Caesar strengthened captured fortifications, built a strategic bridge, and ensured a Roman presence in the region for hundreds of years.

It was then on to Mainz where Gutenberg printed the first books using moveable type; and then to Worms, the site of the 1521 Diet, which produced the notorious Edict condemning Luther as a heretic and announcing a reward for his arrest; and then on to ancient Heidelberg where Twain extended his stay from a day to three months, boated on the winding Neckar River, imagined Huck and Jim rafting down the Mississippi, broke his writer's block, and thankfully resumed drafting his signature work.

The efficient Mr. Gallagher had fortunately arranged the tour so that I wasn't constantly crisscrossing the continent. After leaving Germany, my itinerary ran clockwise around Western Europe—from Switzerland, to Italy, then to southern France, Portugal, Spain, northern France, Belgium, the Netherlands, and finally up to Denmark, where the tour ended in mid-December. I knew the last few days would be brutal not because of the travel but because of the down time between the last two concert dates. I was really anxious to get back to the States and to Allison, but I had a concert in Helsingør on the nineteenth and a final stop in Copenhagen on the twenty-first before flying home the following day.

But once again I made the most of a difficult situation, passing the time by exploring unique sites of the region in a rental car I had splurged on at the end of my long, modestly successful tour. After flying into Copenhagen, I drove up the scenic coastline to Rungsted on the narrow channel separating Denmark and Sweden and indulged in the privacy and comfort of a charming bed-and-breakfast.

I had chosen to stay in this small, boutique hotel because it was only six miles from Helsingør and was adjacent to Rungstedlund, the rural family estate of the novelist Karen Blixen, who had returned home from Africa at forty-six and penned her strongest works there, *Seven Gothic Tales* and *Out of Africa*. Although the writer had died some twenty-five years earlier, benefactors had stepped in to preserve and continuously maintain the timber-and-stucco main building and the surrounding forty acres of gardens and woodlands, which now served as a bird sanctuary.

After a superb lunch of fresh fish, potatoes, and local beer at an idyllic restaurant directly across the street from the sea, I walked back up the road to the Blixen property and boldly rang the bell. When the caretaker finally answered the door, he politely emphasized in relatively fluent English that the manor house was not open to the public, that there were plans to establish a museum in the future, but I was free to roam the forty-acre sanctuary behind the house. Perhaps it was the effects of the strong beer at lunch but I persisted in trying to get a private tour of the main building. I pleaded my case, explaining I had come a long way, had written essays on Ms. Blixen in graduate school, and would probably never make it back there again. After a few additional minutes of imploring and cajoling, the sympathetic fellow relented, opened the door, and invited me into the forbidden house.

As the caretaker-turned-docent led me down a long hallway, he explained, "The rooms are still pretty much the way Ms. Blixen left them at her death in 1962." He paused, pointed through a doorway, and added, "For example, the decorations there, her African portrait paintings, the furniture, and even the winter flower arrangements." We continued down the hall and entered a large open space, where he focused on two pieces of furniture: "The mahogany wardrobe here belonged to Ms. Blixen's ex-husband." The caretaker then turned and pointed toward the far side of the room. "And that chair over there was her lover's favorite." The caretaker smiled, lowered his voice, as if he didn't want anyone else to hear, and added, "I moved the two pieces in here together for dramatic effect. The juxtaposition adds a certain tension to the space given the, ah, the 'triangular' nature of their relationship."

I nodded and smiled respectfully throughout his conjecture about Ms. Blixen's private life but must admit the longer he spoke, the more uncomfortable I became. He was hitting way too close to home.

We moved quickly through the drawing room where the novelist entertained guests and conducted her popular radio broadcasts in the 1950s and then entered the dramatic study, "Ewald's Room." My guide continued his invaluable lecture: "During Ms. Blixen's last years of failing health, she slowly transformed the study here into a memorial for those whom she had loved or respected very much. The bust on her father's gun cabinet over there is the likeness of the great Danish poet and dramatist Johannes Ewald. The painting of the toucan here on the south wall—Ms. Blixen painted the picture while in Africa and presented it to her lover not long before he died in a plane crash in 1931. And the weapons and shields on the north wall there above the lowboy bookcase were a part of her brother's extensive African collection."

When we reached the back of the manor house, the caretaker announced, "Well, that's the end of your tour, sir."

I extended my hand and said, "Thank you. You can't imagine how grateful I am. I'll remember you and your tour for the rest of my life."

He then escorted me to a private entrance; and as he unlocked the door, he reiterated, "I highly recommend that you visit the sanctuary, especially now that the snow has begun to fall."

I thanked my host once more for his hospitality and followed his detailed directions, strolling along a narrow, winding path past a small pond to a dormant orchard and flower garden, which the caretaker had explained supplied many of the seasonal arrangements for the manor house. I continued walking along the trail, crossed a small wooden footbridge, and gradually climbed to the highest point on the property, called Ewald's Hill.

I paused for a moment to enjoy the panoramic view and then searched for a special beech tree located somewhere near the bottom of the knoll. After spotting the ancient tree, I walked on down the path toward it and stopped at a large solitary flat black marker facing south toward Africa. The snow had already begun settling into the block letters carved in the smooth surface of the dark stone. I broke off a sprig of holly at the base of the massive beech, moved to the foot of the large rectangular marker, and placed my modest offering just beneath the name, KAREN BLIXEN.

The snow was coming down heavier now, and a cold, biting wind had begun blowing in off the sea. I raised the collar of my light corduroy jacket, cast a brief prayer into her blessed solitude, and quietly repeated her reassurances I had read so long ago: "For God does not create a longing or a hope without having a fulfilling reality ready for them. But our longing is our pledge, and blessed are the homesick, for they shall come home."

By the following afternoon, the heavy snow had tapered to light flurries, so I ventured out onto the roads and skidded the six, white-knuckle miles north to Helsingør. Storm clouds still hugged the landscape as I parked the car and walked over a long moat bridge leading to the strategic sea fortress protecting the strait into the Baltic Sea. I must confess I drove there that day in the dead of winter before the concert not to see the renowned chapel, the tapestries, or the Renaissance towers but just to walk the lonely bastions in the fading December light and relive the ghostly exchanges reverberating within Elsinore's haunted walls:

BERNARDO
It would be spoke to.

MARCELLUS
Question it, Horatio.

HORATIO
What art thou that usurp'st this time of night,
Together with that fair and warlike form
In which the majesty of buried Denmark
Did sometimes march? by heaven I charge thee, speak!

After visiting the snow-covered ramparts and the dark vaulted casemates beneath the defensive walls, I headed back to the car quietly repeating Francisco's opening lines on the platform at Elsinore: "'Tis bitter cold, and I am sick at heart." I drove over to Axeltorv, the main square in Helsingør, parked on a side street, and walked to the "authentic Irish pub" where I would be playing later that evening. As I entered the old establishment, I immediately sensed it was the ideal place for an acoustic solo concert—a small, intimate space surrounding a tiny stage; timbered, whitewashed ceilings; a roaring fireplace to the left; and a spacious, well-stocked bar with at least a dozen colorful draft beer taps to the right.

I introduced myself to the portly, middle-aged bartender. "Good afternoon, sir. I'm Sam Lynch. I'm scheduled to play your place this evening. Is the owner handy?"

Knowing enough English to understand but not to converse, the bartender raised his index finger and turned away, indicating that he would be right back. Within seconds he returned with a burly, pipe-smoking fellow of ruddy complexion, who extended his hand and enthusiastically welcomed me in perfect Queen's English. "So, Sam Lynch, welcome to the København Pub, one of the oldest, most renowned in Denmark!" He laughed and added, "I'm Aksel Olesen, the biased owner."

I extended my hand and replied with a well-deserved compliment, "Well, your place sure looks the part. And if it's not one of the most renowned pubs, it should be."

Mr. Olesen smiled approvingly, put his arm around my shoulder, and said, "Let's go over by the fire there so we can chat." As we neared the table, he shouted back at the bartender, "Two beer, Bjart!" He motioned for me to take a seat; and when our beers arrived, the owner got down to business. "I have a confession to make."

"What's that?" I asked.

He looked down at his glass, turned it slowly in his hands, and answered, "I've only sold about half the tickets that I thought I could sell. Only about a hundred. It's been tough. I mean with all the recent storms. And then there's also the time of the year. You know, being so close to Christmas and everything, I guess people are just a little low on funds."

"We'll make do," I said, not wishing to reveal that a hundred attendees was a multitude when compared to the number attending some of the small venues in which I had performed over the past seven months.

Despite playing to a half-capacity crowd that evening in Helsingør, I believe it was one of the most enjoyable concerts of the tour. It was the Christmas season. I knew I would soon be going home to Allison. And the crowd really got into the music, especially enjoying the surprise I had for them at the end of the second set. Before the concert, I had spent several days rehearsing the melodies to several well-known Danish Christmas songs: "Jeg er så glad hver julekveld," "O Jul med din glede," and "Jul, jul, strålande jul." I realized early on trying to learn both the melodies and the Danish lyrics was a bridge too far; but I felt that if I showed goodwill playing the melodies, the friendly Danes would spontaneously chime in with the words to the familiar songs.

And that is exactly what they did, but only after they gave me a pit-in-the-stomach scare. I tuned my guitar and began playing the opening chords of "Jeg er så glad hver julekveld." Silence. I continued playing the carol. Silence. But then a lone voice at the back of the room started singing. And then there were two… three… four. And it wasn't long then until everyone was singing along in the warm, glowing ambience of our refuge from the bitter, blowing wind.

That night, for one of the few times during the tour, I felt lucky to be sleeping upstairs in a cramped, third-floor bedroom above the family quarters. After consuming all the free rounds of Christmas beer, I was in no condition to drive anywhere. And the next morning was not a pretty sight. I did my best to play the appreciative guest, but the horrible throbbing and sensitivity to light had made me nauseated. All I really wanted to do was down some double shots of espresso, say a polite thank you and good-bye, and then get on the south coastal road to Copenhagen.

While I had earlier groused about the two-day layover in the capital before flying home to Tennessee, I now felt relieved the schedule had worked out the way it did. Frankly, I was in no shape to perform that night. The one-day respite would allow me to recuperate, to further polish the Danish Christmas carols, and to telephone Allison to discuss my travel plans.

Over the past seven months our communications had been both limited and asymmetrical. Since I was traveling from city to city almost daily, I was in essence a moving target, which precluded Allison from telephoning or corresponding with me on a regular basis. For my part, however, every two weeks or so I would mail her an international money order of half my earnings along with a brief note updating her on the tour. Because of the excessive charges for overseas calls, I had only telephoned her twice since May—once on her birthday and then again on that most meaningful and personal of days for me, Thanksgiving. I looked forward to hearing her voice again at the end of the night.

I didn't have any trouble finding the charming bed-and-breakfast in the quaint seventeenth-century building across the street from the Royal Danish Theater. As I unpacked the car, I noted Drachmann's classic fairytale comedy, *Der var engang* (*Once upon a time*), would be finishing its run on Christmas Eve. The neighborhood surrounding the theater was quite attractive with narrow streets, small, cozy shops, restaurants, and coffee bars; and the boutique hotel itself was the most luxurious place I had stayed since sleeping at the Pension Jansen in Cologne seven long months ago.

The luxury apartment in Copenhagen had a fully equipped kitchen, bedroom, living room, and private bath. It didn't take me long to figure out the method to Mr. Gallagher's madness. I had earlier speculated he had booked me into the upscale Cologne pensione to set a positive tone and get the tour off on the right foot. And here I was now on the last leg of my journey, and my agent had booked me into only the second boutique hotel of the entire tour. He knew he would be seeing me over the holidays to discuss a follow-on project beginning in mid-January, and he wanted to leave me with a strong, positive impression to soften me up for the pending negotiations.

After a much-needed afternoon nap, I strolled the few blocks over to the picturesque Nyhavn canal lined with seventeenth-century façades of historic townhouses, restaurants, cafés, and bars painted bright yellow, fire brick red, and vibrant cerulean blue. I wanted to get something good to eat, meet the owner of the club I would be playing the following evening, and buy some handcrafted Christmas gifts for Allison and the boys. Unlike Helsingør, Copenhagen had only received a trace of snow, which had completely melted once the sun had reached its zenith in the winter sky. As I turned off Kongens Nytorv onto Nyhavn Street, I was surprised to see how many people were dining alfresco toward the end of December. It appeared most establishments had made the outdoor experience unique and enjoyable by offering thick blankets to their customers and scattering propane heaters throughout the seating areas.

While it was a bit tricky, I located the club hosting my concert in the cellar of a large commercial building. I wended my way through the cluster of outdoor customers, descended the stairs into the darkened space lined with exposed stonewalls, and stopped a waitress as she carried a tray laden with drinks. "Excuse me, miss. The proprietor? Where could I find him?" The young woman made a pointing gesture, which I took to mean she would fetch him for me.

When the proprietor arrived, a Mr. Seitz, he invited me to sit a moment to review the contract, the proposed sound equipment, and the physical layout for the concert. Seitz was an affable man, and when we had concluded our business I asked to be seated outside in the crisp sea air. "Of course, of course," he said and showed me to a table set for one. For the next hour and a half I enjoyed an open sandwich, a salad, and several cups of strong black tea.

Before returning to the hotel, I walked along the canal and peered into the lighted shops looking for the perfect handmade Christmas gifts for Allison and the boys. And when I finally left the lively area long after dark, I was loaded down with hand-crafted jewelry, scarves, gloves, ornaments, and an exceptional assortment of fine local cheeses.

Because of the time difference between Denmark and the States, I waited until after midnight to telephone Allison to firm up my travel plans. She picked up on the third ring. "Hello. Summerfields."

"Allison?"

"Yes."

"It's Sam—calling from Copenhagen."

"Sam! Is that you?"

"Yeah…. It's really great hearing your voice, babe! I missed you so much! I'm coming home. Flying out of Copenhagen early on the twenty-second. Connecting through New York and landing in Nashville late in the afternoon."

"I'll try meeting you in Nashville, Sam. I say 'try' because we're supposed to get a winter storm sometime during the day on the twenty-second."

"No, don't risk it. I'll hop the late train, and maybe you could pick me up at Warfield Station."

"I'll check the time and be there," she said.

"How's everyone doing? Zach? Beau? The Squire?" I asked.

Allison paused and replied, "I have news."

"News? What news?"

Another pause and then she responded, "You're really going to rack up the charges. It can wait. You'll be home day after tomorrow."

12

THE GODS WERE charitable the day I left Denmark. Despite a brief weather delay in Copenhagen, everything else proceeded like clockwork, and my train pulled into Warfield Station on schedule at a quarter past eight. As the sleek stream-liner slowed to a stop, I gazed out the window eagerly searching for Allison and found her huddled near the depot away from the stiff December winds. God, it was really good to see her. I had missed her so much. She was wearing tight jeans, tall winter boots, a fur-trimmed parka, and a beige beret sweeping down over the left side of her forehead. On first glance, she appeared to be alone; but as I stared beyond the lights, I saw a shadow within the shadows. Perhaps Zach or Beau had come along to keep Allison company while waiting for my train.

I gathered my earthly belongings and piled out of the coach car onto the platform. Allison called out my name. I turned to look at her and she began walking toward me, smiled, and gave me a big hug. While lying in bed every night on the road, I had dreamed of this moment when I would hold her in my arms again. But as we embraced, I saw King Hamlet's ghost appear out of the darkness, extend its arm, and ask, "Remember me?" I involuntarily recoiled from Allison's arms, feigned a smile, and hesitantly responded to the apparition, "My God, Squire, is that you?" I spontaneously moved past Allison, approached the specter, embraced him, and respectfully whispered, "It's good to see you."

As she drove us back to The Afterlife, Allison described the Squire's partial road to recovery. "After experimenting unsuccessfully with a number of antidepressants, the doctors recommended electroshock therapy as 'the preferred treatment of last resort.' Over the course of twelve rigorous sessions, we all sensed the gradual improvement. The Squire had more energy and appeared to be much more upbeat. The only downside to the therapy was some memory loss related to events months before and weeks after the physicians had administered the shocks.

"The doctors say they don't know for sure how the Squire will react to the therapy over the long haul; but they have assured us the memory deficits have been temporary in many of their patients. The Squire and I knew the risks going in and were willing to accept them. We felt the memory loss was a small price to pay, if the Squire got at least some semblance of his life back. That's right, isn't it, dear?"

She looked over toward her husband, who had been sitting motionless in the front passenger's seat listening to his wife's recounting of his medical history. The Squire turned stiffly toward Allison and quietly nodded his head in agreement. Allison then continued her assessment. "We're not a hundred percent yet, and we're not ready to go back to the office. But we're really working hard on it. Aren't we, sweetheart?"

Again she glanced over toward the Squire, and again he quietly nodded yes. As we pulled into the long driveway leading up to The Afterlife, she ended the news on a positive note. "One good thing that's happened out of all of this, we've both been able to attend every concert and every baseball game Zach and Beau have played in."

I leaned in over the front seat, patted the Squire on the shoulder, and said cheerfully, "Sounds like you're well on the road to recovery, sir!" I then slumped back into my seat, sighed heavily, and thought to myself, "Is there still a place for me here?"

Christmas arrived and disappeared as quickly as the fast-moving storm that had dressed the holiday landscape in a thin, feathery layer of picturesque snow. On the surface everything was perfect—the impeccably decorated seven-foot fir, the familiar carols on the stereo and the radio, the brightly wrapped humorous and thoughtful gifts, the exquisite five-course Christmas dinner, and the evening storytelling near the roaring fire—but I must admit I felt stymied and frustrated. Tension percolated beneath this tranquil surface. Since my return home, Allison and I hadn't shared a single moment alone. I didn't know how the Squire's recovery would affect our relationship or how she felt about me after spending all those months apart.

Our first real chance to express our feelings didn't occur until New Year's Eve. Zach and Beau had been invited to a sleepover at a schoolmate's house, and the Squire had excused himself early "to ward off the flu," which had been making the rounds. Just as the year before, I made us a drink, sat down beside Allison on the curved sofa, and toasted the future. I desperately wanted to know how she felt about me, but I thought it best to tease the answer out slowly and indirectly.

After an awkward silence, I began, "As you know, Allison, when you travel, you spend a lot of time alone, especially at night lying in bed trying to get to sleep. And night after night these past months, I've played our conversations over and over in my mind. You were a Sphinx, who spoke in riddles. I left for Europe with more questions than answers. You said I reminded you of an early lover, a musician, who left for Paris because the timing wasn't right. How do I remind you of him?"

Allison shrugged her shoulders, paused, and responded, "He was creative… caring… perceptive… and every bit the romantic."

And then another long, difficult silence. I was tempted but nixed the follow-on question about whether the timing was right for us. Perhaps I was afraid to hear an honest answer. So I moved on. "What did you mean when you asked if I thought I was the only artist who had ever sat at a typewriter and succumbed to the longing and the loneliness?"

She paused for an even longer time and then confessed, "I honestly don't remember saying that. I… I don't know what I meant."

Again I rejected asking the natural follow-up question, whether she had ever felt the longing and the loneliness I had felt about her. So again I moved on. "Okay, let's try another question, this one about the 'captivating object' in the room. You said I was in the far corner over there, and you were over here in the opposite corner. You explained we have different angles of vision when viewing the object, but the object itself remains the same—it loses none of its characteristics, its value, or its beauty. So, Allison, what the hell is the immutable object in the middle of the room?"

Allison smiled enigmatically, shook her head, and said, "The best I remember the object didn't symbolize anything. It was just part of an analogy while trying to make a point."

Since the indirect approach wasn't producing the desired results, I spontaneously leaned in to kiss Allison as I had so many times in the past. But she turned her head to the side, firmly raised her arms to block my advance, and whispered, "Please, no."

Feeling hurt, rejected, and confused, I slowly pulled back and asked, "What's wrong?"

"I just can't," she responded. "The Squire's back home. Things are different now, Sam."

I refused an immediate urge to fire back, "My God, woman, do I deserve this kind of treatment after busting my ass for all those grueling months to help feed your family and keep you in The Afterlife?"

But before I could refine my response into something more appropriate, Allison continued, "You know, the Squire, the boys, and I realize how much you've sacrificed to support us, and we'll never forget that. We're still in the same precarious financial condition today that we were in the day you left last May. So by speaking openly and honestly I am risking everything. But I know you deserve an explanation.

"Last Christmas the Squire was under a suicide watch. He wasn't responding to the most advanced medications, and he faced very long odds of ever returning home and resuming his career. Perhaps I was afraid of losing the lifestyle, too focused on picking up the pieces and maintaining the status quo. In retrospect, while I found you unbelievably charming, handsome, and full of life, I suspect the attraction was actually a conflicted mixture of fear, selfishness, love, and... and physical desire.

"When the Squire returned home after the grueling series of shock treatments, I immediately sensed his vulnerability. My protective instincts kicked in, and I've spent most of my waking hours since then caring for him and watching for any signs of depression or suicidal thoughts. So while you've been away, I've had plenty of time to think this through. I know I really do love you, but I can't leave my husband in this condition. I'm sorry, Sam. I'm really sorry."

My heart sank. All I wanted to do was to get away. I remember saying something about moving back out to the lakeside cottage, doing some songwriting, and coming to terms with the reality. But as luck or the gods would have it, I never moved back to the cabin. I only visited it for a brief afternoon the week after New Year's to return the borrowed journals I had just carried all over Europe and to load my scruffy knapsack with a half dozen new volumes of possibilities.

My young, conscientious agent, Mr. Gallagher, was the force behind the change of plans. He telephoned the day after New Year's.

"Hey, Sam, I've got good news!"

"Good news, Gallagher?" I asked.

"Yeah, I've lined you up for an extended winter-spring tour through Ireland and the UK. Trusty sites that I've booked for other artists. Venues in Galway, Dublin, Manchester, London, and the Isle of Wight."

I responded upbeat. "Sounds great, Gallagher! So when do I have to pull up stakes here?"

"No later than the middle of the month, Sam, for sure," he replied.

As he revealed the accelerated timeline, I enjoyed the supreme irony that if he had made his announcement between Christmas and New Year's Eve, I would have perceived his "good news" as bad; but since he was presenting it only hours after Allison and I had spoken, he was indeed informing me of some very good news.

During my "last supper" with the family two weeks later, Allison revealed she had arranged for a neighbor "to come by and keep the Squire company" while she drove me to Warfield Station for the train back to Nashville. So the next morning after a genuine round of bear hugs from the Squire and the boys, I stowed my gear in the trunk and eased into the front seat next to Allison. The ride to the depot was quiet and introspective with every elegiac curve conjuring bittersweet memories of happier times together.

At the train station I purchased my one-way ticket east, and we moved outside onto the deserted platform to spend our last few minutes alone. I unzipped one of my canvas bags, grasped a single long-stem rose, and handed it to Allison. I gazed into her eyes and murmured, "A rose in winter, a symbol. Yes, our time is out of joint, but we'll always have the future."

As my train rounded the last long curve and lumbered into the station, she smiled and repeated my hopeful prayer. "Yes, we'll always have the future."

I embraced her, gathered my bags, and quickly boarded the train. After stowing my gear in the overhead rack, I sat down and stared out the window toward the icy platform. No one was there. All I had left now were the photographs, the memories, and the hollow feeling of what might have been.

13

I'M CERTAINLY NOT a saint, but I did keep my appointment. For all the years I toured I continued mailing money back for Allison's account. From time to time we would speak briefly by phone. Nothing earth-shattering, just "checking in." And occasionally I would send postcards letting everyone know where I was and that I was thinking of them. But like the faithless Mr. Wingfield, I too fell in love with long distance, preferring to stay on the road year-round rather than circling back home. That is, until the gods intervened, snuffing out one poor soul and maiming thirty-seven others, including me.

I had gone to Victoria Station during rush hour on a dreary winter morning to catch a connecting train up to Oxford. I was looking forward to spending three days in the old city hanging out with the undergraduates and playing evenings at the medieval Pentangle Pub. But five pounds of powerful Semtex got in the way. As I rushed through the terminal toward the trains, a violent force lifted me and drove my left side into a wall. Strangely, I didn't see or hear the blast. Everything just went black, and then all I heard was the surreal cacophony of moans, shrieks, and plaintive cries for help.

After struggling to sit up, I looked through the lingering layers of smoke and saw my right hand had become a mangled, bloody pulp of sinews and stubs. I felt no pain; I just sat there staring at what seconds before had been a fully functioning human hand. At the time of the bombing, I didn't panic because I couldn't grasp the severity or the implications of my injury and I had emergency personnel reassuring me all the way to the hospital that "Everything is going to be all right." It was only after many months of useless therapy at a local clinic that I faced the reality that my three-fingered hand would always be grotesquely locked in a cupped position.

Throughout the therapy, the pain was almost unbearable. When it finally became tolerable, I tried strumming; but the deformity affected the clarity of my playing. I would mistakenly hit multiple strings, producing an amateurish, muddy sound. I knew then for sure that my professional career was at an end. So I made a call to my agent. "Hello? Gallagher?"

"Yes, Sam. Is that you?"

"Yeah. I was just calling from London."

"How are you making out with your rehab?" Mr. Gallagher asked. "When you first telephoned after the attack, you said that you felt pretty optimistic about your recovery. Everything still on track, Sam?"

"Ah, that's what I was calling you about." My voice cracked as I struggled to get the brutal fact out. "It's over, Gallagher."

"Over?… You mean the rehab, right?"

"Ah, no. My career, Gallagher. I can't strum without making a mess. No more concerts, no more tours. It's over."

After a pause, the agent said earnestly, "I'm really sorry, Sam. If there's anything I can do…"

"Thanks, Gallagher."

Trying to move the conversation a little away from the pain, Mr. Gallagher asked, "When you coming back home to the States, Sam? Route your flight back through New York, you hear? You can stay at my place on Long Island. I would like you to meet my new wife and some of our closest friends."

I sucked up all the strength that I had in me and replied, "That's really kind of you, Gallagher. I'll keep the invite in mind when I make my reservations. And then I'll give you a call."

Truth be told, though, I never made that call to Mr. Gallagher. I stayed on in London until the following winter. And then as a wounded animal seeking its lair, I instinctively returned to McGill via Atlanta and rented an apartment close to the Pantheon campus. I avoided Allison and The Afterlife. I was embarrassed about the ugly hand, my failure to wire money the past few months, and my inability now to offer the family any help at all. And besides, I had spent a long time healing after Allison had made her decision, and I didn't want to open myself up to more longing and pain.

But I did visit Professor Taylor to trial balloon my plans for the future. I knocked on the office door.

"Come in!" my former mentor shouted. "It's unlocked!"

I eased the door open and stood in the threshold. Professor Taylor raised his head from his papers and jumped up. As he moved toward me, he extended his hand. But when he sensed my hesitation, he stared down at my three-fingered stub and exclaimed, Sam!… Sam!" He opened his arms wide and embraced me. "It's so good to see you." He then held me out at arm's length, gazed into my eyes, and asked, "What happened, Sam?"

To keep from tearing up, I responded in halting words and phrases, "Going to Oxford to play. Victoria Station. Semtex. The IRA… It's ended, sir."

"What's ended, Sam?"

"The concerts, the touring. That's why I'm here. I need your advice, Professor."

He released my arms, motioned for me to take a seat, and responded, "What's up?"

"I'm torn, sir. Torn between writing lyrics professionally and trying to finish a PhD."

Professor Taylor stroked his beard, and after briefly sorting out the possibilities, he replied, "I think you have a win-win here, Sam."

"How's that?" I asked.

"Why not pursue both paths at once."

"Both, sir?"

"What's to keep you from finishing your course work, writing the thesis, and joining a university faculty while continuing to write songs on the side? You would be hedging your bet and ensuring a higher income."

"I… I don't know, sir."

"Why the hesitation, Sam? It seems pretty cut and dried to me."

"Going for the PhD presents some real challenges."

"For example?" the professor interjected.

"For example, I would want to transfer over from English to comparative literature."

"Okay, but why the change? You excelled with the British and American authors."

"I know, sir, but honestly, I've read the major and even the minor writers over and over. I'm afraid that the boredom will set in again and I'll be right back where I was when I made the big leap over to music."

"So you think that you need a change of venue? Hmm...." He smiled and added teasingly, "You think that you need to run away from this decrepit old English mentor and right into the arms of a new comparative literature adviser?"

I managed a smile and replied, "It's not exactly like that, sir. It has nothing to do with you or the English department. It has to do with all the international miles that I racked up while touring Europe. I had plenty of time to experience authors writing in the countries I visited. I fell in love with the likes of Kundera, Coelho, Saramago, and García Márquez. As I said, I had read most of the major British and American authors multiple times. But here was something refreshing, something exciting, something new."

Professor Taylor adopted a business-like tone again and responded, "If that's what you want, Sam, I'll see what I can do. I'll speak with the comparative lit chairman as soon as possible. But, you see, there's not only a matter of getting you into the program but also transferring all your expired English credits from here over there so they'll count toward your comparative lit requirement."

"Thank you so much, sir." I paused and looked down, embarrassed. I then continued haltingly, "But there's one more wrinkle to iron out."

"What's that, Sam?"

"I won't be able to make it financially without an undergraduate teaching position."

Sensing my unease, the professor responded empathetically, "I understand. I'll see what I can do about that too, when I speak with the chairman."

For once everything went according to plan. I finished the course requirements in less than two years and began conducting research for my doctoral thesis, *The Incarnation of What We Can Never Be: Bianca in the American Milieu.* Considering the Portuguese poet's close ties to the university and my keen interest in the American existentialist movement, Bianca became an obvious choice for my thesis.

The rare-book section of the main Pantheon library housed many of the documents and manuscripts associated with the movement's influential quarterly journal, *The Messenger,* which my former mentor had helped edit over the two-year span of its regrettably brief existence. For my research, besides having unfettered access to the primary sources, I could also consult my old mentor, who would provide valuable insight into the published works, explain personal relationships within the movement, and perhaps even offer leads where I might locate some of the journal contributors for in-depth interviews.

I was nearing the end of my exhaustive doctoral research when I stumbled onto an interview that not only raised the likelihood my dissertation would be published but radically altered my professional and personal life forever. One Friday evening after teaching my undergraduate classes, I dropped by the packed Two-Way Café for a drink. I took a seat at the only open table I could find, a seat across from a striking, dark-haired coed. "Man, this place sure is hopping tonight!" I shouted over the din to break the ice. I smiled, looked into her eyes, and then added, "By the way, I'm Sam. And you are... ?"

The beauty extended her hand across the table and replied warmly, "Hi, I'm Marguerite."

"You a student here?" I asked.

"Yeah, working on my master of fine arts in the graduate writing program."

"How's it going?"

"So-so."

I smiled and probed, "Just so-so?"

"Oh, it's not really that bad, I guess. Just working my way through the required courses before getting into the fun stuff next spring."

"The fun stuff next spring?"

"Yeah, for example, I'll be enrolling in an advanced creative writing seminar next semester. It's offered by a visiting lecturer named Danielle. She's a young Iberian novelist who is purportedly the daughter of the late Portuguese poet Bianca."

I set my beer down slowly, cupped my hand near my ear, and said, "With all the noise—I'm sorry—you said who was lecturing next semester?"

Marguerite nodded and repeated, "Danielle, a young novelist, who is supposedly the daughter of the late Portuguese poet Bianca."

"My God," I thought, "with all the research I've done, how did I miss Bianca had a daughter?"

I then began bombarding Marguerite with rapid-fire questions about Danielle and the upcoming seminar and continued the interrogation until I sensed I had gleaned every last bit of information. I then ended the polite grilling, excused myself, and headed home, determined to meet the mysterious Danielle as soon as possible.

When I telephoned to explain my project and express a desire for an interview, Danielle enthusiastically agreed to meet me in the graduate faculty lounge in early March. Filled with anticipation and armed with a legal pad full of notes and questions, I arrived early, quickly downed two espressos, and staked out a private corner at the back of the lounge. Only minutes after I sat down to review my material, a young, statuesque redhead glided into the room, surveyed the instructors seated near the entrance, and then noticed me waving in the back corner. As she neared my table, the green-eyed beauty smiled, extended her hand, and teasingly asked in perfect English, "Samuel, I presume?"

After exchanging pleasantries about the "iconic nature" of the campus landscape, I broached the subject of Bianca. "Isn't it unbelievable that you've come to Pantheon to lecture and research your mother's past in the States, and I'm here in America writing a dissertation on her life and poetry but wondering about the details of her early life in Portugal? Why don't we go at this chronologically? You tell me what you know about your mother's birth, childhood, and days at the university, and I'll follow on with details I've discovered about her triumphant but tragic years here in the States."

"It's a deal," Danielle said, and opened the conversation with some family history. "My maternal grandparents had owned one of the storied vineyards in the Douro River Valley producing some of the finest port wines in Portugal. My mother, Bianca, was born at the quinta and remained there until she left to study literature and languages at the University of Coimbra, where she fell in love with a visiting professor and followed him back to the States."

I nodded, smiled, and quickly picked up the narrative describing Bianca's first years in America. "She shared an apartment with her lover in Hopewell, New Jersey, studying creative writing at Princeton, publishing her first volume of poetry, the Wordsworthian *Serra de Sintra,* and then drafting her first elegiac love poems based on the intense but short-lived affair with her professor. Bianca later met the avant-garde playwright Jeffrey Kline at a party in New York, fell deeply in love a second time, and followed the dramatist back to McGill, where he joined the Pantheon faculty as an adjunct professor teaching dramaturgy and overseeing graduate theater practicums. During her time in McGill, Bianca socialized with the foremost American existentialist writers and even contributed lyrics to *The Messenger*."

The spontaneous duet continued. After reporting Bianca had traveled to Europe that summer with several associates, I smiled and motioned for Danielle to pick up the biographical thread. "My mother returned to the quinta with some American friends to celebrate the sesquicentennial anniversary of the founding of the family's port wine business. Now, I've rummaged through our family's extensive memorabilia surrounding the anniversary celebration and didn't find any mention of a Jeffrey Kline attending the ceremonies."

"But that makes a lot of sense!" I interjected. "He was probably in New York rehearsing his first full-length play, *What Others Only Tell You*, which was to open off-Broadway that September. And at this point the record gets a bit murky. I know your mother returned to McGill after her trip to Portugal, published two volumes of poetry, toured the States conducting readings, and then returned to Europe for an extended period to promote her latest works overseas."

Danielle shook her head and smiled, "That second trip to Europe wasn't to read poems. It was to have me! My mother stayed at the quinta for a little over nine months and returned to the US three months after my birth. Once she left the Douro she never returned. From that point on, my grandparents cared for me at the family estate. And that was the last time Grandma and Grandpa heard anything until some years later when they received the call from the States that my mother had died. I think I was going on eleven."

I reluctantly asked, "You have any idea what happened during that decade?"

Danielle shook her head and whispered, "No. No idea. And regrettably, I never had a chance to meet either of my parents."

I tried as delicately as possible to explain her mother's inexorable descent into madness, her constant moves from city to city, and finally her suicide by hanging. But I wanted to end the narrative on a positive note. I reminded Danielle that her mother's friends had ensured a fourth book of poetry was published posthumously and that her mother's international reputation continues to grow even years after her death.

But I kept the really upbeat news until the end—the news that I had plans to introduce her to an old friend who had known Bianca while she lived in McGill writing some of her best lyrics and contributing regularly to the *Messenger*. I explained the introduction, however, would have to wait until midsummer because the professor was on sabbatical—ironically, touring Portugal and Spain.

During that spring semester, Danielle and I met frequently on campus to discuss the progress we were making on our respective projects—I on my dissertation and she on her second full-length novel, *A Time Outside the Days*, based on the twelfth-century power struggle between Afonso Henriques, the count and future king of Portugal, and his mother, the Countess Teresa, and her lover, Fernão Peres de Trava. But by late spring these academic discussions over coffee in the faculty lounge had evolved first into friendly dates to concerts, movies, and plays and then into sharing more time together probing our pasts, primarily at her guest cottage only two blocks from Redman Hall.

At this point I believe we both would have acknowledged our relationship had progressed from a collegial friendship to an enduring camaraderie. But it was more cerebral than emotional, and it certainly had not escalated to the physical. I don't believe either of us would have used "romance," "love," or "liaison" to describe the feelings we shared. Rather, while we were passionately embracing intellectually, we were holding each other at arm's length emotionally. I could only speculate about her rationale. Perhaps she was thinking, "He's American, and I'm Portuguese. He'll be staying, and eventually I'll be going. He's a graduate student, and I'm a young writer. And we are both facing uncertain futures." But I knew why I had remained guarded as the relationship deepened: I didn't want to relive the pain, isolation, and hopelessness I'd suffered after losing Allison, my first real love.

But sometimes during a deepening relationship, one of the close friends will innocently say or do something that sparks the other to take the first risky steps toward love. As our conversations became increasingly personal, I became more trusting even to the point of comfortably describing the unspeakable, the gloved right hand. While we spent most of our time at her guest cottage discussing world literature, we would occasionally venture into music. On one of those occasions I held my veiled stub into the air and allowed my frustration to declare, "I hate this."

Danielle gazed into my eyes and responded, "'Hate' is a pretty strong word, Sam."

I nodded and whispered, "Yeah, but losing a career to a terrorist's bomb, losing the basic pleasure of either picking up the twelve-string or sitting down at the piano and making music alone—" I stopped midsentence to hide the deep pain and bitterness.

Danielle didn't respond; she rose from the sofa, walked over to the old upright against the far wall, sat down, and began playing. I sat motionless on the couch, stunned to hear the clarity and fluidity of her technique. While she had clearly received professional training, Danielle had never mentioned she played the piano. I slowly got up, moved over to her side, and received a second surprise in less than a minute. All the complexity, color, and expressiveness of that thick, penetrating sound radiated from a single hand, her left. Message sent; lesson learned. I asked, "What is it?" She turned toward me as she played and responded, "Alexander Scriabin's *Nocturne in D for Left Hand*." I closed my eyes and reveled in the lush romantic harmonies and the realization I had just regained the keyboard as a friend.

When Danielle finished the heavenly *pianissimo*, she turned around, smiled, and whispered, "There's a world of solo music out there for you—Reinecke's *Piano Sonata*, Brahms' *Chaconne* after Bach, and even Corigliano's recent *Etude No. 1 for Left Hand*. And that's only scratching the surface. Thanks to Paul Wittgenstein's commissions, the concert pianist who lost his right arm in the First World War, we also have major orchestral works including Ravel's *Piano Concerto for Left Hand* and Prokofiev's *Piano Concerto No. 4*."

I shook my head and asked, "How did you learn to play like that? And why the familiarity with all the pieces for left hand?"

Danielle escorted me back to the sofa and sat down. "In a way," she said, "it's a funny story. Only by chance, my Portuguese grandfather met my German grandmother backstage at the Staatsoper Unter den Linden in Berlin, where she was starring in Berg's new opera, *Wozzeck*. After embarking on a long-distance relationship lasting about a year, my grandmother retired from the stage, married my grandfather, and moved to the Douro estate in Portugal.

"As a child, Grandma had received classical training in piano; but as she matured, the choirmaster recognized she had a stunning operatic voice and recommended vocal lessons with one of the finest instructors in Leipzig. While the earlier keyboard instruction proved invaluable to Grandma's fundamental understanding of operatic music, the formal piano lessons ceased at age fourteen as the focus turned to Wagner and Verdi. So it was only natural, when I turned seven, Grandmother saw the parallels and began instructing me in piano and voice."

When Danielle paused, I jumped in. "But I'm still curious. Why all the interest in pieces for the left hand?"

She laughed and replied, "Oh, that's where the humor comes in. Grandma was a hard taskmaster demanding hours and hours of practice every day. Even though I quickly learned to play well, I must admit I didn't look forward to those long afternoon sessions of perfect pronation, supination, thrust, pull, and claw. So it was not surprising I found the silver lining in a severely broken right arm, which would mean a lengthy reprieve from Grandma's demanding instruction. But Grandma was always about teaching what she called 'life lessons,' and lesson number one was, 'Danielle, you must seek creative solutions to find success.' And the next afternoon promptly at three, I was seated at the keyboard practicing the Scriabin nocturne for the left hand."

Her sensitive response to my frustration and vulnerability was the moment I fell hopelessly in love for a second time. Danielle's journey lasted only a little longer. Since we were spending increasingly more time together, we recognized our projects would suffer if we didn't divide the cottage into her study and my screened porch and allot at least a solid eight hours a day to our professions. It was during one of these self-imposed exiles that I began seriously analyzing Bianca's last thin volume of poetry published posthumously by her friends. I had scanned the book earlier, before drafting an outline for my thesis committee. My overall impression was the descent into madness had robbed Bianca of much of her creative powers. And the addendum, comprising a number of "miscellaneous fragments found on napkins and in magazines," sadly appeared to mirror the psychological chaos she experienced toward the end.

But I sensed "Fragment Four" was something more than schizophrenic flotsam and jetsam, perhaps a moment when the clouds lifted and the world ceased to spin. The poem opens:

> I no longer fear the giants and the pounding drums.
> I no longer hide in the crook of my mother's arm.
> I stand at the base of the public fountain
> And bravely receive Our Lady's blessings.

The three-stanza, twenty-four-line "fragment" goes on to describe a surreal city lined with paths of painted sea salt, hydrangea, and eucalyptus leaves and concludes with a number of unfamiliar Portuguese references, which I suspected were charged with deeply personal meaning.

I reluctantly put the explication on hold and moved on to "Fragment Five," hoping Danielle could shed some light on the mysterious allusions after dinner. We skipped a formal meal that evening and opted to feast on crusty bread, red wine, and Portuguese cheeses. As we sipped a second full glass of *vinho tinto*, I broached the matter of the fourth fragment.

"Danielle, I know it's well past closing hour, but I need your help on one of your mother's poems. It's in the last volume, the one her friends helped publish after her death. The lyric is in the addendum listed as one of the fragments, but I think there's something more going on here. I'm having trouble with the

Portuguese history and place names. Could we run through the lines together?"

Danielle pulled closer to the small book lying on the coffee table and replied enthusiastically, "Let's see what Mother had to say."

When I read the opening lines about the drums, the giants, and the surreal city, Danielle shook her head and said, "I'm not sure; keep going." I continued reading the rest of the first stanza describing "ancient rounds," a "centurion tapestry," and "a basilica high on the August hill." I paused; and Danielle motioned for me to go on. I read the first lines of the next stanza:

> Discovery begets a homecoming.
> I return to frame the youth
> I stowed to make the unknown known.
> I gaze out over the bearded wharves,
> Over the rhythmic tiles toward the arcing Cabedelo,
> And memory becomes reality.

Danielle vigorously signaled for me to stop and exclaimed, "I'm pretty sure I know now what the first lines are about. Cabedelo is an enormous beach just south of Viana do Castelo. My grandparents would take me to Castelo every year the third week in August for the festive pilgrimage of Our Lady of Sorrows. It was a happy time for us. Elaborate parade floats accompanied by plenty of music, eating, dancing, and drinking. My grandfather always reserved the same corner suite in the old hotel on Santa Luzia Mountain, ensuring a stunning panorama of the city—the old port, the Lima estuary, and the sweeping bronze coastline.

"We usually stayed on after the *romaria* ended. This was by far my favorite time of the year. One day we would hike a wooded mountain trail to pastures where wild horses roamed. On the next we would explore an ancient Celtic village where hunter-gatherers thrived for thousands of years before the Romans conquered Portugal and forced them into the valleys to become farmers feeding the Roman forces. And then on another, usually our last, we would take the ferry back across the Lima River to Cabedelo, where Grandfather would read Pessoa while Grandmother and I would sculpt elaborate sand castles for an imaginary prince charged with protecting the citizenry of the southern shore.

"I'm sure my grandparents took my mother to Viana do Castelo for the *romaria* of Our Lady of Sorrows also. Her opening lines accurately capture the pilgrimage, the participants, and the atmosphere. Hundreds of drummers in traditional dress join large, grotesque figures at the front of the procession escorting the statue of the Madonna through the 'surreal' streets decorated with colored sea salt for the celebration."

Danielle picked up the book and read the poem more closely before setting it back down. "Yes, as the poem opens, Mother is now attending the festival as an adult and remembering how as a frightened child she would bury her face in the crook of her mother's arm at the sight of the ugly giants and the ominous sound of the pounding bass drums. Unlike the past, however, she can now stand calmly in Republic Square near the Lopes Fountain and gratefully 'receive Our Lady's blessings.' The remainder of the references in the first stanza are pretty straightforward. The 'ancient rounds' are the ruins of the circular Celtic huts. The basilica is the twentieth-century byzantine-style church on Santa Luzia Mountain. And that 'centurion tapestry' hangs in the old hotel where we always stayed. It's a rather large historic work depicting the Romans crossing the River Lima during their invasion of Portugal two thousand years ago."

"Wow, I'm so glad I asked you. Do you have any insights into the second stanza? Without the history, I'm not sure I can piece it together."

"I believe the key to the second stanza lies in the opening phrase, 'Discovery begets a homecoming.' During the fifteenth- and sixteenth-century Portuguese Age of Discovery, hundreds of carracks and caravels sailed from Viana do Castelo and returned laden with valuable spices, exotic goods, and claims to valuable lands. From here João Velho set sail to explore the Congo, Gonçalo Velho Cabral went to colonize the Azores, and João Alvares Fagundes left to chart the rich fishing grounds of the North Atlantic. When these explorers returned home to Viana do Castelo, they must have paused on Santa Luzia Mountain; surveyed the familiar beauty of the city, the river, and the sea; and whispered a quiet, manly prayer of thanksgiving.

"As the ancient Portuguese mariners before her, Mother set sail on her own long voyage of discovery and has now returned

'to frame the youth she stowed to make the unknown known.'
I believe she is standing at the window in our old hotel room
on Santa Luzia 'framing' the panorama of 'bearded wharves,'
orange-tiled roofs, and the beach at Cabedelo. The 'youth' in
the line is the childhood memory of this striking view, which
she carried with her as she traveled the world physically and
spiritually during her personal age of discovery. And now
that she has returned home to the hotel, the memory of the
cherished view has once again been transformed into reality."
Danielle paused and then asked, "What does the third stanza
have to say?"

I smiled and then began reading the opening lines:

> Emerald blue bursts the night above the liquid Eiffel.
> I savor this last joy before the three step ends
> And I must sail again into the maelstrom.

Danielle motioned for me to stop and eagerly began inter-
preting the mysterious phrases once again. "On the last night
of Our Lady's festival, the citizenry move from the town center
to the marina to enjoy spectacular fireworks arcing above a
double-deck bridge designed by Eiffel. So Mother first captures
the color and rapidity of the pyrotechnic blasts by telescoping
'emerald green' and 'blue' into simply 'emerald blue' and then
introduces the pièce de résistance of the show, the firework
waterfall showering silvery flames into the dark estuary along
the full length of the bridge. From the opening procession
until the fireworks fade, the music and the dancing never cease.

Mother next describes the bittersweet feeling of simultaneously enjoying the familiar sights and sounds of her homecoming while realizing she must figuratively set sail from Viana do Castelo once the *vira* dance ends."

With her face aglow, Danielle signaled for me to continue, and I slowly read the last few lines of the poem, closing with:

Though I've crossed the mythic river,
I know you.
I see you.
And I treasure your brave castles by the sea.

When I finished reading the fragment, I expected Danielle to immediately jump in with a thorough explanation as she had with every other passage before. But this time she leaned back into the sofa, breathed in deeply, and reflected before offering her interpretation. She openly confessed, "I'm not one hundred percent sure about this, but I believe Mother is making a valedictory statement before leaving Viana do Castelo. She's promising the townspeople that no matter where the journey leads, she will always remember their fairytale city of woodlands, rivers, castles, and churches."

I nervously responded, "Perhaps there's a bit more going on here. Your explication of the first two stanzas has actually led me to a much more personal reading of the last verse. While you logically contend Bianca is saying farewell to the townspeople, I strongly believe she's speaking to someone other than the locals. Here's my thinking. You shed some light on the 'centurion tapestry' hanging in the old hotel. You said it depicted the Romans crossing the Lima River during their invasion of Portugal.

"I remember reading a remarkable story about this crossing in one of my undergraduate history courses. I don't know if it's apocryphal; but as the story goes, when the legionnaires reached the Lima, they thought it was the Lethe, the mythological river of forgetfulness. The Roman soldiers refused to cross the river, believing that if they did, they would lose all memory of their homeland, their associates, and their loved ones. Their leader, however, bravely forged ahead on horseback. When he reached the opposite shore, he called out each soldier by name to prove he hadn't lost his memory during the crossing.

"I would argue it isn't a coincidence Bianca mentions the tapestry in the first stanza and then writes in the important closing lines, 'Though I've crossed the mythic river, / I know you / I see you / and I treasure your brave castles by the sea.' But a key question remains—to whom is she speaking? Your suggestion, the townspeople, makes a lot of sense; but I have other information I haven't shared. And I honestly didn't believe it had any relevance until you helped explain many of the allusions throughout the poem."

Danielle sat with one hand resting on her chin, her expression opaque to me. I shifted uncomfortably before explaining more.

"You earlier described taking the ferry over to Cabedelo Beach, where your grandfather would read Pessoa and your grandmother and you would build sand castles for an imaginary prince. Well, a note in the addendum to this posthumous volume says these miscellaneous fragments were found on napkins and in magazines. And the specific annotation for 'Fragment Four' reads, 'Bianca wrote these lines on the cover of a *Life* magazine depicting a mother and child building a sand castle at the beach.' So I believe there's strong evidence the *Life* photograph reminded Bianca of you. In the last verse she's telling you that despite crossing the river, she hasn't forgotten you and envisions you at the beach with her parents building castles as she had done with them so many years before.... Danielle, for me there's no question. Your mother was writing the poem to you."

I closed the book, placed it on the table in front of us, and then turned toward Danielle for her reaction. She shook her head slowly several times, lifted her arms, and cradled my face in her hands. She gazed into my eyes and whispered, "Despite my grandparents' stories, I never really knew my mother until now. You've given me a gift I can never repay." She leaned in and kissed me first on the right cheek and then on the left. She smiled and said, "That's our way of saying 'thank you.'" She then slid her hands up and behind my head, drew me toward her, and gently kissed my lips.

As she gradually pulled away, I teased, "And that's your way of saying what?"

She hesitated, as if lingering to memorize the moment, and then said softly and sincerely, "I love you."

14

THE DAY HAD finally arrived, and it would now be much more than I had envisioned. I thought I would just be introducing my former professor to a new acquaintance, a visiting lecturer, who wanted to learn as much as she could about her mother's life here in the States. I would make the introductions, step back, and allow the professor to share some stories first about his travels and then about his interactions with the lecturer's mother. But because my old mentor had become something of a father to me, and Danielle was now my lover, I knew the dynamics had changed, and we would spend the time not only plotting the past but also charting the future.

We had arranged to meet at Professor Taylor's office in Redman Hall at nine o'clock. Since we had arrived on campus an hour early, we stopped by the Union for coffee and a rare doughnut before walking over to his ivied building, climbing the marble staircase, and standing outside room 311 precisely at nine o'clock. I turned to Danielle and whispered, "Here goes," then knocked tentatively on the door. The professor shouted, "Come on in; the door's unlocked." When we entered, we found my old adviser sitting behind his large oak desk with open books and loose papers strewn all about the room, covering the desk, the tall bookcases that lined the side walls, the checkerboard linoleum flooring, and the two visitor's chairs, where I had assumed we would be sitting.

Professor Taylor sprang from his chair, skittered around the corner of his desk, and cleared our seats as fast as he could without spilling everything. When he had finished transferring the last books to the floor near his desk, he exaggeratedly rubbed his hands down the side of his pants and extended his arms to greet my companion. I opened the introductions. "Professor, I'd like you to meet Danielle, a published novelist, a visiting lecturer teaching creative writing, and, ah, my love. My... my fiancée. She's interested in learning all you know about Bianca."

My adviser laughed before motioning for us to be seated. He responded affably, "Sam, it looks like you've been busy while I've been away."

Somewhat embarrassed, I quickly changed the subject. "So, Professor, we're really interested in hearing about your trip to Portugal and Spain."

Taking full advantage of the invitation, Professor Taylor leaned back in his chair, locked his fingers behind his head, and said, "Okay, but I assure you, only the highlights...." He then eased into a full play-by-play of his trip. "The overnight flight from JFK landed in Madrid, where I spent a glorious week visiting the museums—the incomparable Prado, the new Thyssen, and the Reina Sofia housing Picasso's 'Guernica.' But the week wasn't all about culture. I had plenty of time to stroll through the Buen Retiro Park, shop the boutiques on the Calle

Serrano, feast on the seafood paella at the St. James, and enjoy the tapas and Rijoa wines anywhere I stopped any hour of the day." I could see Professor Taylor relished the rapt attention of his audience. I urged him to continue.

"Let's see," he said. "From Madrid it was on to Barcelona to pay homage to Gaudí, attend the Spanish Grand Prix, and participate in a fascinating but somewhat controversial seminar, *Conflicting Views: Wright, Hemingway, and Stein on Spain*. The following Friday I flew from Barcelona to Lisbon and spent the weekend outside the city in Sintra at the hotel where Lord Byron wrote part of *Child Harold's Pilgrimage*. On my only other trip to Portugal years ago I'd spent a glorious evening there walking along the narrow cobblestone streets, peering into the lighted shops and staring up at the floodlit battlements of the ninth-century Moorish castle. I swore that someday I'd go back, and I finally kept my promise."

"It sounds wonderful," I said. "I hope to be able to return to Europe some day. Did you do anything else while you were overseas?"

"Well, I was invited to conduct a seminar at the University of Lisbon. The topic was *The New Critics' Contribution to the Rise of Henry James on the Iberian Peninsula*. We spent the rest of our time exploring what Saramago called the 'vast and burning lands of Alentejo,' the region stretching southward from the Tagus River all the way to the Algarve. Most of the time I stayed in the state-owned hotels, the pousadas, set in scenic and historic locations. One night it was a thousand-year-old Moorish castle in Alcácer do Sal, the next a fourteenth-century royal residence King Denis built for his wife, Saint Isabella of the Roses. Later on I stayed at a Franciscan convent in Beja, where a young seventeenth-century nun, Mariana Alceforado, purportedly fell in love with a French soldier and had an illicit affair. On the officer's return to France some years later, Mariana wrote five passionate letters to her lover, which became an instant sensation when they were published on the continent as *Letters of a Portuguese Nun*."

Professor Taylor paused, stared transfixed at a point above our heads, and quietly recited some of the nun's lines, which appeared to have a special meaning for him. "What! Are all my hopes to be utterly futile? And shall I never see you again in my room with all the ardor and passion which you once showed?" Then he slowly lowered his head, gazed into Danielle's eyes, smiled, and said, "Well, that's enough about me. So all that Sam would say on the phone was you were a visiting novelist teaching a writing course and you had an interest in learning more about Bianca's years here in McGill. Just curious, are you planning a project? Perhaps incorporating Bianca's life story in a novel, an essay, or the introduction to an anthology of contemporary poetry?"

Danielle replied succinctly, "Oh no, professor, this isn't about academics. It's personal. I've come here to learn as much as I can about my mother, Bianca, and my father, Jeffrey Kline. Samuel said you knew both my parents when they were contributors to *The Messenger* and you were helping with the editing. Since I know next to nothing about my father, perhaps you could begin with what you remember about him."

The professor collected his thoughts, cleared his throat, and responded, "I... I really never knew that much about Jeffrey, but here's a thumbnail sketch. He was an avant-garde playwright who'd temporarily joined the Pantheon faculty to teach dramaturgy and supervise theater practicums. It's been a long time, but I believe he went to a Big Ten school as an undergraduate and then attended the Yale School of Drama in New Haven.

"After being graduated, he worked backstage at a theater on Broadway and began seriously writing plays in his spare time. I liked Jeffrey. He was a charming rare blend of warmth and flair. The flamboyance was not so much about the persona as the way he dressed. In fact, his low-key personality clashed with his vivid yellow, orange, and scarlet fashions. It was as if on the one hand, he was wearing the flashy outerwear to promote his futuristic plays, while on the other hand, he was using the clothing to distract people from his shyness. His rural midwestern background. His conservative social ethic."

Danielle politely interrupted the professor and asked, "What did he look like? I haven't seen any pictures."

Professor Taylor smiled and replied, "Jeffrey was arguably the handsomest fellow on campus. He was tall, maybe six foot three, muscular, long curly brown hair, large brown eyes, thin nose and an angular, clean-shaven chin. And much to Bianca's dismay and mine, no matter where we saw Jeffrey on campus, he was always surrounded by a throng of beautiful, energetic coeds hanging on his every word. But honestly, Jeffrey was a reluctant celebrity who genuinely felt uncomfortable with all the attention."

"Professor, do you know much about my father's work or his career?"

He paused and responded, "I really don't know much about his early plays, that is, the works he completed when he was living in New York right out of college. While he was teaching at Pantheon, I know he contributed three one-act plays to our journal, *Divine Agony*, *Atholton Park*, and *Cradlerock Way*, and completed his first full-length drama, *What Others Only Tell You*, which eventually opened off-Broadway to favorable reviews. Two more plays followed in short order, *Toss the Feathers* and *Forgiven but Not Forgotten*. I read complimentary reviews of both in the *Times*. The latter review mentioned that *Forgiven* was set in New England, where the playwright had taken up residence at some time in the past. And with everything I had going on down here in McGill, that's where I unfortunately lost track of Jeffrey. I'm sorry."

Danielle shook her head. "That's okay, Professor, I know a lot more now than I did just a few minutes ago, and you've provided me some valuable leads to follow up on in the future. So can you now tell me what you know about my mother?"

The professor paused again to collect his thoughts. "I don't know any other way to describe her," he said. "Bianca was a genuine force. She was one of the most beautiful, creative, and intelligent people I've ever met. I'll never forget the first time I saw her. It was at Professor McMasters's legendary Halloween soiree. She and Jeffrey arrived fashionably late, strolled into the room as if they owned it, and immediately became the focus of attention.

"As with Jeffrey, I immediately sensed a duality in her. While on the one hand she was soft-spoken and very feminine, on the other she had a strong undercurrent of passion and volatility. She was in her midthirties and still retained all the appearances of a fashion model—tall; dark, curly hair; high cheekbones; small, straight nose; and large, blue, almond-shaped eyes.

"My first extended contact with Bianca was when we were compiling volume 1, number 1 of *The Messenger*. She submitted three poems."

The professor got up, walked over to the tall bookcase to his left, picked up a book off the crowded shelf, and moved over beside Danielle. He opened the journal and began scanning the table of contents.

"Here's a copy of volume 1, number 1. Let's see. Here are Bianca's poems starting on page ninety-five, 'The Burden of Feeling,' 'The Sacred Instinct of Theories,' and 'The Incarnation of What We Can Never Be.' Having read her earlier published volume, *Serra de Sintra*, I quickly realized these latest lyrics were so much more personal than the earlier poetry. If *Serra de Sintra* was Wordsworth, then these three poems were Keats. She had moved beyond the recollected landscapes of the Douro and was now addressing the immediate needs of her soul."

I looked over at Danielle and saw her eyes glisten. Having not known my father, I recognized how meaningful this brief conversation was to her.

"From that point on," the professor was saying, "our friendship grew, and she made me a generous offer to accompany her, Jeffrey, and a couple other journal contributors on an all-expense-paid trip to Portugal. How could I refuse? Bianca's parents were celebrating the sesquicentennial of the founding of the family's port wine business near Pinhão."

Danielle smiled and interjected, "Yes, I'm familiar with that anniversary celebration. And what's exciting for me is you got to meet my grandparents and visit the estate where I grew up. The quinta is still in the family. I inherited it from my grandparents, and my uncle manages it for me today. Ah, by the way, I have a question that I hope you can clear up for Samuel and me. After my grandparents told me about the celebration and mentioned my mother had invited several guests from the United States, I rummaged through the family records surrounding the festivities and found no mention of my father attending the ceremonies. As a young girl I was hoping to find something, perhaps even a picture. So did my father actually attend the celebration?"

Professor Taylor paused and replied, "Jeffrey was supposed to travel with us. But before we left, he learned his play would open in New York that September. Jeffrey apologized profusely and stayed behind to rehearse *What Others Only Tell You.*"

Danielle turned toward me and smiled. "Well, Samuel, you got that one right. My father was in New York, and that's the reason there were no references or pictures of him in the family files. Please go on, Professor. What else can you tell me about your visit that summer with my mother?"

He nodded and picked up the narrative describing the group's activities from the time they landed in Lisbon until they flew home to the States. "Since we were recovering from our overnight flight to Portugal, Bianca chartered a traditional *barco rabelo* that first afternoon for a leisurely cruise up the Douro River toward Tua, where we then hopped a small narrow-gauge steam train to the medieval city of Mirandela. It's strange. I don't recall much about the place, but I do remember feasting on the city's specialties: the little salt-cod cakes, the flavorful kale soup, and the fried alheira sausage.

"The pre-festival activities continued the following morning with a guided tour of Vila Nova de Foz Côa, where we explored a prehistoric open-air gallery of etchings portraying everything from mysterious signs to primitive representations of goats, oxen, horses, and deer. These petroglyphs ranged in size from six inches to six feet, incorporated existing rock fractures into the line drawings, and often formed a striking series of panels and compositions. I remember one engraving in particular depicting a lone human figure approaching ancient horses and wild cattle and transmitting the artist's striking message of brotherhood across countless millennia.

"Ah, the Sunday morning following the anniversary celebration we began our circuitous journey back to Lisbon for the return flight to the States. Since the old Roman city of Viseu was on our way to the capital, we attended mass in Viseu's Romanesque-Gothic cathedral dating from the twelfth century. As Sam will attest, I am not a religious man; but the combination of the imposing architecture, the superb Renaissance motets, and the priest's masterful homily brought me closer to the divine than anything I've experienced before or since. The text for that sermon was from the first book of John, which has become one of my favorites: 'He that loveth abides in the light, and there is none occasion of stumbling in him.'" As the professor paused to relive the treasured moment, Danielle and I spontaneously turned toward each other and smiled. We agreed with his assessment of the text and sensed a truth in the apostle's words.

The professor regained his focus and continued. "When mass ended in Viseu, we said our good-byes to Bianca's parents and drove southwest to the walled city of Óbidos, where we had lunch at one of Bianca's favorite restaurants and walked along the ramparts encircling that perfect intersection of past and beauty. History was literally piled on top of history there. I understand archaeologists still probe the city's cultural layers from the Portuguese to the Moors, to the Visigoths, the Romans, the Celts, and the mysterious prehistoric tribes emerging from the Old Stone Age. And then there was also the breathtaking beauty of the place: the windmills, the vineyards, and the narrow cobblestone streets lined with white-washed houses sporting either old gold or royal blue accents and window boxes afire with lantana, geranium, and morning glory. It was a remarkable landscape worthy of a Corot, a Sisley, or even a Monet.

"Later that afternoon we reluctantly said farewell to Óbidos and drove on down to Sintra, which became our base for the short time we had left before flying home. Since I've already described my recent visit there, I won't elaborate other than to say I agree with Byron's assessment of Sintra as the most beautiful place in the world. The following morning we drove over to Caiscais, a fashionable seacoast town just outside Lisbon. After lunch and a guided tour of the Guimarães mansion's unique collection of paintings, porcelain, and jewelry, we walked northward along the rugged, windblown coastline toward Guincho Beach, where we had a hearty round of farewell drinks and watched the sun ease into a flaming sea.

"After returning to McGill, Bianca and I immediately focused on the tasks at hand—she on publishing a third volume of poetry and I on completing my doctoral work. When she finished the third book, she flew back to Europe on her extended stay. And it was not long after she returned to McGill that second time that we noticed the first subtle changes in her mood and ability to write, which widened over time into dramatic swings between brightest sunlight and darkest night. In the beginning there was much more light than dark, which produced significant periods of creativity. But as the months passed, the pendulum swung increasingly more in the shadows, which meant considerably less productivity.

"As she sank deeper into depression, we became alarmed and insisted she see a physician. She finally agreed. But little did we know this doctor was only the first of many over the years who would try helping her but ultimately fail. One thing you can say about Bianca is she was brave throughout the long ordeal. Once she agreed to seek help, she was willing to try almost anything to get better, including experimental medications, shock therapy, and lengthy stays in hospitals for testing and observation. And it was this courage that inspired her friends and me to publish a posthumous collection of her final poems. It was the least we could do. She had tried so hard to return to us."

Professor Taylor paused, looked down nervously at his watch, and apologized. "I know you must have a hundred more questions, but I have to leave for an appointment with the department head. I can't leave Smith waiting, especially when it's about one of his pet projects, changes to the undergraduate requirements. But I'm sure Sam will bring you back around again when we have more time." He rose from his chair, escorted us to the door, and extended his hand to both of us. We thanked him for his time and quickly left the room.

Once we had exited Redman Hall and begun walking across the quadrangle toward home, I asked Danielle what she thought of our meeting with the professor. She whispered, "Okay."

I replied, "Just okay? What's wrong? I know something's troubling you. What's up?"

She stopped, turned toward me, and said, "The professor was very kind. But I just wish he'd given us more details, especially about my mother's last days. What was she doing? What was she feeling? Were there any warning signs? Did anyone see it coming? Who found her? Was there a note? Professor Taylor glossed over all this."

Admittedly sounding a bit defensive on my mentor's behalf, I responded, "Danielle, try to put yourself in his shoes. There was a lot going on there, a lot to process. He had never met you before. He didn't know Bianca had a daughter. Since I know him so well, I realized early on in the conversation he was much more comfortable describing your mother's actions than her motives or emotions. And as far as sheltering you from the specifics of your mother's death, I'm sure he was just attempting to practice a bit of decorum and protect you from the hurtful details. Give him time to get to know you. I'm sure you'll learn much more about your parents in due course."

We resumed walking across the campus toward Danielle's cottage. She slid her arm beneath mine, pulled up close, and whispered, "I hope so. It's only natural that I'd want to know as much as I can about both of my parents." She turned toward me and smiled. "I'm Portuguese," she said. "We're fighters. I'll survive anything he has to say."

I gently stroked her arm and said, "Yes, after all you've faced and accomplished, I'm sure you will."

15

WHEN SORROWS COME, they come not as single spies, but in battalions. It was only now, after relinquishing the beloved loft, touring the world, and returning to McGill for good that the Buccaneer finally deciphered the perplexing phrase for me, "I'm doing the Lord's work." I had gotten word that Birmingham's health had deteriorated, and he was now spending most of his time in bed. The onset of the disease had been subtle, first the weakness in the left leg and then the right.

Trying to ignore the advancing symptoms, he buried himself in his work, spending increasingly more time in the gym mentoring fighters and steeling himself in the reassuring glow of athletic camaraderie. But when he began visibly twitching and staggering about, his wife and caring friends insisted he immediately schedule a thorough examination at the highly respected McGill Clinic. The Buccaneer grudgingly relented, received a comprehensive assessment, and subsequently learned the harsh diagnosis: Lou Gehrig's disease. He had waited so long to see a doctor, his time remaining was much shorter than he could have ever hoped or expected.

When I went to visit Birmingham at his home, his gracious wife, Janet, answered the door, sincerely thanked me for coming, and then led me down a narrow hallway to the back bedroom of their aging bungalow. The Buccaneer's thinning, expressionless face was propped up with pillows on a high-tech articulated bed, which the fellows at the gym had purchased with generous donations from fans. As I approached the near side of the bed, I said encouragingly, "Hello, my friend."

He didn't turn his graying head toward me but responded with a weak, "Is that you, Lofty?"

I leaned over the guardrail, privately mourned the present, and then gently hugged the treasured memories and the father I'd never known. For the better part of an hour we reminisced. I say "we," but I did almost all of the talking. Since his breathing had become so labored, I would describe former boxers and past incidents at the gym and then ask Birmingham if my narratives accurately captured the characters and scenes as he remembered them. And he would occasionally acknowledge my question with a faint, "Yes." As the minutes passed, I sensed Birmingham was gradually wearing down and wearing out. I rose from the old lounge chair, returned to the bed rail, and placed my hand on his rigid fingers. The Buccaneer asked softly if I would honor one last request, and I simply answered, "Absolutely, anything."

He then whispered, "Do the Lord's work."

And now we were back in the gym on the bleachers resuming the brief conversation he had abruptly ended that memorable September afternoon years ago. I asked, "How can I do the Lord's work?"

He replied, "Remember me and honor my memory."

I needed clarification. "Honor your memory?"

"Look after our graves."

I struggled to connect the dots. "Do the Lord's work." "Honor my memory." "Look after our graves." Birmingham quickly detected the uncertainty in my silence and directed me over to the maple wardrobe at the far corner of the room. He then asked me to retrieve an old cardboard box from the bottom shelf and examine its contents.

I moved over to the cabinet, rummaged through the pile of shirts and shoes on the lower shelf, and located the Buccaneer's booty. I untied the thick brown cord securing the treasure, slowly lifted the worn lid, and discovered what appeared to be a rolled document surrounded by a number of Catholic medals with likenesses of Saint Sebastian, the patron saint of athletes, and Saint Gertrude of Nivelles, the patron saint of the dead.

Birmingham instructed me to remove the scroll and untie the small gold ribbon. Strangely, there was a pleasant fleeting memory of my youth, lying on the wide planks near the crackling fire, reading Stevenson and marveling at the shadowy, swashbuckling privateers projected on the painted walls of the darkened room. The Buccaneer had now become the Captain, Billy Bones, and I the innkeeper's son, Jim Hawkins, who was about to inherit the Captain's valuable map of Treasure Island.

I managed to loosen the small knot with my good hand and then slowly spread my forearms far apart to completely unfurl the rolled paper on the linoleum floor. It was indeed a map. Not of exotic isles but the mid-Atlantic states from the Tidewater in the South to Pennsylvania, New Jersey, and Delaware in the

North. There were twenty gleaming stars dispersed among these coastal states. I looked up quizzically at the Buccaneer's taut, inexpressive face and humorously asked, "Are these all the places you've buried the treasure?"

Before he could respond, Janet entered the room and saw I was poring over the yellowed map. She approached Birmingham's bed, smiling approvingly of the revelation, and stroked her husband's head with a loving touch. The Buccaneer whispered he preferred she now explain the map, the stars, the saints' medals, and the long-standing mystery of the missing weeks every August.

Janet paused to collect her thoughts and then began relating Birmingham's private journey from agonizing victim to benefactor of the heroic dead. "The Warrior's unexpected offer of employment," she explained, "was the pivot where Buc's growing layers of anxiety and depression lifted and he began developing plans to pay back what he had so generously been given before and after the championship fight. He devised a method of tithing, not to the church but to a savings account; not to help the living but to honor the forgotten heroes who had made his career possible.

"It all began so spontaneously; he happened to have read a lengthy newspaper column describing the indispensable contributions of second-tier boxers to the rapid growth of the sport during the early decades of the twentieth century. One of the fighters highlighted in the laudatory piece was Buc's chief idol, the Bayonne Bomber. This insightful commentary led immediately to biographical research and then to multiple calls to the Bomber's second cousins and an irritable but indispensable great-aunt. During these discursive interviews, Birmingham learned growing dementia had forced the Bomber first into retirement and then out onto the streets, where he ultimately died of exposure, refusing to heed the volunteers' warnings of a bitter subzero night.

"The Bomber's distant relatives vaguely remembered the boxer's burial in a public cemetery somewhere near the Bayonne city limits. With only this limited information in hand, Buc traveled back East the second week of January to visit the three public graveyards most likely harboring the Bomber's remains. While a survey of the first two snowy cemeteries proved unsuccessful, Buc continued his quest in the third memorial park, methodically walking up and down the long rows of monuments and crosses.

"But as sundown approached, Buc resignedly returned to his car and drove back to the front entrance, where a groundskeeper had just arrived to secure the property for the evening. Buc thought it was worth a shot to ask the guard if the Bomber was indeed buried within the walls of the expansive cemetery. Buc slowed to a stop, rolled down the window, and shouted at the caretaker, who was busily unlocking the thick wooden door of a small gatehouse. When the man heard 'Bayonne Bomber,' he smiled and vigorously signaled for Buc to join him in the tiny stone cabin. He pulled the records and determined the specific section and lot where the Bomber was buried, then eagerly offered to hop into Buc's car and help him pinpoint the Bomber's final resting place." She patted Birmingham's hand then and continued with her story.

"They drove along the gently curving road to the top of an inconspicuous knoll near the back wall of the cemetery. The groundskeeper asked Buc to park the car, and they walked over to the modest granite monuments erected for 'Ruth Bynum' and 'Teresa Wagner.' The caretaker pointed to the snow-covered space between the black headstones and declared the small, unmarked lot the Bomber's grave site. The two stood there for several minutes with their heads bowed, silently recollecting the faded exploits of a forgotten hero.

"As they continued staring into the narrow opening between the markers, Buc and the caretaker shared several youthful memories of the flashy, unorthodox lefty who almost made it to a championship fight. In his scandalous heyday, the handsome idol's notorious behavior was thoroughly chronicled, with 'tell-all' stories and action photos appearing in boxing magazines as well as the racy tabloids of the day. But visitors who now pass the graves of the Misses Bynum and Wagner are oblivious of the genuine sport hero resting incognito underfoot."

The Buccaneer's wife paused for a moment as if to add emphasis to what was to follow. "It was during the overnight drive home to McGill that Buc thought up his plan of tithing to purchase a worthy headstone for the Bomber and begin the research to identify the next deserving ringman whose grave should be cleared and whose identity should be admiringly etched in monument stone. And that was the beginning of my husband's annual cycle of financial and personal sacrifice—conducting the laborious research, identifying a worthy candidate, accumulating sufficient funds, leaving me and the family behind, and traveling back East each August to find an abandoned grave, clear the brush, and erect a fitting memorial."

She then looked directly into my eyes and explained, "Buc has often dreamed of finding a reliable replacement to continue his activities. I mean, he never expected the new recruit to carry on the burdensome practice of conducting annual research and discovering new honorees; he just wanted someone to maintain the sites he had already improved—visit several graves a year to inspect the headstones and trim back the surrounding grass and shrubs." Janet glanced over at the large map I was holding, smiled warmly, and declared, "It looks like Buc has settled on his man."

Before she could formally ask the obvious question, I returned the smile and assured both of them, "I'd be honored to carry on the tradition."

As I rolled up the map and returned it to the bottom of the box layered with the saints' medals, I explained I regrettably had to be leaving; I had an appointment in downtown McGill. I embraced Janet and encouraged her to telephone me if I could help in any way. I then moved over to Birmingham's bed, leaned in, and whispered, "Thank you for all you've done for me over the years. I love you. Rest easy. I'll continue the mission. I promise I won't let you down."

It was early the following month that I learned I would be "doing the Lord's work" for twenty-one grave sites, not the original twenty starred on the Buccaneer's map. Janet telephoned with the news her husband had died peacefully that morning in his sleep. She said according to his wishes there would be an ecumenical service at the McGill Fight Club the following Friday afternoon. I thanked her for calling, expressed my genuine condolences, and promised I would definitely attend the funeral at the Warrior's old gym and then join the family for the private interment ceremony at the Mount Olive cemetery between Warfield and McGill.

The memorial service was scheduled for two o'clock. I arrived a half hour early to greet old friends but primarily to ensure I had my special seat in the bleachers where the Buccaneer and I had sat those late summer afternoons when I first arrived on campus. As I drove up to the fight club, members of the press, town fathers, former and current boxers, rival trainers, and fight fans from all over Tennessee were milling outside the front entrance where years earlier I had fortuitously noticed the posted sign announcing the Warrior's loft was for rent.

Following my game plan, I said hello to a former boxer and a trainer I recognized from my days on campus, then quickly entered the gym. The Buccaneer's open casket rested on a large catafalque uniquely elevated at a forty-five-degree angle in the center of the ring. (This strange positioning must have been Birmingham's idea. During his career, he had never been knocked down, and he was not about to enter the afterlife lying flat on his back.) On either side of the coffin were impressive life-size photographs of the Buccaneer landing stiff punches to the champion's head in the early rounds of the title fight that ultimately ended his career.

At exactly two o'clock the public murmuring ceased as the procession of family mourners solemnly filed out of the Warrior's old office and proceeded toward the reserved seats nearest the ring. The Most Reverend Jeremiah Sparks, the acknowledged benefactor of the homeless and roving shepherd to resident boxers, followed several steps behind the family members until he reached the corner of the ring, where he angled off to his right and mounted the three wooden stairs onto the wide apron. One of the gym's professional trainers, dressed for the somber occasion in his rarely worn pinstripe suit, separated the bottom ropes with his hand and foot to allow the Reverend to gracefully stride into the ring as boxers are accustomed before a big fight. Even the Reverend's black pulpit vestments with deep purple and bright yellow trim oddly echoed the boxers' flashy robes worn when first entering the ring.

As the "official timekeeper" rapidly rang the bell usually signaling prefight introductions, a large silver microphone dropped quickly from the rafters. The Reverend strode to the center of the ring, pulled the mike close to his lips, and raised his deep baritone to the Lord and the assembled mourners in the gym. "Brothers and sisters, we are gathered here this late summer afternoon to celebrate the life of our beloved friend, Birmingham, the Buccaneer. We all know he was not a church-goer; and we can't even be sure he believed in the divinity of

Jesus Christ our Lord. But who here today could deny the Buccaneer was a true Christian in every respect? The prophet Micah explains what Jehovah expects of us: 'He hath shown thee, O man, what is good; and what doth the Lord require of thee, but to do justly, to love mercy, and to walk humbly with thy God?' Is there anyone here today who believes our brother, Birmingham, treated them unfairly?"

The Reverend paused; and after several seconds of silence, the "timekeeper" rang the bell again. The minister continued with the same tone and intensity, "Is there anyone here who has ever questioned Birmingham's honesty or his trustworthiness?" Another pause, silence, and then another ringing of the bell. The booming voice carried on, "Is there anyone here today who has ever witnessed our brother arrogantly recounting his many achievements?" Another pause. Again the brief silence. And then the ringing of the bell.

"Is there anyone here who questions the Buccaneer's generosity? Has he ever refused a helping hand to families in need? And since moving to McGill, has he ever missed a Thanksgiving or Christmas working the soup kitchen from morning to night?" Pause. Silence. A ringing of the bell. "Is there anyone here who believes the Buccaneer would be denied entrance to a heavenly afterlife because he didn't attend church or profess his belief in the divinity of the Christ?" A pause. A silent acknowledgment with a shaking of heads. And then another ringing of the bell.

"Isaiah tells us, 'They that wait upon the Lord shall renew their strength; they shall mount up with wings as eagles; they shall run, and not be weary; and they shall walk, and not faint.'

Is there anyone here who believes Birmingham is not seated at the right hand of God?" Pause. Silence. Another sounding of the bell. "Did our brother suffer great disappointments in this life? The lost championship, the blindness, the early retirement, his most promising contender called home to the Lord only weeks before a title shot, and the awful paralysis which strangled the very life from his being.

"What does the Lord say about those who suffer and triumphantly surmount immeasurable disappointments? The Lord assures us, 'He that overcometh shall inherit all things; and I will be his God, and he shall be my son.'" Pause. Silence. A ringing of the bell. "And John prophesies in Revelations about the final days before the Christ returns, 'And I saw three unclean spirits like frogs come out of the mouth of the dragon, and out of the mouth of the beast, and out of the mouth of the false prophet. For they are the spirits of devils, working miracles, which go forth unto the kings of the earth and of the whole world, to gather them to the battle of that great day of God Almighty, gather them together into a place called in the Hebrew tongue Armageddon.'

"Does anyone here deny there will be a cataclysmic battle between the kings of the earth and the King of Kings at Armageddon?" Pause. A few audible "Amens" rise from the gymnasium crowd. The timekeeper strikes the bell again. "Is there anyone here who believes the Buccaneer is not helping prepare the angelic forces for a final victory before the Christ returns to earth?" Pause. Silence punctuated now with several loud, unprompted "noes." And then the ninth ringing of the bell.

"In closing, I would like to share a few final comforting thoughts of reassurance from our brother. I visited the Buccaneer only hours before he died. I believe he sensed he was about to cross the threshold. There was no fright or foreboding. Nothing but calm acceptance. Birmingham was at peace with himself and his life. He drifted in and out of consciousness during the hour I was at his side. The Buccaneer murmured, 'Arena.' I knew immediately he wanted me to read a favorite excerpt we'd shared in the past, a passage from the president's speech at the Sorbonne in 1910: 'The credit belongs to the man who is actually in the arena, whose face is marred by dust and sweat and blood... who at the best knows in the end the triumph of high achievement, and who at the worst, if he fails, at least fails while daring greatly, so that his place shall never be with those cold and timid souls who neither know victory nor defeat.'

"Some fifteen minutes later, Birmingham awoke again and whispered, 'Paul.' I quickly surmised he was referring to a favorite passage in Paul's letter to Timothy, which concludes: 'For I am now ready to be offered, and the time of my departure is at hand. I have fought a good fight, I have finished my course, I have kept the faith.' These were the last thoughts our brother shared with us. As the final round ended, the arms were heavy, the lungs bursting, and the legs burning with fire. But the Buccaneer was satisfied. He knew he had given life everything he had to give. Our brother now felt the peace of God, which passeth all understanding."

The Reverend bowed his head. And as the timekeeper rang the bell repeatedly, signaling the end of the ten-round memorial service, the crowd rose to its feet and cheered loudly for the Reverend's inspired remarks and the brave life of their own Buccaneer.

The following morning I drove out to Mount Olive to assess the work of the burial crew and to have a few last words with my longtime friend. It was relatively easy locating Birmingham's grave site despite the heavy morning mist that had settled overnight into the broad flat valleys between the undulating knolls. The Buccaneer's scenic burial plot stood prominently in the widest of the hollows beneath one of the tallest cypress trees scattered about the vast public cemetery.

I pulled off the road and walked over to the polished marker at the head of a fresh mound of earth, which was covered with two large funeral sprays from yesterday's service, one with an indigo ribbon and silver script, "Birmingham," and the other with an emerald band and gold lettering, "The Buccaneer." Having grasped the painful lessons of his mid-Atlantic map with the twenty gold stars, Birmingham had left nothing to chance. He had ordered in advance his own simple headstone, containing his name, his birth date, a circular carving of a pair of Everlast gloves, and his own arrangement of lyrics from the Simon and Garfunkel folk ballad, "The Boxer."

I stood silently for a moment at the foot of the Buccaneer's new grave, bowed my head, and offered up a few private thoughts to the alleged worlds beyond. Some may consider my solemn act a prayer. I would describe it more as the random launch of memory and hope into the inscrutable, unresponsive mystery surrounding us all. I moved to the right of the floral displays, approached the marker, knelt, and placed the customary Sebastian and Gertrude medals at the base of the headstone. I whispered my sincere thanks for accepting me when I first arrived on campus, for helping me sort out a conflicted future, and then subtly guiding me to accept a lover's generous offer to join her, her husband, and their young children in the idyllic Afterlife.

16

No one called. I read the disturbing report in the *McGill Gazette*. It was big news around here; it was on the front page above the fold. The Squire had died suddenly. No cause of death was given. "Suddenly" and without cause. I immediately suspected the Squire had finally succeeded in stopping the pain. And it wasn't surprising the publishers had honored him with such high-profile reporting. After all, he had survived the deadly assault on Normandy, had deep family roots in the community going back well over a hundred years, had been a major landowner in the county, and had invested millions of dollars in local philanthropic activities, including the Food Bank, the Jobs Bank, and the Venture Bank for gifted entrepreneurs.

I decided to skip the wake but attend the services at Saint Paul's Episcopal, where we had spent memorable Thanksgivings serving the poor. After all this time away from the family, I thought it best I keep my distance while showing my love and respect for Allison and the boys. And why not ask Danielle to go along? She had heard so much about how the Squire had encouraged me to pursue a music career. And wouldn't seeing Danielle send a clear message to Allison that I had healed and moved on?

Danielle agreed to accompany me to the funeral at Saint Paul's. By the time we arrived, all but the last few rows of the vast space were filled, a testimony to the Squire's standing in the community. Danielle and I took a seat on the far right side at the back under the Chagall stained-glass masterpiece. Bright March sunlight angled in through the rose, cerulean, and brilliant white window. As the pallbearers entered carrying the Squire's casket, the organist launched Mendelssohn's majestic *Sonata in C Minor*. Allison, wearing a traditional black shift dress and sweater, followed the coffin with her stepsons supporting her on either side. My God, Zach and Beau were now handsome young men, and I had once built Christmas toys for them.

When everyone had been seated, the Reverend Berkley climbed the stairs to the elevated lectern and offered a simple prayer: "Lift us, O Lord, into the joy and peace of thy presence. We ask in Jesus' name. Amen." And after the renowned soprano and Memphis native Elizabeth Archer offered an angelic interpretation of Schubert's *Ave Maria*, the priest faced his most challenging assignment: providing comfort and absolution to grieving family members of a loved one who had taken his own life.

He raised his head from his text and opened his sermon with an admission: "Sorrow is never an easy burden to bear, especially when it hits us so suddenly. It ironically raises doubts about our own past actions. For example, what could we have done differently to prevent this? And swirling about this doubt are our feelings of anger, grief, and crushing pain. Do the scriptures offer us any reassurance, any consolation?"

Reverend Berkley constructed his convincing response around only two biblical passages, one a familiar reading from the New Testament and the other a little-known scripture from the Apocrypha. He first quoted Saint Mathew in which Jesus makes a promise to his disciples:

> Come unto me, all ye that labor and are heavy laden, and I will give you rest. Take my yoke upon you, and learn of me; for I am meek and lowly in heart: and ye shall find rest unto your souls. For my yoke is easy, and my burden is light.

And then he turned to the Wisdom of Solomon, in which the prophet offers solace for this specific situation:

> But the souls of the righteous are in the hand of God, and there shall no torment touch them. In the sight of the unwise they seemed to die: and their departure is taken for misery, and their going from us to be utter destruction: but they are in peace. For though they be punished in the sight of men, yet is their hope full of immortality. And having been a little chastised, they shall be greatly rewarded: for God proved them, and found them worthy for himself.

When Reverend Berkley finished his brief sermon, he asked the congregation to stand for a final prayer. And with the last "Amen" the choirmaster raised his hand to signal the recessional had begun:

Sing with all the saints in glory, sing the resurrection song!
Death and sorrow, earth's dark story, to the former days belong.
All around the clouds are breaking; soon the storms of time shall cease;
In God's likeness we, awaken, knowing the everlasting peace.

Out of respect for Allison and the boys, Danielle and I attended the interment service. We secured a place about twenty cars from the front of the impressive motorcade stretching back at least half a mile along Main Street. After only ten minutes into the ride to the cemetery, Danielle and I realized it was not only the right thing to do, but unbeknownst to us, the Squire's family and friends wanted the procession to be a final tribute. As we approached a meaningful landmark in the Squire's life, the motorcycle escort would slow to a brief stop and then resume our journey to the cemetery. First the Food Bank, then the Jobs Bank, the Venture Bank, the McGill Auditorium, and the most poignant stop of all, The Afterlife. We then continued on down the McGill-Warfield Pike toward the Mount Olive cemetery, where we had just buried the Buccaneer months before. It would be a proper resting place for someone of the Squire's stature; a number of the county's luminaries had been buried in the prestigious cemetery over the past one hundred and fifty years.

But as we neared the entrance, the motorcade maintained its speed, passed Mount Olive, and headed on toward Warfield. The plot thickened as we drove through town, reached the major intersection between McGill-Warfield Pike and the Nashville-Memphis Highway, and continued south into a sparsely populated section of the county. I looked out the windshield to the right and saw a brown highway marker indicating historic Graves Bend was only a half mile ahead.

I remembered reading that the immediate area around Warfield was the "hornet's nest" of guerrilla resistance in Union-occupied Tennessee. A couple thousand horsemen, loosely associated with the Confederate army, "entertained" forty thousand Federal troops here for more than three years. Many of the rebel cavalry who died during the war or passed on later of old age received the community's highest honor—burial at the hallowed guerrilla stronghold, Graves Bend, on the wide, meandering Duck River.

I couldn't believe what was happening. We made a left turn into the park and followed every sign leading to the rebel cemetery near the riverbank. My God, what were they thinking? This would be the last place the Squire would want to be buried. I knew he had strong feelings of guilt about his ancestors' actions during the Civil War.

As we rounded a long gentle curve echoing the bend in the river, the first of many rows of small headstones appeared on both sides of the road. My worst fears were then confirmed. I spotted the telltale chapel tent less than fifty yards from the car. How could Allison let this happen? The funeral director exited his sleek, gleaming limousine and signaled the pallbearers remove the casket from the hearse and follow the priest over to the grave site. He then motioned for all of us to leave our cars and join the family near the large green tent.

Reverend Berkley opened the brief interment ceremony with a prayer and a reading of the familiar psalm:

> The Lord is thy keeper; the Lord is thy shade upon thy right hand.
> The sun shall not smite thee by day, nor the moon by night.
> The Lord shall preserve thee from all evil; he shall preserve thy soul.
> The Lord shall preserve thy going out
> And thy coming in from this time forth and even for evermore.

During the committal part of the service, the priest spoke directly to the Squire's spirit. "We now commend you into the Lord's keeping. Trusting in his great mercy and his promise of the resurrection, we commit your earthly body to this hallowed ground. Earth to earth; ashes to ashes; and dust to dust. All glory to the living God for your triumph over death." The priest then addressed all of us during his benediction. "Go forth in peace. Care for one another. Share with one another. Forgive one another. May the Lord bless you and keep you. May he make his face to shine upon you and be gracious unto you. May he lift up his countenance upon you and give you peace both now and for evermore. Amen."

When the service ended, Danielle and I stayed at the back of the tent until the crowd had thinned. We then joined the circle of mourners still waiting to pay their respects to Allison and the boys. I admit I was a bit anxious; I knew this could be awkward. I hadn't seen Allison in years, and Danielle was now standing at my side. Given that Allison's friends and relatives were within easy earshot, I believed the less said, the better; ambiguity would be an ally here.

When it was our turn to step forward, I motioned Danielle to lead the way and formally introduced her by name only. I hugged Allison and whispered, "I'm so sorry."

As we separated, she tenderly touched the side of my face and responded, "I'm so happy you were here today."

I then gave Zach and Beau big bear hugs. "Hey, you two. Take good care of your mother, you hear?" They murmured something agreeable, and then Danielle and I moved out of the way so others could express their condolences.

I suspected after all the laughter and tears we'd shared over the years, this formal, distant meeting at the Squire's interment celebration would be the last time Allison and I would ever speak. But the gods were a bit more generous and caring. A month after the funeral, I discovered a note from Allison in my departmental mailbox thanking me again for attending the services and asking me to telephone her to arrange a meeting the following week. After confirming the conference with Allison, I played it straight up with Danielle. I explained Allison had requested a meeting. I didn't know what it was about, but I promised to share the details of what transpired.

Early the following Wednesday morning, I climbed the familiar stairs to the third floor of Redman Hall, walked slowly down the empty hallway to the last door on the right, took a sharp left on entering the dimly lit room, and headed back toward the espresso machine. But Allison startled me again with a soft "Good morning, Sam" from the opposite end of the room.

I wheeled around, laughed nervously, and joked, "Well, you've done it again; and twice is unforgiveable." I switched on the rest of the overhead lights and walked toward the corner table at the back of the room.

Allison rose from her chair, moved to the front of the table, and embraced me. She held me at arm's length and whispered, "It's really good to see you again. Thanks for coming." After a shared silence of reminiscence, I suggested the customary double espressos, and she heartily accepted. When I returned with the coffees, she pointed to a chair opposite hers. I sat down, sipped the soothing liquid up through the rich foam, and gazed into her sensuous dark eyes. She was as beautiful as ever.

Allison smiled. "A penny for your thoughts," she probed. I laughed and replied ambiguously, "A Shakespearean sonnet," the actual lines racing through my memory: "But thy eternal summer shall not fade / Nor lose possession of that fair thou ownest." I quickly changed the subject and the tenor of our meeting. "Allison, before we go any further, there's something I have to confess. I remembered you telling me the Squire felt a great deal of guilt about his ancestors' actions during the Civil

War—smuggling contraband and most importantly executing slaves at Fort Pillow.

"While I was living out at the cabin on the lake, I found a trunk in the attic that debunked the battlefield fiction that the plantation owner's son had executed two of his father's runaway slaves. I had every intention of telling the Squire, but...."

Allison put her finger up to her lips, signaling for me to stop. She smiled, shook her head, and responded, "Sam, you are one of the worst handymen I've ever seen. You really made a mess of the bedroom ceiling. After the Squire returned home from the hospital and was feeling stronger, we drove the wagon out to the cabin to spend some time together in the fresh air and to check on things. When we went into the bedroom, the Squire almost immediately spotted the damage to the ceiling, grabbed the ladder from the side of the house, and removed all the bent nails you had hammered into the attic door. To make a long story short, we found the trunk, the uniform, the weapons, and the journals. Piece by piece we carried each treasure down out of the attic and loaded it onto the back of the wagon. You would have been pleased to see how overjoyed the Squire was reading the journals. And yes, he did find and understand the implications of the critical passages about the alleged executions.

"Believe me, Sam, it was not the ancestral guilt that drove my husband to take his life. In the note he left at the cabin where we found him, he spoke of an overwhelming and endless sense of gloom. He also spoke of a personal guilt. He asked Beau, Zach, and me to forgive him for letting us down financially. He said he tried so hard to get better, but nothing the doctors tried worked for very long. It was heartbreaking. The only request he made was to be buried at Graves Bend. For some reason I'll never completely understand, he believed it would be fitting to lie next to the ancestors whom he had renounced for so many years. But after finding the memorabilia in the attic, he said he felt 'as if he were now riding with them.' And, Sam, he shot himself with the Confederate revolver we found in the trunk. I thought long and hard about this. The only thing I could imagine was he saw a similarity in their fate and his. They had fought nobly in battle but ultimately lost the war."

Allison paused for a moment and then continued, "Enough about the past; let's talk about the future. You seem to have moved on. You and Danielle make a beautiful young couple. I could see the love in your eyes. Well, it's time for me to move on too. Beau and Zach have received full scholarships to Stanford, both of them in premed. While they loved growing up here, the boys are ready for a change and have no interest in maintaining The Afterlife. I've already found an apartment in Menlo Park. I'll be close to them and can perhaps hook up with some folks in the San Francisco music scene, play small venues throughout the Bay Area, and make a little spending money singing your old songs and hopefully some new ones.... You're so damn good, Sam."

She opened her purse, retrieved a business card, handed it to me, and continued, "So, Sam, I've decided to put The Afterlife on the market. Please understand. It would be so difficult for me to maintain the property. It's just too much. I just hope someone will buy it who'll love the land as much as we have and never let the plantation fall into the hands of developers. You know, they're always looking for farmland. It wouldn't be long until it was wall-to-wall houses all the way from here to Warfield. But I'll do everything I can to avoid selling to the builders."

She paused and displayed a nervous smile, waiting to hear my reaction to her revelation. I slowly looked up from my empty cup and responded haltingly, "Allison, that's a lot to take in all at once. The Squire gone. You and the boys leaving for the West Coast. The Afterlife up for sale. I understand the situation, but so much at once.... I don't know what to say."

She jumped in with a lighthearted, "How about 'good luck.' You know, I'm going to need a lot of it to get everything to work out just right."

I laughed. "Okay, then, good luck."

As Allison reached under the table to retrieve something from the chair next to her, she said, "I have something for you." She extended her arm across the table and handed me a package wrapped in blue foil with a silver bow. "Thank you," I said, and slowly opened the gift. It was her copy of Capote's *Other Voices, Other Rooms*, which I had returned to her after our first meeting in this room so long ago. Fighting back a tear, I repeated my earlier response: "I don't know what to say."

She smiled and replied, "How about promising me you'll read the inscription?"

As I started to open the cover, she reached across the table, grasped my arm, and said, "No, not now. Perhaps this evening after we've said so long. But I promise you this time there will be none of your lame excuses. My name and new address in Menlo Park are just below the inscription. You can't miss them."

Allison stood up and said she would have to be going. We walked over to the door, stopped, turned toward each other, and embraced. She then drew back, gazed into my eyes, slowly leaned in again, and kissed me softly on the lips. We stood at arm's length for just a moment and stared into each other's eyes. There was no need for conversation or explanation. We knew what the embrace and kiss meant for both of us—deep love, ill timing, and a wistful feeling of what might have been. And I now understood why she wanted to meet there again that day in the dimly lit, nondescript faculty lounge where we had first met and I began falling in love with her. It would provide symmetry, an alpha and omega to our star-crossed lives. We walked down the empty staircase arm in arm, exited Redman Hall, and embraced one last time before entering our afterlives.

When I returned home late that evening after burying myself all day in my dissertation, I discovered Danielle had already gone to bed and fallen asleep reading Camões's *The Lusiads*. After quietly undressing, I moved over to her side of the bed, carefully rescued the open book, and kissed her softly on the cheek. I retrieved Allison's gift from my briefcase, climbed into bed, and read her inscription: "Sam, although we'll now hear other voices in other rooms, still let every breath we take be hallelujah." I placed the book on the nightstand, switched off the light, and then held Danielle tightly until I slept.

17

EXCLUDING THE PERFUNCTORY "Good morning, Samuel," I knew exactly what Danielle would say when she awoke the next morning. And I nailed it. As she entered the kitchen and headed directly for the pot of espresso, she said, "Good morning, Samuel," which was followed by a long pause and then the pièce de résistance, "What did Allison have to say?" I didn't brag about my clairvoyance. I just paused to savor the moment and then responded seriously, "Well, it wasn't good news. Allison is moving to California with her stepsons and is putting her property on the market. While she says she will do everything she can to avoid it, I suspect the odds are much greater than fifty-fifty the plantation will end up in the hands of developers.

"You know, I stayed out there for some time in a cabin on a lake. It was an absolutely stunning place to write music. The mountains, the forests, the fruit trees, the pastureland. And that's to say nothing about the history surrounding The Afterlife. To think all of it could be buried under asphalt and three-acre country estates. It would be a travesty. Having grown up on that enormous, terraced quinta in the Douro, I'm sure you know what I'm feeling. I just wish you could walk the land before someone buys it and puts their bulldozers to work."

"Well, let's do it then," Danielle enthusiastically replied. "It's supposed to be nice over the weekend. Let's stuff our backpacks with bread, cheese, maybe even a bottle of wine, and ride our ten-speeds out there. Make a day of it. What do you say?"

As I pulled my wallet from my jeans pocket, I said, "Sounds like a plan. Allison gave me the real estate agent's card. It should be right here…. Yes, here it is. I'll call the agent. I'll be right up front with him. I'll tell him we could never afford to purchase the property, but if he would be so kind, we would love for him to escort us through the main house and allow us to walk around the plantation after he leaves. Maybe we could offer to buy him lunch to reimburse him for his time."

"Oh, Sam, that's a great idea. How wonderful to see the place where you wrote 'Missing You.' I can't wait."

The following Saturday morning we rolled out of bed before eight o'clock, loaded our backpacks with muffuletta sandwiches, real Swiss emmentaler, crisp apples, and half bottles of red wine, and began our ten-speed journey to The Afterlife. The gods were with us that day: perfect weather, no tire changes, and an on-time arrival just as Mr. Jeffcoat wheeled his red Corvette onto the plantation's long, winding driveway. By the time we made it up to the mansion, Mr. Jeffcoat had already unlocked the front door and was leaning against one of the thick columns gracing the antebellum porch while puffing on a long cigar. We climbed the majestic front steps, introduced ourselves, and thanked Mr. Jeffcoat for generously agreeing to show us around.

As we entered the grand foyer, I realized Allison had already moved everything into storage. Our footsteps echoed in the emptiness. But for me the rooms were full of voices. Walking down the central hallway I heard, "Oh, that's my father there, another Daniel who had survived the fiery furnace." In the kitchen, "Well, while you eat that biscuit, let me tell you about our former pastor and the elder's second wife." Next the ballroom, "I believe the pieces deserve a hearing. How about you?" Then the family room, "Do you believe you are the only isolated artist who has ever succumbed to the longing and the loneliness?" And finally the master bedroom, "Show me."

After Mr. Jeffcoat had finished the tour, locked the place up, and headed back to McGill, I led Danielle up to the Squire's scenic overlook to experience the panorama of gardens, pastures, rolling hills, and small ponds dotting the landscape. A soft wind blew through Danielle's auburn tresses, pushing the long curls down over her forehead. As she raised her hand to sweep the hair back from her tanned face, she said, "This is breathtaking. It reminds me of the quinta. The only thing missing is the Douro."

From there it was on to the summit walkway and then the dappled pinewood path leading out to the cabin on the lake. Nearing the daylight at the far end of the woodland tunnel, I playfully put my hands up over Danielle's eyes, guided her out onto the craggy shoreline, lowered my arms, and announced, "Welcome to paradise!"

I took Danielle's hand and guided her up the shore along a familiar but precarious path between the wet, jagged boulders and the wild blackberry brush, which had reclaimed its territory once a perennial nemesis had left McGill for Germany and the Emerald Isle. After walking up the shoreline about a hundred yards, I stopped and pointed eastward toward the two-story log house standing on a slight rise perhaps twenty-five yards back from the large waves crashing against the rocks below. I motioned for her to follow me up the large slate flagstones leading to the porch, which wrapped completely around the front of the cabin.

After attempting to peer through every accessible crack and shuttered window on the front porch, I suggested we take a seat on the top step. "I'm sorry you can't see the rustic beauty inside," I said. "On the first floor to the left there's a large fieldstone fireplace. To the right there's an antique blue enamel wood cooking stove. And all along the back wall there are tall shelves lined with hundreds of biographies, histories, and top-notch fiction.

"My bedroom was on the second floor. Whitewashed walls. Plenty of furniture surrounding my bed and a door leading up into the attic where I found an old trunk full of heirlooms belonging to the Squire's ancestor—a Civil War uniform, weapons, and a host of journals describing life here and around the county, which was home base for the rebels fighting Lincoln's army. The journals provided inspiration for many of my songs." I paused, looked down at my watch, and said, "Hey, it's going on three o'clock. Let's just sit here, enjoy the view, and eat our sandwiches."

Danielle replied, "What better place than this? Here amid the beauty, the history. and your memories."

As we finished off our half bottles of full-bodied syrah, I broke a long silence. "Danielle, while we are here in this special place, why don't we discuss the future. You and I both know we've been avoiding it, perhaps afraid we'd destroy the magic we've shared over the past months. Why don't I just lay my thoughts out on the line and you respond openly and honestly to them. Danielle, I love you, and I'm willing to live anywhere in the world as long as I have you at my side. I've never been happier in my life. It just feels right for us to be together. Let's take the next step.... Let's get married."

Danielle slowly turned, gazed into my eyes, and replied, "Only in the afterlife."

I asked, "The afterlife? Not now but perhaps some time in the distant future?"

She smiled, gently wrapped her arms around my neck, and teased, "No, silly, not when we're spirits, but now, while we're very much alive. Let's buy the plantation, get married, and live here in The Afterlife. I have plenty of money in my trust account to purchase the property from Allison. With our strong backgrounds I'm sure we can both find permanent positions at the university, which will provide a steady income. And we'll find sharecroppers to farm the land and cattlemen to lease the pastureland."

I just sat there shaking my head and finally managed a stunned phrase, "I don't know what to say."

Danielle replied, "Just say yes. We'll call Mr. Jeffcoat in the morning and get started with the planning."

I have no recollection of the return walk through the woods, the bicycle ride back to the city, or much of anything else that transpired the rest of the night. All I know is, the next few weeks were truly heaven on earth. Everything was brighter, sweeter, and more alive. But as philosophers learned long ago, for every yang there's the yin.

I had gone over to the comparative literature department for a meeting about my summer teaching assignments. On my way out of the office after the conference, the department secretary stopped me and explained she had something for me. She reached into the top drawer of her reception desk and retrieved a small wrapped package secured with thick twine. She then explained, "Sam, this didn't come through the regular mail. A gentleman appeared at the desk several days ago, confirmed you worked in the department, and asked me to deliver the package to you when you dropped in the office. Since there didn't appear to be any sense of urgency on his part, I decided to hold on to it until you stopped by. I knew you would be coming in soon to finalize your summer schedule with Doctor Snyder."

I turned the package around so I could read the return address: Graham, Stewart, Watkins & Dupree, Attorneys at Law, 521 East Main Street, McGill, Tennessee. The secretary nervously twirled her hair, smiled, and probed politely, "Any idea who could be sending you a present this time of year?" Distracted, I deflected her prying query with a "I haven't got a clue" and quickly left the building for Danielle's cottage.

I dropped my briefcase off on the sofa and rushed down the hallway toward the kitchen for a pair of scissors to cut the string and packing tape. After extracting the nine-by-twelve-inch box from the wrapping paper, I moved over to the kitchen table, where I found a loving note from Danielle reminding me she would be home late that evening because of a makeup seminar.

I set the note aside, then slowly lifted the lid off the box and discovered a sealed envelope addressed to me lying on top of another sealed package below. I carefully opened the envelope, which contained an audiocassette with a barely legible label dated less than two months ago. I quickly fetched Danielle's portable cassette player, loaded the tape, and with a pounding heart, hit play:

"I'm sorry, Sam. I would've sent a letter, but my hands are shaking too much now for writing. I've instructed my estate attorney to deliver this tape and enclosed package only after receiving word from the funeral director that I have passed on and been buried near my mom in Louisville." I paused the tape, took several deep breaths allowing my mind to absorb the shock, and then pressed play again. *"Several months ago, I began suffering excruciating headaches with strong seizures. After an extensive battery of tests, I received a diagnosis of advanced Glioblastoma multiforme, a lethal brain tumor with a very short life expectancy.*

"The specialists offered me the standard combination therapy—surgery, chemo, and radiation. But since the docs admitted nothing really worked for long, I have refused treatment and opted to live independently as long as I can before turning to the caretakers at the Odyssey Hospice not too far from where you and I grew up. Before I become completely incapacitated, I have some things I need to say.

"During our first meeting in Redman Hall, we discussed my old high school classmate with whom you shared a last name. It wasn't a coincidence. I knew your mother. I knew Catherine very well. We had been lab partners in our senior year. After going away to college, I lost track of her for a time… but we reconnected during a five-year high school reunion just as I was about to enter graduate school at Pantheon. She explained she hadn't begun college because of family obligations, taking care of her sick mom, while her dad traveled for business.

"After her father made the painful decision to institutionalize his wife, Catherine decided to make the break and enter Pantheon as a freshman in premed. One thing led to another, and over time, Catherine and I became lovers and remained close until I met a woman who haunted my soul. Your mother and I had a heartrending last meeting at the hometown cemetery the day after my mom was buried. And then I lost track of her again. She never returned to Pantheon to finish her degree.

"I tried calling her several times over the years, but no one answered. I returned home to attend reunions in 1963, 1973, and 1983. I thoroughly checked the crowds each time, but Catherine never appeared. I asked high school buddies if they had seen her around town; and they said it was as if she had vanished. And I heard no more about your mother until you appeared at my office door for your first graduate school interview.

"If you remember, I began our conversation asking biographical questions. You said you never met your father. Your mother told you when you were a teen he had been recruited by one of the US intelligence agencies, left Pantheon, and later lost his life in the line of duty. You said your mother also told you that when your father shipped out under deep cover, he had no idea your mother was pregnant with you. I then asked you to speak about your mother. You explained she had also been at Pantheon but had returned to Louisville once your father had left for Europe and she had indeed confirmed she was pregnant.

"You described how she made many sacrifices for you working as a hotel clerk and attending nursing school at night. I then asked you how she was doing at that point in '83; and you explained she had died in the late 1970s after a long battle with breast cancer. You said she had willed herself to live until you were graduated from high school.

"But unbeknownst to you, there was a lot more going on during our first meeting than you could have ever imagined. Throughout our conversation, I glanced furtively from you to a framed photograph facing me on the desk. It was a picture of your mother and me arm in arm, standing outside the football stadium after our team had won an important victory. I quickly became convinced the young man in the photograph and the young man sitting across from me were identical—the same eyes, nose, lips, and auburn beard.

"And with the similarities in our appearances and the timing of Catherine's pregnancy, I knew without a doubt you were my son. After you left our meeting, I understood why your mother never returned to Pantheon to finish her degree; why she never attended any of the reunions; and why she just dropped off the face of the earth. I'm sure you're asking, why didn't I just tell you then or at least at some point over all the years?

"Sam, I struggled with the dilemma but reasoned that if I explained who I really was and debunked the story that your father had died heroically serving his country, you would have cruelly lost both your parents again. I believed I was doing what was best for you then, and I believe I am also doing what is best for you now. After you left the university to pursue a music career, I didn't get to see you very often. But when I did, I always cherished the few moments we had together. And when you returned after the horrible injury, I did everything I could to help you resume your academic career. After all, you were my son.

"And I was pleased when you telephoned and said you had someone you wanted me to meet. Despite your explanation that this visiting lecturer had an interest in Bianca, for some reason, perhaps something in your voice, I believed it was actually more about you and your feelings for her; and as it turned out, I was right, at least in part. Seeing the two of you together for the first time, I could tell you cared so much. I was so happy for you; Danielle was so beautiful and vibrant. Everything was going so well until I asked that damned question, if she were planning a project based on Bianca's life or works.

"When Danielle answered that her visit was not so much about academics but to learn as much as she could about her mother, Bianca, and her father, Jeffrey Kline, I knew I'd again have to ask, 'What is best for you, Sam?' I want you to know that everything I said about Jeffrey Kline was true. He was a playwright. He and Bianca were lovers. He had a play opening in New York; and because of the play, he didn't travel to Portugal.

"And everything I said about Bianca was also true. She offered me a free trip to Europe for the sesquicentennial celebration. She finished her third book of poetry and returned to Europe. She came back to McGill and began a downward spiral. And I published a fourth volume of her poetry in her honor. But I confess there were some things I didn't tell you. During our stay at the quinta, Bianca and I became lovers. When we returned to the States, she stopped in New York to break off her relationship with Jeffrey Kline.

"Concerning her trip back to Europe, she led me to believe she was going on an extended tour promoting her third volume of poetry. I had no idea she was pregnant and was planning to stay at the quinta until after the birth. I don't know whether the childbirth or leaving the child behind with the grandparents had anything to do with it, but she did begin showing signs of instability not long after returning to McGill.

"And those years following her return were so difficult for both of us. We moved around a lot from city to city seeking help and satisfying her compulsion to continually be on the move. But what I don't regret is holding back on my description of Bianca's last few weeks. I just couldn't discuss it with Danielle. It was really bad—the isolation, the paranoia, the deep depression, and finally the suicide. I just couldn't tell Danielle I was the one who found her mother hanging out the bedroom window.

"A final thing, Sam. I can tell you for sure Jeffrey Kline was not the father of Bianca's baby. She never saw Jeffrey again after meeting him in New York to break it off. Following her first return to McGill after our trip, Bianca and I shared an apartment for about two years. So according to the timing of everything, she was pregnant when she left for Europe on her purported promotional tour.

"And until Danielle was sitting across the desk from me that day, I never knew I had a daughter. But my God, given the circumstances, what could I say? 'Things were in the saddle and ride mankind.' Sam, I wouldn't venture telling you what to do with this revelation, but I hope you'll think it through and do what's best for you and Danielle. Notwithstanding your decision about revealing the identity of her real father, there are three things you may want to share with her: first, the fact that Bianca and I became lovers after Jeffrey was out of the picture; second, the enclosed package of letters Bianca wrote me during her extended stay in Europe; and third, the location of her mother's grave in our hometown cemetery. Son, forgive me. I loved you from the moment I realized you were my son, and I will love you until my last dying breath."

I stopped the cassette player, lowered my head, and stared at Danielle's loving note lying on the table next to the package of letters. The tectonic plates had just shifted. North was now south. Left was right. Up was down. Incoherent half thoughts raced through my head. There were no answers. Just life-changing, existential questions: Why this? Why now? Tell her? Her response? The marriage? The Afterlife?

In a strange way, the tape was my father's last will and testament. He was passing his secrets, his guilt, and his endless quest for resolution to his offspring. It was Christmas, Easter, and more than thirty years of birthdays all rolled into one. He had wrapped everything up in a small, tidy package and had it hand-delivered to the executor of his spiritual estate for final disbursement, if and when I saw fit. And for several days I wrestled with the pros and cons; but in the end, I relied solely on my love for Danielle to chart a course.

When she returned home from the library early the following Friday afternoon, I asked her to pack a casual bag for the weekend and to ask no questions about where we were going or what we were going to do. She would just have to trust me on this one. And an hour and a half later, we were boarding a train at Warfield Station headed for an elegant hotel in downtown Louisville.

It was like a homecoming for me. I had made many visits there in my youth. Everything was as I remembered it: the long rectangular skylight, the soaring ceilings, the giant marble columns, and the colorful pioneer murals ringing the walls. Danielle gazed at the gilded chandeliers and the marble registration desk spanning the width of the room and said, "On the train you finally confessed we were going to a hotel, but, Sam, this is a castle! Why come here, Sam? Why Louisville? Why now?"

I raised my finger to my lips and replied, "Remember now, no questions. I'll just say that everything will be much clearer tomorrow. I promise."

As we rode the elevator to the top floor, I took several deep breaths and thought to myself, "There are minefields directly ahead, Sam. What will you say or do after you return from dinner? How will you delay— No, how will you avoid the expected lovemaking? Here you are in an opulent hotel. You're on a surprise getaway and no lovemaking? You give Danielle every right to expect it and nothing happens? What can you do? Extend dinner? Feign illness? No. I'll just be straight up with her without revealing the truth. I'll pull her in close to me, hold her tightly, and reassure her as before, 'You'll just have to trust me on this one until tomorrow morning. Get some sleep, my love.'"

Despite conventioneers reveling in the hallway past two o'clock in the morning, I slept surprisingly well the rest of the night. Perhaps it was the calm of inevitability that Dostoyevsky and Boleyn had felt. I ordered up room service for breakfast, a regional specialty Danielle had never experienced before, Kentucky Benedict with red-eye hollandaise and sourmash bourbon biscuits.

As we ate our home-style breakfast, I revealed that I had visited the hotel a number of times as a boy. "My mother worked here as a clerk. When she had to come in for a half day on the weekends, I'd load up my backpack with books and ride the bus uptown with her. I didn't mind it; the folk working here were nice. They made sure I had plenty to eat and entertained me with tales about the place. A lot of famous people stayed here, even some of our presidents, like Wilson, Taft, Roosevelt, and Truman. But for a teenage boy, the politicians couldn't compete with the mobsters, Remus and Capone, who used the hotel's secret passageways to escape the police.

"But since I'd fallen in love with stories early on, even the gangsters paled in comparison to the fictional characters who roamed these halls." I paused and asked, "Have you ever read Fitzgerald?"

Danielle smiled and replied, "Yes, of course, almost everything he wrote for an undergraduate seminar."

I continued, "Well, Tom and Daisy Buchanan probably stayed in this very room on their wedding night."

Danielle laughed and responded skeptically, "Samuel, I don't remember a racy bedroom scene. How can you make that claim?"

"Well, there's method to my madness," I said, smiling. "The hotel staff told me years ago this was the very room Fitzgerald demanded when he came to town. You're a novelist. Just extrapolate. If he used the hotel ballroom as the setting for Tom and Daisy's reception in *Gatsby*, wouldn't he also incorporate the familiar into their wedding night? Yes, I know he didn't include it, but I'm damn sure he must have thought it."

After this lighthearted intermezzo, it was now time to play the final act. We picked up the rental car late morning and headed toward the east end of town. Everything looked pretty much as it had decades before, when we followed my mom's hearse to the same cemetery. And just as the boulevard rounded a large curve and split, I spotted the familiar limestone tower rising above the golden raintrees lining both sides of the avenue.

I drove through the main gate and stopped at the administration center. I turned to Danielle and said, "Why don't you wait in the car while I run inside to get directions." As I entered the office, a very pleasant elderly lady sitting behind a small oak desk greeted me and asked if she could help. I explained I was interested in getting a map of the grounds and the location of a specific grave. When I mentioned the professor's name, a booming voice rang out from the back corner of the room: "If you hold on a minute, I'll drive up that way with you and show you exactly where we laid the professor to rest. I've got some work to do up there anyway." The caretaker fetched some tools from a small annex, joined me at the front door, and instructed me to wait outside in my car while he pulled his truck around from the back.

It was as if the fellow were taking a slow, circuitous route to the grave site to proudly exhibit his handiwork of rolling hills, exotic ponds, and sloping terraces of magnolia, hemlock, willow, and spruce. As we approached a formal garden of rhododendron and azalea, the caretaker thrust his arm out the window and motioned for us to pull off to the side. I parked the car, and we joined the caretaker where he stood in the middle of the road pointing toward the crest of a hill. "You see that wooden and wrought-iron bench up at the top of the hill? Well, if you draw a line straight down the slope, that's where the professor's buried. It's not hard to find. There's still a lot of fresh dirt around where the grass hasn't sprouted."

I politely interrupted, "Excuse me, sir, for asking, but you refer to our acquaintance as 'the professor,' as if you knew him fairly well." The caretaker responded directly, "I did. I'd known him for years. I remember the first time he came by the office. He needed a grave lot for a loved one whose body would be shipped up here the following week. He said he first wanted to visit his own family's grave site with its available lots. You know his mother, the violin virtuoso, is buried up the hill there among our community luminaries—the city founder, most of the mayors, Keats's brother, and on and on. After visiting the family lot, we walked along the summit for a few minutes. He just kept shaking his head and finally said, 'The family lot isn't right. Do you have other plots?' I pulled the maps out of my satchel and found several single-space graves. Ironically, they were just down the hill from his mother, albeit on the 'busy side' of the grounds where you could occasionally hear the traffic from the highway.

"When we reached the designated area, the professor asked if I could find him two lots together. I reiterated that these were single-space graves and then proceeded to point out the available lots. There was one near the summit and one down the slope toward the stream over there. He said he would take both lots. The one at the top of the hill would be for his friend, and the one in the valley near the water would be for him. I asked the professor if he was sure he wanted to be buried down here away from his mother and his family. And I'll never forget his response: 'I think I should be down here among friends; and besides, I'll still be able to hear the music.'

"After his friend's burial, the professor would show up here with a bouquet from time to time and would sit up there on the bench near the grave site until just after sunset. The routine remained the same until one day some years ago, he dropped by the office and asked if I would search the files for another party he suspected could be buried here. I conducted the search; and sure enough, the name was there. We grabbed the maps, drove out to the perennial garden here, and found the unmarked site not too far from the summit and just paces away from his friend's grave. I'll never forget. We went back to the sales office, and he bought a granite marker on the spot.

"Once the headstone had been inscribed and positioned at the site, the professor reverted to his previous routine—showing up from time to time and sitting on the wood and wrought-iron bench up there until a little past sunset. The only difference was he now brought two identical purple-and-white bouquets of hyacinth, snowdrop, periwinkle, and forget-me-nots. Yes, he came from time to time; and then the visits stopped. And it wasn't too long before my worst fears were confirmed. We received the call from the mortuary asking us to prepare the site down at the stream."

The caretaker lowered his head and added, "He was a good man, and I'm going to miss him a lot." Sensing he was beginning to express too much emotion, he extended his hand to each of us and explained he had to get to work across the road in the arboretum. We thanked him for his help and stood there in the middle of the road until he disappeared beyond the crest of the nearby hill.

I knew the moment was now at hand. I put my arm around Danielle's waist, and we walked that way until we reached the freshly turned soil. We stood at Professor Taylor's grave for several minutes, reminiscing about the only time the three of us ever met. My pulse quickened as I tugged at Danielle's arm and then guided her up the hill toward the other graves. As we walked along the path, I tried to ease the shock of what I knew was coming. "Danielle, I'll have to explain how the professor led me to your mother's grave."

When we reached Bianca's headstone, Danielle knelt down beside the marker, folded her hands, and whispered a prayer. Tears streamed down her cheeks as she read the inscription, which stated Bianca's full name, her birth and death dates, and several verses from one of her poems that appeared in the first issue of the *Messenger*.

After several minutes of reflective silence, I helped Danielle to her feet and led her up the hill to the professor's customary bench on the summit. It was easy to see why he loved sitting up there. From his vantage point looking west and framed by massive hemlocks reaching more than eighty feet in the air, he could clearly see the sun setting behind the shimmering skyline of boyhood memories and dreams. And in the immediate foreground, he could trace the telling pyramid floating amidst a sea of granite white caps below. Bianca's headstone on the left and Catherine's on the right formed the base of the inverted isosceles whose sides extended down the hill to the professor's grave at the apex near the intermittent stream. A lovers' triangle surrounded by strangers. Close and still so far away. Found and lost. Death imitating life and the afterlife.

I turned toward Danielle, gazed into her eyes, and said, "There are some troubling things I've learned which I must share with you now. As you know, several days ago, I received a package from the professor's executor containing a cassette and some letters. That's how I found out he had passed away. What I didn't tell you is that, on the tape, the professor said he was dying and wanted us to know the mysteries behind his life. He explained he knew my mother, Catherine, in high school; and they became lovers while attending Pantheon. When he broke off the relationship, my mother dropped out of college and just disappeared. He swore he had no idea that she was pregnant when they separated. Years later and unbeknownst to me, my long-lost father became my graduate school mentor.

"During our first meeting, he deduced I was his son and asked warily how my mother was doing. I told him my mom had died. He then found her unmarked grave here—I didn't have enough money to buy a headstone at the time—and he purchased that fine granite marker just down the hill there on the right. Can you make it out? That's my mom's grave. I hadn't been able to get back here for so long, I never knew about the headstone.

"The professor also had some revelations about his relationship with your mother. He said that during the trip to the quinta for the celebration, they became lovers. When they returned to the States, your mother stopped off in New York to break off the affair with Jeffrey Kline. The professor asserted he and Bianca lived happily together for two years in McGill before she left on the purported book tour. The professor said he had no idea Bianca was pregnant or that you existed."

I reached down into my backpack to retrieve the package of letters. "The professor wanted you to have these letters your mother wrote to him while she was in Portugal.… Given the timing of everything, the professor insisted there was no way Jeffrey Kline could have been your father."

As I discussed the question of her parentage, I sensed Danielle was locking the last pieces in place. She first looked toward Catherine, next to Bianca, and then down the hill toward Professor Taylor. The geometry of the landscape offered clues—Catherine and Bianca's congruent sides met at the professor's grave. She clearly understood now the professor was our father, which meant there was only one conditional statement remaining: "If the professor is our father, then you, Sam, are my half brother." Danielle shuddered, turned away, and stared out over an exotic pond of lotus plants. The longer the silence continued, the more the pressure built to ask, "What about the future? What about The Afterlife?"

But finally, after several minutes, Danielle turned back toward me and spoke calmly and resolutely. "Sam, you remember Professor Taylor's account of attending mass in Viseu on his way back to Lisbon?"

I nodded. "Yes."

"He said the experience brought him closer to the divine than anything before or since. Do you remember the text for the homily?"

"First John, I believe. Something about love. It's strange. The words escape me, but I remember exactly how I felt when he quoted them."

Danielle responded, "The professor said it was one of his favorite texts. I wonder if he was trying to send us a message. During our meeting, you introduced me as your fiancée; and by the time the professor quoted the passage, he must have known I was his daughter and you were his son. And despite knowing our situation, he still quoted the scripture, 'He that loveth abides in the light, and there is none occasion of stumbling in him.' So, Sam, let's abide in the light."

I embraced Danielle and whispered approvingly, "Yes… abide in the light. Let's say so long to everyone here and get back to The Afterlife. We've got songs to write and stories to tell."